W9-DDM-525

THE SECRETS OF BONES

THE SECRETS OF BONES

KYLIE LOGAN

THORNDIKE PRESS
A part of Gale, a Cengage Company

Fountaindale Public Library District
300 W. Briarcliff Rd.
Bolingbrook, IL 60440

Copyright © 2020 by Connie Laux.
A Jazz Ramsey Mystery.
Thorndike Press, a part of Gale, a Cengage Company.

ALL RIGHTS RESERVED
This is a work of fiction. All of the characters, organizations, and events portrayed in this novel are either products of the author's imagination or are used fictitiously.
Thorndike Press® Large Print Mystery.
The text of this Large Print edition is unabridged.
Other aspects of the book may vary from the original edition.
Set in 16 pt. Plantin.

LIBRARY OF CONGRESS CIP DATA ON FILE.
CATALOGUING IN PUBLICATION FOR THIS BOOK
IS AVAILABLE FROM THE LIBRARY OF CONGRESS

ISBN-13: 978-1-4328-8280-8 (hardcover alk. paper)

Published in 2020 by arrangement with St. Martin's Publishing Group

Printed in Mexico
Print Number: 01   Print Year: 2020

For all the dogs who have been part of our lives . . .

Woofer, the little gentleman in a dog suit

Hoover, who could — and did — eat anything, including doors and rocks.

Oscar, who tried his best to teach me patience. It didn't work.

Ernie, my boyfriend

Casey, the old lady who trusted us until the end

Hooligan Apollo, here for a heartbeat but always in our hearts

Lucy, my familiar

Eliot, the crazy boy who makes us laugh

CHAPTER 1

Wally the puppy was a nineteen-pound ball of boundless energy with more sass than a three-year-old kid, and more common sense than one, too. He came when he was called, knew the names of his toys and fetched them on command, and he could sit and stay. At least when he felt like it.

He loved morning walks, afternoon hikes, and a jog around the neighborhood after dinner as long as it wasn't too hot, too rainy, or the John Coltrane wannabe who played his saxophone over at the gazebo in the center of Lincoln Park wasn't around. Wally wasn't fond of bebop. He was mostly house-trained, except when he didn't feel like going outside, mostly polite, except when a visitor didn't scold him for chewing on fingers and clothing and Wally knew he could get away with it, and he was mostly well behaved.

Except when he wasn't.

In the month since she'd gotten him, the puppy had become the light of Jazz Ramsey's life, the dog of her heart she thought she'd never have again when Manny, her beloved golden retriever, died a little over a year earlier. Wally was also a constant reminder that though her relationship with Nick Kolesov, her former lover and the homicide detective who gave her Wally, was still rocky, as long as there were waggly tails and puppy kisses there was always hope.

Wally was square nosed, long legged, and as smart and smart-alecky as Airedales always are. He had a personality bigger than his puppy-sized brown and black body, and an interest in everyone he met and in everything within range of his sensitive nose or the reach of his paws or his mouth.

He was sleeping through the night now, thank goodness, but Jazz swore she was still catching up on the shut-eye she'd missed that first week when he carried on in his crate, sometimes for hours.

She was young, and thanks to the rigorous and rewarding work she did with human remains detection dogs, she was fit, too, but she was also exhausted.

She couldn't remember a time she'd been happier.

The thought in mind and a spring in her

step that hadn't been there in the year before Wally made an appearance in her life, Jazz dropped her purse on her desk outside the principal's office at St. Catherine's Preparatory Academy for Girls and took a deep breath.

New day.

New beginnings.

Life was good.

"Well, I guess the little beast slept last night or you wouldn't look so perky."

Jazz had been so busy smiling at the framed photo of Wally on her desk, she hadn't seen Sister Eileen Flannery sail into the school's admin office. As usual, Eileen was wearing a dark suit and the TOMS shoes she swore were the only things that kept her feet comfortable enough to negotiate miles of school hallways every day. Her filmy cream and black scarf had just enough touches of rust in it to bring out the coppery highlights in Eileen's short, stylish hair. At the same time Jazz admired her boss's panache, she told herself her own black pants, white shirt, and beige linen jacket were professional enough for the day's special occasion. Her shoulder-length brown hair was scooped back into a neat ponytail, her nails were polished (something she hardly ever did) with an understated, pinkish shade called Hawaiian Orchid, and her shoes . . .

Jazz glanced down at her black flats and cringed, then rubbed the toe of her right shoe against the back of her left pant leg. Yeah, like that would help buff out the marks left by a certain puppy's needle-sharp teeth.

In the hopes that Eileen wouldn't notice and think less of Wally because of it, Jazz ducked behind her desk and checked the time on her computer screen. She wasn't surprised by the principal's earlier-than-usual arrival. It was nearly the end of the school year and Assembly Day, an annual event and one of the highlights of the year, was upon them. In just a few hours the school would welcome women prominent in business, education, and government, speakers who'd talk to small groups of girls about everything from careers in science to summer job opportunities. Eileen and Jazz, the principal's administrative assistant, would be running all day, and it was never too early to start.

"He's a great dog," she told Eileen, ignoring her shoes and adjusting the picture of Wally so it sat at just the right angle next to her computer. "He's so easygoing, he's great with people. My brother, Hal, and his

10

girlfriend, Kaitlyn, stopped over last night and Wally treated them like long-lost friends."

"Can finding human remains be far behind?"

Eileen was kidding, but she should have known better. Jazz had every hope Wally would be certified in human remains detection, just like Manny had been. "It might take a while until he's completely trained," she said. "But you know I'm going to try."

"Don't tell me; let me guess. You've already got the little guy sniffing decomposing body parts." Eileen's expression teetered somewhere between *I'm trying to be interested* and *don't tell me; I don't want to know.* Jazz couldn't blame her. People were often uncomfortable hearing the details of Jazz's volunteer work with cadaver dogs and Eileen, especially, had a reason for being queasy. Just two months before, Jazz and a dog she was training had found the body of a former St. Catherine's student in an old building not far from the school.

It was that, more than anything, that made Jazz determined to put Eileen at ease.

"At this point I'm just exposing him to different scents," she told the nun. "Teeth, bones —"

Eileen help up one hand to stop her from

11

going any farther. "I get it."

"Let's hope Wally does. I'd love to work with him in the field. Fingers crossed he's got the right temperament." Jazz didn't even need to think about what that meant. After ten years of working with HRD dogs, she knew Wally would have to meet all the requirements — loyal enough to follow her commands, independent enough to go off on his own to work a search, flexible enough to handle both urban and rural scenes, hardy enough to work in the field for hours at a time, in all kinds of weather. She'd teach Wally to be an air sniffer for those times the smell of decomposition was in the air, and he'd learn ground tracking, too, to trace cells that might drop from a body or be blown to the grass or soil by the wind.

The other handlers Jazz trained with came in as many shapes, sizes, and backgrounds as their dogs did. When it came to a cadaver dog, breed and pedigree didn't make one bit of difference. What mattered most was that dog and handler alike were committed to the important work of finding the dead.

"He's smart enough," Jazz said, back on the subject of Wally because since the day she got him he was pretty much all she wanted to talk about. "He's going to be the best!"

On her way into her office, Eileen patted Jazz's shoulder. "You'll make sure of that. For now —"

"The coffee and bagels should be here in just a couple minutes." Jazz shook away the Wally infatuation and got down to business, motioning toward the tables set up along the wall at the far side of her office. Last thing the day before, she'd covered them in red and yellow tablecloths — St. Catherine's school colors — and arranged white plates from the cafeteria on them along with red and yellow paper napkins, flatware, and bouquets of flowers that included red carnations, yellow daylilies, and purple irises, just for a little pop. "We'll be ready by the time our speakers arrive."

"And I know you've got the day's schedule worked out down to the minute."

It was printed and waiting on Jazz's desk and she retrieved the list and waved it at Eileen. "Our speakers should start arriving in . . ." She checked the time on her phone. "One hour and thirteen minutes. I've got the speaker from NASA in the gym, the woman from Case medical school in the science lab, the attorney in the library, the yoga instructor in the art room. Sarah said it would provide the right vibe."

Sarah Carrington was the art teacher at

St. Catherine's and Jazz's best friend, and since both Jazz and Eileen knew she was also the most ethereal free-thinker on the planet and a big believer in things like the mojo of a place, they exchanged knowing smiles.

"All the other speakers and their rooms are listed, too," Jazz told Eileen and handed her the paper. "We've got a full house, not one room open in any of the time slots."

"The girls will love it." It was what mattered to Eileen. That and the fact that she was helping in the formation of intelligent, independent, and confident young women. "You did . . ." Eileen's smile thinned with skepticism. "You managed to get some of the girls to sign up for the talk in the chapel, didn't you?"

"Religious vocations?" Jazz sighed. "Not the hottest topic on the agenda."

Eileen's grin was one-sided. "What? They don't all want to grow up to be me?"

"They should be so lucky. But you've got to admit —"

"Yes, I know. Believe me, I get it. Obedience is bad enough. But the whole chastity thing . . . Well, it's harder today than ever to get girls to think about religious life. There aren't many of them anymore like —"

Eileen didn't need to finish the sentence.

They both knew who she was talking about, Bernadette Quinn, a teacher who'd left the school three years before.

"Bernadette should have been a nun," Jazz reminded Eileen even though she didn't have to. "She was —"

"Obsessed?"

"I was going to say devoted, but now that you mention it . . ."

It was all they needed to say about the subject. They both remembered the last, uncomfortable weeks Bernadette had taught religion at St. Catherine's, the complaints from parents, the uneasiness of the other teachers who had to deal with Bernadette, the tears of the students who couldn't live up to Bernadette's impossible standards.

But then, Bernadette had never been able to live up to those standards, either.

"I wonder what ever happened to her." The words escaped her before Jazz could stop them and she could have kicked herself. Assembly Day was all about energy, all about excitement. Thinking about those last weeks and the discord holier-than-thou (or anybody else) Bernadette caused at St. Catherine's should have had no part of it.

Talk about mojo!

Jazz swished away the bad vibes with the wave of one hand and offered a confession.

15

"I got girls to sign up for the religious vocation talk because I convinced Tina Carlson to offer extra credit in Religion to anyone who agreed to attend the chapel talks."

If she expected Eileen to criticize the strategy, she was wrong. A knowing smile, a wink, and Eileen went into her office.

The next hour was as hectic as early mornings always were at St. Catherine's, with parents calling girls out for sickness, girls stopping into the office to retrieve lost items, others running late and rushing past the office just as the last bell was about to ring. By the time it had and the girls were in their homerooms, the coffee and bagels were delivered and their speakers were gathered. The sounds of their conversation echoed back from the fifteen-foot-high ceilings of Jazz's office.

St. Catherine's was located in the Cleveland neighborhood of Tremont, once the home of dozens of different ethnic groups, people from all over the world who'd come to Cleveland at the end of the nineteenth century to labor in its factories. The building had once been a Russian Orthodox seminary, and though it had been remodeled when Eileen spearheaded its transformation into the most prestigious girls' school in the area, it still retained its old-world charm. The scientist from NASA chatted with the attorney and Eileen near the bookcases with leaded-glass doors. The yoga instructor and Sarah, who was the one who'd recommended her as one of the speakers, laughed together over near the windows that looked out across the street and Lincoln Park, the eight-acre green space in the center of the neighborhood.

It was the perfect setting and everything was going well. Except . . .

Jazz took a look around the room, did a quick tally, and caught Eileen's eye, and the principal excused herself from her conversation and came over. "What?"

"Sister Dorothea Baker." Jazz poked a finger against the nun's name on her list of speakers. "No sign of her."

Eileen chomped down the last of a cinnamon raisin bagel, freeing up her hands so she could give Jazz an unconcerned shrug.

"The ditzyest nun I've ever met. And that's saying something!" Eileen flashed her a smile. "Don't worry. I guarantee you, once she shows up, you'll hear all about how she was running late and ended up getting lost. But she'll show up."

Only she didn't.

By the time each speaker was met by a host teacher and escorted to the room where she'd spend the day and the girls would rotate in and out in forty-five-minute shifts, there was still no sign of Sister Dorothea. The girls who signed up to hear her speak about religious vocations might actually be relieved, but that didn't keep Jazz from worrying.

Before she had a chance to mention it to Eileen again, the phone on Jazz's desk rang. It was Dorothea Baker.

"It's not a bad accident." On the other end of the phone, Sister Dorothea's voice was high and tight with tension. "Just a fender bender, but —"

Jazz heard a man somewhere nearby bark out "turn signal," "brake lights," and "watching where you're going."

"I won't be able to make it to St. Catherine's," Sister Dorothea announced, her voice wobbly.

"She won't be here," Jazz repeated, because just as Sister Dorothea abruptly ended the call Eileen glided back through the office. "Sister Dorothea. Minor accident."

Eileen's mouth thinned. "And a forty-five-minute slot where we're going to have to entertain a lot of girls." She tapped one foot against the hardwood floor.

"I'll tell you what we're going to do,"

18

Eileen said at the same time she picked up the phone and called down to Maintenance. "Frank, it's me. How soon can you get the fourth floor straightened up?"

Frank, the head of the maintenance department, like everyone else at St. Catherine's, didn't argue. What Eileen wanted Eileen got, only by the time she ended the call Jazz wasn't sure what it was she wanted.

"What are you planning?" she asked the principal.

"Don't worry about me, you've got work to do." Eileen put her hands on Jazz's shoulders and turned her toward the door. "We can't have a dog demonstration in the chapel, so Frank's going to clean up the fourth-floor space. Nobody's been up there in years, so it shouldn't be bad except for some dust. By the time he's done, it will be time for the girls to switch speakers and you'll be back with that puppy of yours."

It took a second for the reality to sink in. "I will?"

"Uh-huh. A little cadaver dog demo, that should keep them interested."

"But Wally's not —"

"Get moving," Eileen told her. Jazz didn't argue with her, either.

CHAPTER 2

As far as Jazz could see, the only thing Wally could give a really good demonstration on was the inconvenient art of peeing on the floor.

Something told her that wasn't exactly what Eileen was looking for.

With that in mind, she zipped home to get the puppy, and on her way she made a phone call. Margaret Carlson lived nearby and she had a retired HRD dog, a chocolate Lab with a great temperament and a keen nose who Jazz hoped would enjoy a change of pace and a little work. She'd bring Wally along for the cuteness factor.

With Wally and Gus in their crates in the back of her SUV and a bone and tooth she'd retrieved from the refrigerator in her garage in sealed bags and on the seat next to her, she raced back to school.

She had just arrived on the third floor with bone, tooth, and dogs when she ran into

Eddie Simpson from Maintenance. He was waiting outside the locked door at the bottom of the stairway that led up to the fourth floor.

Eddie was the nephew of Loretta Hardinger, the woman who was in charge of St. Catherine's cafeteria. He was a rangy, dark-haired kid with blotchy skin and Jazz clearly remembered the day four years earlier when Lorraine had come into the office to ask if Eileen and Jazz couldn't find some way to give him a job. ("Because I'll tell you what, if he doesn't keep himself busy and find a new bunch of buddies to hang with, that boy's going to end up in prison.") Since then Frank, his supervisor, was pleased enough with Eddie's work.

Eddie caught sight of the dogs and froze. His face turned the same dull gray as the pants and neatly tucked-in shirt he was wearing and he clutched the broom he was carrying, his knuckles white, and held it front of himself like a shield. His left eye twitched.

Gus was trained. As soon as Jazz stopped four feet from Eddie, he sat down beside her. Wally, not so much. Sensing the opportunity to make a new friend, or maybe just interested in chewing on the broom, he bounded closer to Eddie at record speed.

Eddie retreated, hopping backwards down the hallway and toward the closed door of the chapel.

"No!" Jazz told Wally, and gave his lead a little tug. "Sorry." This time she was talking to Eddie. "I didn't know you didn't like dogs. They're friendly," she assured him, but Eddie wasn't buying it.

He gulped and his Adam's apple bobbed. "You're not . . . Is that why Frank wants me to sweep upstairs? You're taking them dogs up there?"

"Orders from Eileen."

It was all any of them ever needed to hear. Eileen's school. Eileen's orders. Eileen's wishes were their commands.

Which was why Jazz was surprised when one corner of Eddie's mouth pulled tight. "I bet it's awfully stuffy up there," he said. "I'd hate to see those girls be all hot and uncomfortable."

"They'll live," Jazz assured him. "And they won't be up there long. Forty-five minutes at the most. Then the next group comes in."

His gaze slid to the dogs. "And they're gonna do . . . ?"

"Just a little demo," she told him. "Just to keep the girls occupied." She moved a step closer to the door, and when Eddie didn't get the message she asked, "What are we

22

waiting for?"

"Uh . . ." He pulled his gaze from the dogs. "The key. Sister Eileen, she —"

"Of course!" Jazz felt guilty for being impatient. The door to the fourth-floor space was always kept locked, and Eileen was the only one with the key. "Sorry to be pushy," she told Eddie. "I just need to get up there before the girls show up. To hide my bait."

Like most people, he didn't ask what the bait was. He slid another look at Gus, who thumped his tail, and Wally, who saw it as an obvious invitation for a lifelong friendship and bounded forward again. "And those dogs —"

"Well, Gus here will find the bait. At least I hope so. Wally's still learning."

Eddie blinked and thought about it. "Okay. Sure, Jazz, only how about you . . ." He poked his thumb over his shoulder. "You . . . uh . . . maybe you can wait over by the chapel door with them dogs until the door gets unlocked and —"

"Sorry! Sorry!" Out of breath, Eileen arrived at the top of the stairway that led from the second floor to the third. "I got buttonholed by the basketball coach speaking in the health room and couldn't pull myself away." She was carrying the ring of the school's master keys and they jangled when she lifted it. "I'll get the door opened for you in a jiffy and you two can do what you need to do. Oh, it's Wally!"

Unable to resist — Jazz knew she was right about the cuteness factor — Eileen bent and scratched a hand over the puppy's head. He rewarded her efforts by chomping her thumb.

When Eileen yelped, Jazz cringed. "Sorry. Puppy teeth."

"And I should know better." Eileen went to the door and flipped through the keys, counting low under her breath. "Let's get going here so you two can be ready and —" Her hands stilled over the keys and her brow furrowed.

"What's wrong?" Jazz asked.

"Wrong? Nothing." Eileen flipped the keys back to their original position and started counting again. "One, two, three, four, five, six —" Her mouth thinned. "These are the old keys, the ones we hardly ever use, and I've got them arranged exactly the way I want them." She sorted through them again. "Number one is the garden shed back by the parking lot." As if to prove it, she showed Jazz a heavy metal key with a long shank, its color dulled by age. There was a sticker on it that identified which door it opened. "Number two is for the old furnace room in the basement that's been closed off for years. Three, four, five, six," she finished the count below her breath. "The sixth key on the ring is supposed to be for this door, but it's not. This key . . ." She held up key number six to demonstrate. "This is for the sacristy door in the chapel." Her nose crinkled, she looked through the rest of the keys and finally smiled when she got to the end of the keys on the ring.

"There it is! I must be losing it. Whenever I used it last, I must have taken it off the ring and didn't put the key back where it was supposed to be." She unlocked the door and stepped back. "You two are all set to go. Come and see me, Jazz, when you're all done today and I'll come up and lock the door again."

Before Jazz could even agree, Eileen hurried back down the stairs.

"You or me first?" Jazz asked Eddie.

He shot the dogs a look. "Let me get up there and see how bad it is. Give me a few minutes. Then I'll . . ." He thought about it. "I'll tell you to come up and I'll wait at the side of the room by the old roof access door. How about that?"

It was a good plan. At least when it came to making sure Eddie and the dogs stayed far away from each other. The roof access door was nowhere near the stairway.

The fourth floor of St. Catherine's had once been the dormitory where the men in training to be priests lived. It was a vast, drafty space with a sloping ceiling and windows tucked into the small space between slanted roof and floor. There was only this one stairway leading up to or down from the room, so in addition to it being noncompliant when it came to safety regulations, the space was inconvenient, and it had never been used in the time St. Catherine's occupied the building.

It was unheated in the winter, not cooled in the summer, and good for pretty much nothing except that roof access door Eddie had mentioned, nailed shut for longer than Jazz had been alive, and another access door, also never used, that led to a labyrinth of pipes from the old steam heating system.

At the top of the stairs the room opened up left and right, and Jazz thought about the photos she'd seen from back when the seminary occupied the building. Fifteen beds on one side of the aisleway in the center of the room, and fifteen on the other. Thirty priests in training to the left of the doorway. Another thirty to the right.

Jazz couldn't contain a cynical smile.

These days, Eileen couldn't even convince a few girls to go to the chapel to hear a talk on religious vocations.

Philosophical thoughts aside, Jazz softened the edges of her smile and looked at Eddie. "Once you give me the go-ahead, I'll bring the dogs up and take them over to the other side of the room," she told him. "Then when you're finished, you can go down and you won't have to deal with them."

He ran his tongue over his lips. "Thanks, Jazz. But I dunno." He opened the door and they were met with a puff of stale air. "I don't think this is a good room for the girls to be using. It's got to be pretty dirty up there."

"Dirty or not, it's our only choice." She waited for Eddie to get a move on. "And the girls are going to be here in just a couple of minutes."

As messages went, it wasn't exactly subtle, but it still took a bit for it to sink in, and when it finally did Eddie clambered up the stairs and Jazz waited for his signal. It didn't come, not right away, and she caught herself tapping her foot. Eddie was sweeping, she reminded herself. He wanted the room to be as clean as possible before he called Jazz up. And she needed to chill. She still had plenty of time to hide her bait.

"It's okay now, Jazz!" he finally called to her, and she took the dogs up the stairs and found Eddie waiting a safe distance from the door. He'd already given the room one quick sweep. There were cleaned, curved tracks in the dust on the floor and Eddie had worked up a sweat. His shirt was untucked; there was a sheen of sweet on his forehead.

Jazz let him finish, crossing thirty feet or more of empty attic space to stay far out of his way, her shoes slapping against the hardwood floor. She tied the dogs' leads to a steam radiator not used for a hundred years, and once they were secured Eddie finished up. The small windows up there protested and refused to budge until he gave them a shove, and once they were open a stream of fresh air flowed into the room and Eddie scurried out of it, and Jazz hid the bait she'd brought along.

A tooth in an open container in the crook where wall and ceiling met at the far side of the room.

A metacarpal behind the radiator on the opposite side of the room from where the dogs waited.

Passing one of the windows, Jazz couldn't help but shiver, thinking about how cold it gets in Cleveland in the winter. "What do you think, guys?" she asked the dogs when she headed back their way, and they tilted their heads and listened as if they understood every word. "Two radiators in a room this size? It must have been like the Antarctic up here. I wonder if the priests fought over who got to sleep closest to the radiators."

Before she had a chance to consider it, she heard the first sounds of footsteps scrambling up the stairs.

Wally heard them, too, and hopped up on his back legs, eager for this next adventure, and Jazz waited for the first group of girls to arrive at the top of the steps.

These were seventh graders, the youngest girls in the school, and just about to step into the old dormitory the two girls leading the pack stopped and looked around, their eyes wide, their cheeks flushed.

Jazz was just about to tell them to get a move on when she realized what was going on.

There's nothing like a locked door and an unused room to spark rumors. Over the years, stories had emerged about the old dormitory. Jazz had heard girls whisper that it was haunted. Some of them even swore they'd heard footsteps up there. Then there was the urban legend about how a homeless

29

man snuck into the school every night and slept there. Jazz had even heard rumors about a cult that gathered in the old dormitory every month when the moon was full, sneaking in, she supposed, the same way that homeless man snuck in, though how either cult or homeless man outwitted St. Catherine's state-of-the-art security system no one ever bothered to explain.

"Lucky you, huh?" She smiled at the girls at the top of the steps. "None of the girls at St. Catherine's have ever been up here, not even the juniors or the seniors. You're getting to see something none of them ever have."

It was enough to put them at ease — at least these two, at least for now — and the two girls in the lead climbed the last step and into the dormitory, their gazes darting left and right, looking, no doubt, for ghosts and homeless men and cult members wearing long black robes with hoods.

Jazz waved them to a spot on the floor that looked at least relatively clean and had the rest of the girls and their homeroom teacher, Cissy Kaski, sit in a semicircle.

It didn't take long for the girls to catch sight of the dogs, and after that Jazz knew all thoughts of how spooky the space was flew out of their heads. They squealed with delight, and a couple times Cissy had to remind them to sit down.

There were twenty girls in the group, and once they settled, Jazz asked how many of them had dogs at home.

A few hands went up.

"And how many of you would like to have a dog?"

This time, a couple more hands were raised and one girl blurted out, "Puppies are so cute!"

Far be it from Jazz to argue with that. "But they're also a lot of work," she told the girls, and she went over and untied Wally's leash from the radiator.

He loved being the center of attention and the oohs and ahs from the girls only made him even more excited. Airedales have a way of prancing when they walk, a combination of runway strut and goofy clowning around.

When Jazz brought him to stand in front of the girls, the oohs and ahs intensified.

"Does anyone know what it takes to take care of a puppy?" she asked the girls.

"Picking up a lot of poop," one of them announced, and the rest of them groaned.

"And feeding them," another one put in.

"And cleaning up the floor!" one of them wailed because of course Wally picked that moment to pee.

Jazz had come prepared. She'd brought along a tote bag of supplies, and she pulled out paper towels, a plastic grocery bag, and a disinfectant wipe and cleaned up before she continued.

"There's training, too," she told the girls.

"Like the way you trained that dog that found that dead girl, right?" somebody asked, undeterred by a look from Cissy that told her it was a subject she wasn't supposed to bring up.

"We'll talk about that," Jazz promised. "And I'll show you how some of that training is done. But before a dog is ready to do that kind of work, it has to know basic commands. Even if you have a dog that isn't going to be a cadaver dog, you're going to want it to listen to you. Not just so you can show the dog who's boss, but so you can keep it safe. One of the first things you're going to teach it is to come."

She unhooked the lead from Wally's collar, signaled him to stay and was stunned when he actually did it, and took ten steps back, then opened her arms and called, "Wally, *come*!"

He did, and Jazz pulled a tiny dog biscuit from her pocket and gave it to him along with a whole bunch of praise.

"You see what I did there?" she asked the

girls. "I told him what I wanted him to do, and when he did it, I told him what a good boy he is."

"My dad yells and screams when our dog doesn't listen," someone in the back row said.

"It's only natural to get frustrated with a dog that doesn't obey." Jazz swallowed down what she would have liked to add, which was more in line with what a jerk the girl's dad must have been. "But you never want your dog to be afraid of you. And a dog . . ." She bent to scratch Wally's head. "All a dog wants is to make you happy. So you always have to be positive with a dog. You're always going to be upbeat. When it does what you want it to do, you give it a reward and a great big smile. Does anyone want to try it?"

A dozen hands shot up.

Jazz scanned the group. She knew one of the girls was particularly shy, and though her hand hadn't gone up, Jazz called on Bella Tamarin.

"Bella, would you like to give Wally a command?"

The girl's cheeks paled, but with some urging from the girl next to her, she pulled herself to her feet.

"Right here," Jazz told her, and stepped

33

aside so Bella could take her place while she re-hooked Wally's leash and walked him ten feet away. "Now look right at Wally, smile, and tell him what you want him to do."

Bella's voice was no more than a whisper. "*Come.*"

"A little louder," Jazz told her. "And make sure you smile."

Bella did. "Come, Wally!"

And when he did and he got the treat Jazz handed to Bella, the other girls applauded.

Red-faced, Bella sat down, and Cissy gave Jazz a thumbs-up.

"Besides *come,* you're going to want your dog to know how to sit and stay and lie down." Because Wally wasn't especially good at any of those things, Jazz didn't demonstrate. "And once your dog is good at obeying you, then you can train it to do other things. Some people like to do agility with their dogs. Anybody know what that is?"

"Running and jumping over stuff," one girl answered, and Jazz nodded.

"And some people train their dogs as therapy dogs. They visit people at hospitals and nursing homes and they offer comfort and companionship. And search and rescue dogs . . ." She couldn't help herself; Jazz's

34

voice choked over the words. Her dad had been, in her humble opinion, the best search and rescue dog trainer and handler on the planet. A firefighter, he'd died in an arson blaze a little more than a year earlier, and she missed him, especially when she was working dogs.

She cleared her throat. "Search and rescue dogs find people after disasters like a tornado or a flood. They alert first responders so they can get those people to safety. Then there are human remains detection dogs."

Jazz hooked Wally to the radiator and brought the other dog to stand in front of the girls. "This is Gus," she told them. "And Gus is retired now, but when he was working, he had a very important job. Gus helped find dead people."

She expected the "Ewwws" and twisted faces, so she didn't take it personally. "Why do you suppose that's important?" she asked the girls once they'd settled down.

Not one of them had an answer, but then, Jazz wasn't surprised. Death was something a lot of adults didn't even want to think about. She couldn't expect it from seventh graders.

Cissy stepped in. "Every life is precious. And when they lose a loved one, every family deserves closure. So if someone you knew went walking in the woods and never came back, wouldn't you want to find out what happened to them?"

"Or if somebody got murdered," one girl said. "Like that girl who went to school here and Ms. Ramsey found her."

"But murder isn't the norm," Jazz was quick to point out. "It's more likely that we're sent out to find someone who fell and got hurt out in the park and no one knows where to look for them. Or a person has a heart attack and never makes it home. So when something like that happens, the police call in volunteers like me, and the volunteers, we bring our dogs. Gus is one of those dogs, and once he's trained Wally will be, too."

She slipped Gus's red "service dog" vest on him and the dog stood at attention, his ears pricked and excitement vibrated through him. "Did you see that?" she asked the girls. "As soon as I put on his vest, Gus knew it was time to work. What Gus doesn't know is that I hid a couple things here in this room for him to find. A bone and a tooth."

She ignored another round of "Ewwws."

"So now I'm going to tell Gus what I want him to do. When the lady who trained him worked with him, she had certain words she said to Gus, and I'm going to use those words, too."

She unhooked the dog from his lead. "Gus" — Jazz swept a hand along her thigh — "find!"

The dog took off like a shot, crossing the room in a zigzag pattern, his nose going up to sniff the air, then down to the floor in the hopes of catching a scent. It took him less than a minute to locate the tooth on the other side of the room, sit down next to it, and bark three times. He waited there patiently and didn't touch a thing (Jazz prayed Wally was watching) until she went over and got the tooth.

The girls applauded, and Jazz rewarded Gus with a lot of praise and his favorite tug toy.

"What do you think?" Jazz asked them. "Think Gus can do it again?"

They agreed that they wanted to see him try, and with another command to *"Find,"* Jazz sent him on his way.

Jazz watched Gus sweep the room as he'd done the first time, all business, and getting closer and closer to the radiator on the other side of the room where she'd stashed the metacarpal.

And then he stopped.

Jazz stifled a groan. She was eager for the

girls to see how capable a cadaver dog was, and she didn't want Gus to blow it. She forced herself to keep her place, reminded herself that giving Gus a hint was as good as cheating.

Gus had his own ideas. He lifted his head, pulled in a scent only the sensitive nose of a dog could detect, and went straight to the access door for the old heating system, where he barked three times and sat right down.

"Is that where the bone is?" one of the girls asked.

Jazz managed a smile. "No, Gus is a little off. But he's pretty excited being here with all of you. Maybe we should try again."

She called him over.

Gus didn't budge.

How Jazz managed to keep smiling she wasn't sure. But then her blood was suddenly frozen and maybe her expression was, too. She took two steps in Gus's direction, then forced herself to stop and turn to the girls.

"Looks like he's just not feeling the magic anymore," she told them. "Which means our demonstration is over." She hoped the look she sent to Cissy told her she needed a little help, and it apparently worked. When their homeroom teacher stood up, the girls did, too.

"Wally and Gus are glad you were here to meet them." Was that Jazz's voice, too high and too tight? Another silent plea in Cissy's direction and the homeroom teacher went to the stairs and stepped back so the girls could start heading down.

What is it? Cissy mouthed the question.

Jazz shrugged. "Could you have Eileen come up?" she asked.

Cissy didn't question her, and one by one the girls filed down the steps, the sounds of their footsteps retreating along with the echoes of their voices.

It wasn't until they were gone that Jazz wiped her suddenly sweating palms against the legs of her pants and crossed the room to where Gus waited.

Not a squirrel.

Not a raccoon.

Not a dead rat.

Gus knew better than to signal on an animal.

Gus had been trained to detect only one scent.

Human death.

CHAPTER 3

"The dog could be wrong."

Eileen's voice was small and hushed. Her words settled in the dust at the corners of the attic room.

Jazz stared where Eileen was staring, at the closed access door that led into the maze of heating pipes, a door that hadn't been opened in years. She would have liked to agree with her boss, but she couldn't lie, and the realization sent a cold shiver up her back. "Gus is really good at what he does."

"But he's retired, right? Maybe he's a little rusty."

"Maybe." Jazz glanced at the dog sitting at her side patiently waiting for her to keep her end of the bargain. His eager look told her exactly what he was thinking — he'd followed the scent, just as she'd asked him to. He'd alerted her to it. Now it was her turn to come through.

Open the door.

Take a look.

To be sure she made a complete and accurate record, she dug her phone out of her pocket and took a picture of the closed door before she turned on the flashlight app. "If he's wrong, no one ever has to know," she told Eileen, and reached for the door.

Eileen clamped a hand on Jazz's arm. "And if he's right?"

Jazz did her best to swallow down the dread that made it feel as if her throat was filled with sand. She'd trained for this moment, with Manny and with other dogs from her HRD group. She knew the drill.

Except she never thought she'd have to use it inside the walls of St. Catherine's.

"If Gus is right . . ." She bobbled her phone and caught it up before it hit the floor. "I'll secure the scene, call the cops, stay here until they arrive. That's the procedure. If he's right . . ." She drew in a breath. "If he's right, I'll follow procedure."

Eileen squeezed her eyes shut for a minute and, when she opened them again, explained, "Praying. Hoping. It's got to be some kind of mistake."

There was only one way to find out.

Jazz grabbed the handle of the door and tugged.

It didn't budge.

"Well, that proves it." The words left Eileen on the end of a whoosh of relief. "That door hasn't been touched in years. There's no way there could be . . ." She swallowed hard. "No way anything . . . anybody . . . It's been so long, there's just no way . . ."

Eileen was looking for reassurance Jazz couldn't provide. "Properly trained HRD dogs have been used on archaeological sites. They've found the remains of graves in Roman hill forts that date back to —"

"Okay, okay, I get it." Eileen waved away the rest of the information with one trembling hand. "So what's inside there . . ." She slid a wary look at the closed door. "It could be very old."

"It's possible." And before she could convince herself otherwise, Jazz tried the door again.

It creaked, budged, flew open.

It was pitch-dark inside the room and Jazz slanted her light at the maze of pipes and the strings of rotted wiring that hung from the low ceiling like fat spiderwebs. She'd just about talked herself into the fact that Gus was, indeed, rusty and wrong to boot when her light flashed against something smooth and pale.

She leaned forward for a better look and

42

her breath caught and her heart bumped against her ribs.

A skull with strands of leathery, desiccated flesh hanging from it looked back at her from a mound of plastic wrapping, its eye sockets black and empty, its mouth gaping.

"He's not wrong," Jazz told Eileen, and when the principal stepped forward and saw what Jazz had discovered she let out a little whimper.

Jazz didn't have that luxury. A cadaver dog that's done his job and done it well deserves praise, and she turned away from the horror of the gaping skull so she could pat Gus and take a chew toy out of her back pocket, the one toy his owner said he loved above all else. "Good boy, Gus! You're a good, good boy."

She smiled when she said it and felt like a fool when she turned to Eileen and saw tears on the principal's cheeks. "I'm sorry. I've got to be upbeat. That's how Gus knows he's done a good job."

"You don't need to explain." Eileen sniffled. "You do what you need to do. I'll stay out of your way."

Jazz hooked the leash to Gus's collar and handed the leash to Eileen. "If you'll take him over with Wally, I'll make the proper call and make sure everything's secure."

Again she swept her light over the scene. She couldn't say she was used to death; she was pretty sure no one could be. But she'd seen it a time or two, and it didn't creep her out or disgust her. There was a certain stillness to it that always struck Jazz as profound, a quiet that hovered over it and around it. She wasn't afraid of death. She wasn't in awe of it. But she gave it its due and met its silence with her own.

Still, when the beam of her flashlight highlighted a scrap of orange-and-brown-plaid fabric beneath the plastic, she caught her breath. And when the light winked against something metallic, she couldn't help but gasp.

"What?" Eileen had just turned with Gus and she stopped and spun around. She had been calm enough, all things considered, sure enough that what Gus and Jazz had found were probably the remains of some long-dead Orthodox priest that had stayed hidden in all the years since St. Catherine's took over the seminary and all the years before that when the building was empty and silent. Now she picked up on the tremor of recognition that sent a cascade of goose bumps up Jazz's arms, and when she saw what Jazz saw she caught her breath.

It was a gold cross, maybe three inches

long, bigger than the ones people typically wore around their necks. The gold probably wasn't any more real than the jewels in each arm of the cross. A red ruby at the head. A blue sapphire at the feet. An emerald on the right. A diamond on the left.

It was ugly. Gaudy. Which had always struck Jazz as odd, because the woman who wore it every day was anything but.

The cross and the chain that held it hung loose around the skeleton's neck, tucked half in and half out of the plastic that contained the woman they both knew.

"Dear God!" Eileen clutched Jazz's arm with both her hands. "It's Bernadette Quinn!"

"And so what makes you think the deceased is this . . ." The detective who'd arrived in response to Jazz's phone call to the Cleveland police was a man she didn't know. He was middle-aged and middle-sized, with a receding hairline, a wide nose, and a square jaw that made him look like he had no sense of humor. He smelled like coffee and cigarettes and he chewed on the end of his pencil while he paged through his notebook for the information she'd given him only minutes before.

45

Jazz found herself wishing Nick was there instead.

Nick would be more efficient. And he'd certainly be better dressed. Nick would be cool and professional, but underneath it all, she knew Nick would care.

This man, Detective Gary Lindsey, was simply going through the motions.

"Bernadette Quinn," he said, and just hearing the name made Jazz flinch. "What makes you think it's her?"

"The clothes for one thing." The crime scene techs had already arrived and they were in the cramped attic access space with what was left of the body, blocking her view, but Jazz looked that way anyway, picturing all she'd seen before they arrived — the scraps of plastic that had been torn by small animals, the shredded pieces of flesh still clinging to the bones, the places where the animals had feasted and nothing was left but bone. "Bernadette was famous for white blouses and plaid skirts. And then there's the cross." She swallowed down the horror of the memory of the gaudy cross that seemed less sacred and more of an abomination wrapped in plastic and nestled in rotted flesh and bone. "Bernadette always wore that cross."

"And she's been missing how long?"

46

Detective Lindsey wanted to know.

The answer was better coming from Eileen so Jazz looked her way.

Eileen, always so self-assured, always so calm, had aged a decade since they made their discovery. There were deep creases at the corners of her mouth and her eyes were dull. But she was, after all, the powerhouse who made St. Catherine's tick and she knew she didn't have the luxury of giving in to the shock or the slap of grief that had overwhelmed both Jazz and Eileen while they waited for the police to arrive.

Eileen pulled back her shoulders and scrubbed her hands over her face. "She wasn't missing," she told the detective. "Not as far as we knew, anyway. Bernadette taught here for one term and she resigned a little more than three years ago."

"Right after Christmas," Jazz added. "That's when we received her resignation letter. It was in the mail when we got back from break."

"And you didn't think that was odd?" the detective wanted to know.

"There was a lot about Bernadette that was odd." Jazz felt guilty the moment the words were out of her mouth.

"She had the potential to be a really good teacher," Eileen admitted. "She was willing to try new classroom techniques and she wanted so badly for the girls to be involved in their learning experiences. Exactly the kind of professional we look for here at St. Catherine's. Unfortunately, students don't often appreciate that teaching is a special talent. And it was Bernadette's first year on the job. She had some problems adjusting."

One of Detective Lindsey's eyebrows slanted. "Problems?"

"Classroom discipline wasn't her strong suit," Eileen said, and it wasn't Jazz's place to contradict her. Not in front of Detective Lindsey. Discipline was a challenge for Bernadette, but it was the least of her problems. "As good as she was in the classroom, she had a difficult time connecting to the girls when she wasn't actually teaching. She prepared up one side and down the other for each and every class. She had that kind of commitment. But when she had to talk to the girls or their parents without a prepared lesson plan in front of her, well, she was uneasy and tongue-tied. She didn't relate well to our students, and they . . ." Eileen drew in a long breath and let it out slowly. "They had a hard time relating to her."

"And we got a postcard from her!" The memory popped into Jazz's head and she blurted out the information. "After she was gone, she sent us a postcard. Maybe . . ." She looked to Eileen for confirmation. "Six months? Nine months after we received the resignation letter? Bernadette sent a postcard from Florida, said she was visiting friends, that she was fine. Only . . ." Jazz couldn't help herself. Again she glanced at the access door and at the techs who worked there, their backs bent and their heads ducked. She heard the crinkle when they rolled back the plastic that covered what was left of the body. "Only it looks like she wasn't fine, doesn't it?"

"You still have it?" the detective wanted to know.

"The postcard?" Jazz really didn't have to think about it, but she pretended to just to give herself a moment to let her heartbeat slow and the whooshing of the blood in her ears settle. "I tossed it," she admitted. "There was no reason not to. But her resignation letter would still be in her file."

"I'll need it."

"Of course," Eileen told him.

"And a list of everyone who has access to this room."

"There hasn't been anyone up here in years," the principal told him. "As you can see, the space is inconvenient."

"But you're here today, why?"

"The dogs." Even though Wally and Gus were already gone, Jazz looked toward the radiator where they'd been tied. She'd called the police first, Margaret Carlson right after that, and Margaret had come for the dogs. Jazz imagined that by now Wally was ensconced on Margaret's couch — just as Gus always was when Jazz stopped in — chomping bits of raw carrot. She only hoped Wally didn't get any ideas about dogs on furniture and try it at home.

She shook away the thought and got back down to business. "I was giving a demonstration," she explained to the detective, "about human remains detection dogs and —"

"I dunno. Yeah, I've seen those cadaver dogs work and their handlers make it look pretty impressive. But I'm saying they've got what . . . a fifty-fifty chance of finding a body? Heck, I could do better than that with a good search team." He emphasized his opinion with a snort.

It was the wrong time to get offended, but as soon as the words were out of his mouth Jazz felt a prickle of annoyance. She lifted her chin. "Gus found the body."

"Why didn't somebody find it before now?" Lindsey turned and paced as far as where the ceiling sloped and he was too tall to stand. "She must have created quite a smell."

It wasn't a detail Eileen needed to think about, so Jazz jumped right in. "The space isn't heated in the winter and if she disappeared right after we saw her last, right when we broke for Christmas vacation —"

"Then how did she write that resignation letter? Or the postcard?" the detective asked.

She was tempted to remind him that he was the detective and it was his job to figure it out. If Nick was there, it's exactly what she would have told him. Then again, if Nick was there, he never would have asked anything that stupid.

"If Bernadette was in the building any time after she sent the resignation letter," she told Lindsey, "someone would have seen her. We have a security system and teachers and staff need to swipe their cards to get in and out. I'd say the answer is pretty obvious. Bernadette didn't write that letter. She didn't send the postcard, either."

"You think whoever killed her did." Lindsey made a note of this, looking up at her from beneath his bushy eyebrows when he was done. "Makes me wonder how you know so much about it."

"I don't know anything about it." Jazz felt

51

like throwing her hands in the air, a commentary on the man's logic, his reasoning, and his people skills. She controlled herself because she knew that was exactly what he was waiting for and she wasn't about to give him the satisfaction. "I'm just guessing, that's all. Just thinking that's what makes sense."

"Like that dog finding the body."

"That makes plenty of sense. Gus is well trained and he's certified. He's got a great nose."

"But if you knew where the body was to begin with —"

"Really?" This time, she didn't care what Detective Lindsey thought of her or her reaction. The single word flew out of Jazz along with a snicker of disbelief. "I killed Bernadette three years ago and kept her body hidden all this time just so I could use a dog to find it and impress a bunch of seventh graders today? Doesn't make much sense, does it?"

"Murder usually doesn't," Lindsey said.

Jazz begged to differ. From what she'd seen of murder, it made plenty of sense, at least to the murderer. This . . .

She looked around at the unused attic space, at the access room where Bernadette had remained hidden for so long. It made sense, all right. Perfect sense. So did the resignation letter that explained Bernadette's absence after break and the postcard that pretty much guaranteed she and Eileen wouldn't try to contact Bernadette. Wrapped in plastic, frozen, forgotten, decomposing in a place where no one would notice the smell or the scurrying of the small rodents that had obviously found Bernadette early on.

It made sense, all right.

Except for the part about how Jazz could have had anything to do with it.

Before Jazz could remind him, Eileen stepped forward. "I know you have questions to ask both of us. Maybe we should start with that resignation letter Jazz told you about. It would be in Jazz's office, in the personnel files."

"Yeah, that's good." Lindsey tucked his notebook in the breast pocket of the black sport coat that didn't match his navy-blue pants. "There's nothing else we can do here." He led the way back to the stairway and waited for Eileen to go down ahead of him, and Jazz brought up the rear. "So tell me, Sister, you know everyone here at this school. Tell me, who could have had a reason to kill this Bernadette Quinn?"

At the bottom of the stairs, Eileen waited

53

for him and for Jazz to step out in the hallway, too, before she twined her fingers together in front of her and set her mouth in a firm line.

"Well," she told him, "me for one."

CHAPTER 4

Detective Lindsey got a phone call just as they were all about to walk into Jazz's office and he took it out in the hallway.

That was just fine with Jazz; it gave her a chance to sidle up to Eileen and hiss, "Are you crazy? You can't say things like that to a cop. You had a reason to kill Bernadette? What's he going to think?"

Eileen brushed her off and went into her own office, where she kicked off the pumps she'd put on in honor of Assembly Day and slid back into her TOMS. By the time she got back, she looked more like herself. More comfortable. More in control. "If he didn't hear it from me, he was going to hear it from someone else," she told Jazz. "That would make me look even more suspicious."

"You're not suspicious at all." Jazz didn't want it, but she poured a cup of coffee for herself from the to-go container the caterers had brought at the start of the day. It seemed like a million years ago. While she was at it, she poured a cup for Eileen, too, added cream and sugar, and handed it to her. "Anybody who thinks you could kill someone would have to be totally nuts."

"You've got to admit . . ." Eileen took a healthy glug of the coffee. "There were days there at the end of the term when Bernadette gave us all reason."

"You don't say." Detective Lindsey stepped into Jazz's office. If he was impressed by the leaded glass, the high ceiling, or the rich oak flooring, he didn't show it. In fact, he settled his weight back against one foot, and when he crossed his arms over his broad chest, the plastic bag he was holding crinkled.

"She was going through a hard time," Jazz told him, eager to back up Eileen's assessment. Just as eager to — Jazz hoped — get Lindsey's mind off what he'd just heard — she crossed over to the filing cabinets, unlocked the proper one, and took out Bernadette's file. Page by page, she made copies of everything in it, but when she got to the resignation letter — the last thing in Bernadette's file — she knew better than to touch it. She glanced over it and the words that had seemed so normal, so mundane.

"It is with the greatest regret that I inform

you that as of today . . ."

Rather than go on, Jazz looked over her shoulder at Lindsey, pointed.

He set down the evidence bag he was carrying on Jazz's desk, and from inside it Bernadette's big gold cross caught the light and winked at Jazz. All that was left of Bernadette. Cross and bones.

Jazz's heart clutched, but before she had a chance to give in to the sadness that wrapped around her like a dark cloud, Lindsey closed in on her, slipped on a pair of latex gloves, and dropped the resignation letter into another evidence bag.

"Fingerprints," he explained. He really didn't have to. Jazz had seen enough cops shows on TV. She knew the drill.

Jazz glanced at the other evidence bag, the one he'd set on her desk. "What about fingerprints on Bernadette's cross?"

"If we're lucky," he conceded. "Now, you were saying . . . ? About Ms. Quinn being difficult?"

Jazz knew she'd get nothing else from him. Not about the cross. Not about anything else they might have found up in the attic. "I was saying that Bernadette was good at what she did. When she was in front of a class, she was really on, if you know what I mean. But it was her first year teaching and

57

she still had a lot to learn about working with the staff and the other teachers, about keeping that connection going with the girls even when class wasn't in session. She didn't think that was a problem. Maybe that's why it was so frustrating dealing with her."

The detective turned a look on Eileen. "So that's what you meant when you said you could have killed her?"

"I didn't say I could have killed her," she reminded him, her voice as even as the look she gave him. "I did say if I was a different sort of person, I might have had reason. The last day Bernadette was here . . ." She considered her words. "We had an argument. About how the school was trying to help Bernadette adjust and Bernadette didn't think she needed help. Our *talk* . . ." She put a spin on the word that should have told Lindsey exactly how ugly it got. "It was loud and it was long. Maybe if I'd been more patient . . . Maybe if I'd been more understanding . . ."

Jazz hated the tremor of remorse that vibrated through Eileen's words. "It's not like Bernadette got upset about the argument and committed suicide."

At which Detective Lindsey gave her a look.

Jazz stopped herself just short of clicking her tongue. "She didn't kill herself, then wrap herself in plastic and stuff herself up there in the attic," she told him, although he surely already knew that and was just waiting to gauge her reaction.

Now that she'd given it to him — full-blown and packed with outrage — she turned back to her boss. "You have nothing to feel guilty about," she told Eileen.

"But you did say you had a reason to kill Ms. Quinn," Lindsey put in.

"No one who knows Sister Eileen would ever believe she could do such a thing," Jazz said, adding the *Sister* designation she hardly ever used when speaking about the principal because she figured it wouldn't hurt to remind this man that Eileen was religious, devoted, dedicated.

"And someone who does not know you well?" he asked the nun.

A spurt of anger coursing through her veins at the same time her sense of justice demanded they clear up this craziness right there and then, Jazz stepped forward. "Bernadette was committed to her work. Sometimes too committed. She could be stubborn. Sister Eileen tried to reason with her. She tried to work with her."

"We all did," Eileen added.

"And Ms. Quinn, how did she respond? Like she didn't hear you?"

"Oh, no. She heard us, all right," Eileen told him. "She just made it clear that we were wrong and she was right. That's why . . ." The realization still stung. Jazz knew that. There was nothing Eileen liked less than failure. "We finally had no choice. We . . . the board and I . . . we decided to put her on probation. She had until Easter to turn herself and her attitude around."

"And if she didn't, she was out the door?"

"We offered her another job," Jazz said. "We created a position, assistant in the library."

"And how did Ms. Quinn feel about that?"

Eileen inched back her shoulders. "She said her life was all about teaching. She threatened to sue."

The detective considered this. "Which is why you said you could have killed her."

More than one girl at St. Catherine's had been on the wrong end of the look Eileen shot at Detective Lindsey. "A lawsuit would have been . . . difficult. At the time we were in the middle of adding to the back of the school. A botany lab and other classrooms. The money was earmarked and we couldn't afford to lose it."

"So Ms. Quinn disappearing, that was sort

of a good thing."

Jazz hoped the one-sided sneer she sent in Lindsey's direction sent a clear message. "We thought she'd come to her senses. That she'd lighten up and relax. She never did. That's why no one was surprised when she resigned," Jazz put in. "Well, when we thought she resigned."

Lindsey sucked on the end of his pencil, thinking this over. "You expected her to be what . . . obedient?"

He couldn't have known it, but with that single question, Detective Lindsey had pushed one of Eileen's hot buttons.

An obedient teacher? Robot students? The notion was so far from Eileen's way of thinking, she actually had to stop for a minute and consider the question. When she finally digested it, she leveled her shoulders.

"I expected her to be professional. It's exactly what I expect of all my staff."

"And she was . . ." He waited for Eileen's answer.

Jazz knew Eileen well enough to know she nearly sighed. She also knew Eileen would consider that a sign of weakness. Now that they were removed from the horror on the fourth floor, now that she was in her TOMS and back in command, there was no way

61

Eileen would reveal that much of herself. Not to a stranger. "She was determined that every girl in her class would live up to impossible standards. I'm not just talking about good grades and homework assignments that were turned in on time. Of course we expect that of all our girls, and if they can't deliver, we work with them so their grades and their habits and their attitudes improve. But Bernadette . . ." Eileen chose her words wisely. "She wanted to make sure the girls stayed on the straight and narrow in their personal lives, too. She asked them too many questions about dating and boyfriends and —"

"She cared." Lindsey dared the comment.

"If that was all it was, I wouldn't have objected. But she offered advice, and most of the advice went along the lines of how the girls shouldn't date, how they should break up with the guys they were seeing."

"A man-hater, huh?"

"It wasn't so much hate as it was . . ." Jazz searched for the right word. "I think it was more of a distrust."

"Not a good attitude for young women to have. Not across the board," Eileen added. "Ms. Quinn was a teacher, not Dear Abby. Some of the girls thought she was sticking her nose where it didn't belong. Many of their parents agreed. It's one thing to have high standards for yourself. It's another when you think other people need to live up to them, too."

Eileen took another drink of coffee. "Not that we don't think high standards are important. One of the things we hope our students take away from St. Catherine's is the ability to think and make decisions based on logical input. Every girl here knows we have a code of ethics and a certain . . . let's call it maturity . . . that we expect of our young women. But Bernadette taught eighth grade, and eighth graders are . . . well, they wouldn't like to hear me say it, but eighth graders are still little girls. We like to ease them into their roles as students and as young women and we all work hard to provide them the proper example. We don't expect them to be perfect. None of us are. Unfortunately, Bernadette had a hard time understanding that. Her expectations could sometimes be too high. She wanted them to sit a certain way, and walk a certain way, and think a certain way."

"So she made enemies," Lindsey said.

"*Enemies* is a strong word." As long as she was holding a cup of coffee and had no intention of drinking it, Jazz offered it to

Detective Lindsey, and he took it and swallowed it down, hot and black, and while he was doing that, she tried to explain what she thought he'd need to know in terms of his investigation. "Some of the teachers were jealous of Bernadette's talents. She made teaching look easy and we all know it isn't. Some of the parents thought Bernadette demanded too much from their kids when it came to homework and special projects, but to Bernadette, that's what learning was all about. Some of the girls . . ." It was something Jazz had thought was behind them and she hated bringing it up. "The girls thought Bernadette was too strict. Some of them weren't very nice to Bernadette."

Lindsey brightened at the thought and pulled out his notebook. "So . . . student enemies."

"Little girls," Eileen reminded him at the same time Jazz's phone rang.

She answered it with her usual "St. Catherine's," but caught her breath when the caller identified herself as a reporter from a local TV station. She should have expected the media frenzy; she just hadn't had the time to think about it.

"We have no comment at this time," Jazz told the reporter, and looked at Eileen to make sure that was the right thing to say.

The principal nodded and Jazz hung up.

Detective Lindsey tapped his pencil against his notebook. "You're going to need to talk to the press sooner or later," he said. "And I'm going to have to talk to them, too."

"I'd appreciate it if you waited until we've spoken with our board members," Eileen told him. "We need to —"

"Get your story straight?" he wanted to know.

Eileen's lips pinched and Jazz held her breath. If ever there was a time for Eileen to bring out of the big guns of her intellect and her outrage and her iron will, this was it.

Instead, the principal smiled, her voice as smooth as melted butter, but her look stony. "I'm sure you understand, Detective, that we need to let our girls know what's going on before we release any information to the media. Jazz . . ." She looked her way. "If you could start making those calls to the board now, we'll have a statement prepared for the girls before the end of the day. Then, Detective . . ." She swung back his way. "You can tell the media anything you like. I'm hoping that will include the fact that you're conducting an expedient investigation and are expecting a quick wrap-up and the arrest of whoever did this terrible thing."

He was a middle-aged man.

He was an officer of the law.

Under Eileen's withering look, he turned into a seventh grader.

"Yes, ma'am, I am certainly going to do my best," he told her, and he backed out of the office.

Jazz didn't even realize she was holding her breath through their entire encounter with the detective. Not until it gushed out of her and her spine accordioned and her shoulders sagged.

"No time for that now." Eileen gave her a pat on the shoulder. "You make the phone calls; I'll start working on that statement. If any of the board members want to be here for the news conference —"

Jazz's head had been spinning since they made the discovery on the fourth floor, but she thought she would have remembered. "News conference? When did we schedule —"

"We didn't. Not yet. But of course there will be a news conference," Eileen said.

"And what will we tell the media?" Jazz wanted to know.

Eileen settled her mouth into a thin line. "Exactly what they want to hear. Bernadette was brilliant and dedicated."

"True," Jazz conceded.

"She loved being a teacher. She did her best every single day. We are shocked and we are saddened and we will have counseling available to the girls. We offer our sympathies to her friends and to her family."

"Do you think she had any friends?" Jazz asked.

Eileen didn't have an answer. She steepled her fingers and tapped her nose. "I think we have to be careful. I don't want to keep anything from the police that might help with their investigation, but St. Catherine's has a reputation and we can't let this turn into a sideshow. I'd rather manage our side of the story than handle damage control." She checked the time on the computer on Jazz's desk. "The girls will switch classrooms in another fifteen minutes. As soon as they do, let's leave them with our guests and have all the teachers in here for a quick meeting. They need to know what's going on."

"And you'll tell them not to talk to the media?"

"I can't tell them what to do," Eileen admitted. "But I can make the suggestion."

"They don't all know. Not the whole story."

"No, but enough of them know bits and pieces and it wouldn't take a smart reporter too long to put two and two together."

"What about Maddie?"

Eileen considered the question, but only for a moment. "There's nothing to tell. Bernadette was a teacher; Maddie was one of her students. No way anyone should glom onto that, but even if they do, it's all they need to know."

"So we're not going to tell them the truth?"

"Oh, we're going to tell them the truth, all right," Eileen said. "But not the whole truth. Not unless we absolutely have to."

Jazz made the phone calls and five out of the six board members said they were jumping right into their cars and heading to St. Catherine's to offer their support. The sixth board member was out of town, but when she spoke to him he told Jazz to let Eileen know he'd be back first thing in the morning and would talk to her before then.

That done, Jazz took care of getting all the teachers into her office during the next period and Eileen delivered the news.

Their shock dulled into grief and their grief morphed into grim expressions and shared hugs, and some of the more sensitive teachers cried, even though they hadn't known Bernadette well. Eileen explained about scheduling a news conference, read a copy of the statement she'd written up for the media, and told the assembled teaching staff — much to their relief — they would be spared telling their students the news. At the next break, all the girls would be ushered into the gym and Eileen would make the announcement herself. There would be a short prayer service, a moment of silence, a chance for the girls to ask questions. While all that was going on, Jazz would trigger the school's emergency notification system and each girl's parents would get a call along with a recorded message about Bernadette's death and the promise of updates as they became available.

It took Jazz two tries to record the statement without sounding either too dramatic or too uncaring, but she made herself do it, finally, because she knew Eileen was counting on her to be the face (or at least the voice) of St. Catherine's in this instance and it was a duty she took seriously.

Finished, she sat back, wondering what was going on in the gym and glad she wasn't there to witness it. In her experience, there was nothing more devastating than young people coming to grips with death, especially when it was the death of someone they knew. As she knew from the recent death of a former student, as she certainly learned when her dad died, the aftershock of today's news would continue to rock their worlds. She also knew that over the next weeks, she'd be asked plenty of questions and have plenty of opportunities to talk to the girls, listen to their concerns, try to allay their fears.

Someone had been killed in their school.

At least that's the way it looked, and Jazz couldn't imagine Bernadette's death had happened any other way. If she'd been killed outside, off campus, it didn't make any sense for her body to be brought back to St. Catherine's, swaddled in plastic, hidden.

No, she had died here.

The realization froze Jazz to the core.

An atrocity had occurred inside the walls of their school. A life had been snuffed out.

They would all — teachers and students, administrators and staff — need to come to grips with the reality.

They would all need to learn to deal.

Jazz was jarred out of the thought by the sound of something falling in the hallway outside her office door.

She jumped, sucked in a breath, pressed a hand to her heart.

All the girls and their teachers were in the gym. All their guest speakers had agreed that, of course, they'd stay around and join the school for prayer and contemplation.

So who was hanging around in the hallway?

Jazz got up from her desk, but by the time she got to the hallway the only sign of life there was another door down the hallway, just swinging shut.

At the same time she reminded herself she was being too jumpy — and that the girls of St. Catherine's deserved more from their administration than frazzled nerves and imaginations that could all too easily run wild — she went back to her desk and sat down to wait for the board to arrive.

They would all need to try to find some peace.

The words settled somewhere between her heart and her stomach, in a place that was still icy.

Peace.

Jazz drummed her fingers on her desk and listened to the echo of the sound fly back at her from the high ceiling.

Peace was something they had never had much of when Bernadette Quinn taught at St. Catherine's.

CHAPTER 5

Fall, three years earlier

"What is it? What's wrong?" Jazz was carrying an armload of T-shirts to the gym to hand out to the cross-country team, and she set them down next to the lost-and-found basket on the table outside the office. It was Thursday and just the third week of the school year and already the basket overflowed with glasses, pencils, hats. She hurried down the hallway and closed in on Bernadette Quinn where she stood outside her classroom door weeping so hard, her chest heaved and the big gold cross she wore that day with a white cotton blouse and an ankle-brushing plaid skirt wobbled up and down, winking at Jazz in the early-morning light. "Are you all right?"

"I'm . . ." Bernadette was older than Jazz and taller than Jazz's five-feet-two. She was heavier than Jazz by at least forty pounds and she had shoulder-length hair darker

72

than Jazz's medium brown and a face that was pudgy and, some people would say, still cute. Her nose was turned up slightly at the end. Her lips — always free of lipstick — were bowed. Her eyes were dark and intense. Right then, they were also swollen and red. "I'm f-f-fine," she stammered.

"You don't look fine. Why don't we . . ." Jazz hooked a hand around Bernadette's arm. "I've got coffee brewing in my office. Would you like a cup?"

Bernadette hiccupped. "Coffee is . . ." She sniffled. "That would be . . ." She gulped. "I . . . I can't. The bell is going to ring and I wouldn't want to not be in my classroom when my girls show up."

"We've got forty minutes until the first bell rings. And your classroom isn't going anywhere, and neither are your girls." Jazz tugged Bernadette into her office and deposited her in the guest chair in front of her desk. "How do you take your coffee?"

"Just milk," Bernadette said, and Jazz breathed a sigh of relief at having corralled her, at having distracted her. Jazz may have only worked at St. Catherine's for a year, but she knew beyond a doubt that the first month of the school year was not the time to let the girls see a teacher in total meltdown. Especially not a first-year teacher.

The girls of St. Catherine's were generally well behaved and sweet, but girls were girls. Jazz remembered her own school days. Any sign of weakness from anyone in authority was the equivalent of an open invitation to attack.

Jazz poured the coffee, added a dollop of milk, and delivered it to Bernadette.

"Want to tell me what's going on?" she asked.

Bernadette's gaze shot to Eileen's closed office door.

"Sister Eileen isn't here today," Jazz told her. "She's got a meeting with the board off-site. You worried she'll find out what you're upset about?"

Bernadette wiped a tear from her cheek. "I think she's a kind woman."

"She is."

"But I know there are rules."

Jazz sat back against her desk. "Rules about . . . ?"

When Bernadette sighed, the red stone above Jesus's head on her cross winked at Jazz.

Bernadette set her coffee cup on Jazz's desk, the better to grasp her hands together on her lap, her fingers tight, her knuckles as pale as skeleton fingers. "I saw him when I was coming in this morning," she said.

74

"Over by the garden shed."

"And he's . . . ?"

"A kitty. A little gray and white kitty. I've named him Titus. Titus, he was a companion of Paul the apostle, you know."

Jazz took Bernadette's word for it.

"And Titus . . ." Bernadette's chest rose and fell. "I think there's something wrong with him, Jazz. When I saw him, when I went over to check on him, he barely moved, the poor thing. He's awfully skinny, too. Do you suppose he belongs to anyone?"

This early in the school year, Jazz didn't know Bernadette well. They'd met at new-teacher orientation. They'd sat next to each other for lunch the first day all the teachers gathered at St. Catherine's to talk about their plans and their hopes for the new school year. They'd passed each other in the hallway any number of times, and every time Jazz was struck by how quiet Berna-dette was, how shy. Jazz had dared to ask Eileen about her decision to hire Bernadette and she wasn't surprised when she got a lecture — delivered politely, of course, but clearly meant as a lesson for Jazz — that Bernadette was sincere, and Bernadette was intelligent, and Bernadette had real poten-tial. Of course Eileen had hired her. Berna-dette would be a brilliant teacher someday, and Eileen believed everyone needed the chance to prove themselves.

For all Jazz knew, that's why Eileen had hired her, too.

The thought was enough to make Jazz tread carefully, but it didn't make her any less down-to-earth. She made sure she offered Bernadette a soft smile, but she told her, "There are a lot of feral cats in the neighborhood."

Bernadette nodded. "But Titus, he's different. He seems so . . ." Her shoulders rose and fell to the tempo of her rough breathing. "He's so lonely."

Far be it from Jazz to dispute the impressions of a fellow animal lover. Still, if Bernadette went to pieces about every homeless animal she encountered in their urban neighborhood, it was going to be a long year.

"The Animal Protective League has a shelter not far away," she told Bernadette. "We could get Titus and —"

"Oh, no! He'd be so unhappy there." Bernadette sucked in her bottom lip. "I thought . . ." Again her gaze darted in the direction of the principal's closed door. "If I gathered up some old blankets . . . if I got him something to eat and kept him warm and found a box where he could sleep behind my desk . . . I could watch out for

76

him. And then Titus would get better."

With Eileen gone for the day, Jazz was in charge, and she was okay with that. She was smart, and she was savvy, and she was prepared to handle whatever administrative situations came her way.

She was not ready to handle kitties. Or teachers in kitty crisis.

Jazz cleared her throat. "You can't bring the cat into the building," she told Bernadette.

"But —"

"Like you said, there are rules. And there's the health department, and the diocesan office, and I'm sure we have students with allergies."

Bernadette sniffled. "Titus is so frail and cold."

"He's not cold." Jazz didn't mean to snap, but really, there was only so much she could take. Like most schools in the area, St. Catherine's year began in August. It wasn't even Labor Day and it was still summer hot. That day, the air sizzled and even the old men who played in the Thursday-morning bocce league in the park across the street and usually showed up early to sit and talk and drink their coffee were nowhere to be seen.

She bit back her impatience and added,

"But I bet he is hungry. How about . . ." She leaned way back so she could see her computer screen and check the time. "How about you finish your coffee, then go get cleaned up and get into your classroom. I'll shoot down to the cafeteria and get some food for Titus. And I bet Loretta has some old towels we can use as bedding, too."

"But where —"

Jazz expected the question. She hopped off the desk and ducked into Eileen's office long enough to find the ring of keys Eileen kept in the top drawer of her desk. Most of the school's doors had electronic keypad locks on them. But there were a few other doors — doors to places long unused — that weren't worth re-keying. When Jazz walked back into her office, the keys that jangled in her hand were big and heavy, as old as the building itself.

She flipped up the first one for Bernadette to see. "I'll open up the garden shed for Titus. How about that?"

Bernadette's smile didn't last long. "But how will he get out when he needs to?"

Since Jazz didn't have the answer, she scrambled. "I'll ask Frank in Maintenance what he suggests. Of course once Titus is better, we're not going to be able to keep him around," she told Bernadette in no uncertain terms. "A little food, a little water . . . he's better off staying here for now because there are more of us to keep an eye on him, but when he's feeling better, maybe you'd like to take him home?"

"Yes, yes of course!" Bernadette bounded to her feet. "In the meantime, I'll have the girls pray for him. That will work. That will surely work." She finished the last of her coffee and headed to the door and it wasn't until she got there that she turned to Jazz, her expression joyful.

"You're very kind, Jazz," she said. "I'll tell the angels. They'll be so pleased."

When she passed Bernadette's classroom door the next day, Jazz heard Bernadette telling her students about Titus, leading them in prayer to Saint Francis of Assisi, the patron saint of animals.

And Titus?

Jazz looked in on him throughout the day, and since she lived close by, she walked Manny over on the weekend, brought the cat food and treats, and checked out the ingenious temporary cat door Frank had rigged.

But Titus, she was sure, was on his last legs.

Malnourished, flea-bitten, jittery. Thanks

to her dad's work with search and rescue dogs and Jazz's own training with cadaver dogs, she knew enough about basic animal first aid to know not even a trip to the vet was going to make Titus well. She decided that on Monday after school she'd take Titus in and she had no doubt the vet would put him down. She couldn't stand the thought of the cat being in pain.

How would she tell Bernadette?

Jazz wasn't sure, but she was confident she'd think of something.

As it turned out, she didn't have to. She arrived at school that Monday morning to find Bernadette already there, standing outside the office waiting for Jazz, dancing from foot to foot, wreathed in smiles.

Jazz poked her security code into the keypad outside the office door. "What's up?" she asked Bernadette.

"Nothing short of a miracle!" Bernadette beamed. "He's better, Jazz. Titus is much, much better this morning."

He wasn't better the evening before when Jazz brought over a can of tuna that Titus ignored.

"That's . . ." She shoved open the office door and went inside to turn on the lights and deposit her purse. "That's terrific," she told Bernadette. "But last night, he wasn't well at all. How —"

"There's no mystery there!" Bernadette's sallow cheeks flushed. "It's a miracle, of course. Saint Francis heard us. We received a miracle! Oh, the girls will be so happy. And I'm happy, too. Not just because Titus is well, but because this will show the girls the power of prayer. What a wonderful lesson!" She clapped her hands with excitement and then kept them in front of her chest, palms together in a prayerful pose. "Thank the Lord!"

It wasn't that Jazz wasn't happy to hear of Titus's recovery. And it wasn't like she didn't believe Bernadette's assessment of the cat. But if there was one thing she'd learned about herself in the time she'd worked with Manny in human remains detection, it was that seeing was believing.

As soon as she was able to get away that morning, she ducked out to the garden shed at the back corner of the school's parking lot.

And there she found exactly what Bernadette had promised.

The gray and white kitty was better — healthier, fatter, livelier.

There was only one problem.

The healthy happy kitty in the shed was a female.

It wasn't Titus at all.

Jazz spent all that day trying to decide what to say to Bernadette.

It wasn't easy.

When she listened in at the doorway on Bernadette's first-period class, she heard the prayer of gratitude Bernadette led the girls in saying and the heartfelt talk she gave them about the power of positive thinking, and the joy of giving troubles over to the Lord, and the wonderful, undeniable fact that God was listening. When she stopped by the classroom again during Bernadette's lunch period, hoping to catch her at her desk where she routinely ate the brown-bag lunch she brought from home, Jazz found a note saying Bernadette was up in the chapel, giving thanks. When she ran into Bernadette just after the final bell rang and saw the smile on Bernadette's face and the bag of cat treats in her hand, she realized she didn't have the words — or the heart — to disappoint her.

"I know about the cat." While Jazz stood watching Bernadette practically skip down the hallway toward the door that led into the back parking lot, Eileen had come up behind her, and when Jazz turned she saw the principal looking where she was looking.

"Of course you do." Jazz wasn't the least bit surprised.

"That's because I'm way nosier than anyone realizes."

Jazz smiled at her boss. "Good to know."

"Don't spread it around," Eileen told her. "People have this mistaken impression that nuns are all Zen about everyday things. They think I'm in my own little world when I'm actually just keeping quiet so I can listen and find out what everyone else is up to. You . . ." She led the way back into the office. "You are exhibit number one — you brought cans of cat food to work with you today."

There was a grocery bag next to Jazz's desk and the cans were inside it, visible to anyone who bothered to look. Because there was always a need at the Animal Protective League, she had planned to donate the food when she went to have Titus put down that afternoon.

"You got me there," Jazz admitted. "But how did you know Bernadette had anything to do with it?"

"She's been praying. Even more than usual. And now she's smiling. And I've seen her out by the garden shed during her

83

breaks. You think I didn't check?"

Jazz laughed. "I would have been disappointed if you didn't."

"I actually don't mind if the cat stays around," Eileen said. "But it could get tricky during pickups and drop-offs. Too many cars and drivers aren't on the lookout for a cat." She drifted into her office. "Maybe we could make sure the shed stays locked early and late. Hey, and while we're at it, he could always be the school mascot."

"Except he isn't he," Jazz informed Eileen.

"I thought his name was Titus."

Jazz made a mental note — it wasn't just a story; Eileen really did know everything that happened at St. Catherine's.

"The name of the cat out in the shed all weekend was Titus," she told Eileen. "But the cat out in the shed now isn't Titus. They have the same coloring. And they're about the same size. But the cat outside now is a female."

"And Titus was —"

"Definitely male."

One corner of Eileen's mouth pulled tight. "What do you suppose it means?"

"I've been wondering the same thing." In keeping with her job, Eileen's office was larger and grander than Jazz's. Jazz sat down in one of the wing chairs in a seating group near the door and Eileen took the chair opposite hers.

"You don't suppose Bernadette switched the cats, do you?" Eileen asked.

Jazz had considered it. "If she wanted to show the girls the power of prayer, I guess she might have done that. But she's awfully happy about the whole thing. Like she really believes."

"Oh, yes, she really believes." Eileen's sigh rippled the air. "Maybe that's part of the problem."

It wasn't something Jazz thought she'd ever hear from a nun, and Eileen knew it because she laughed. "A lot of people think nuns are praying machines," she said. "They think our heads are always filled with sacred thoughts, our hands are always busy over our rosary beads."

"You wouldn't get much done if that were true."

"Exactly." Eileen nodded. "Bernadette is more nunny than any nun I've ever met. She's convinced she's seen God's hand at work here."

"And you're not."

Eileen's eyebrows rose a fraction of an inch. "Are you?"

Jazz's laugh was uncomfortable. "I feel like I'm back in religion class in high school."

"I'm not giving out grades," Eileen assured her. "I'm just asking you to think. What do you suppose happened?"

Jazz had to admit she wasn't sure. Just like she promised Eileen she was going to find out.

In keeping with her promise, the next morning, brighter and way earlier than usual, she was out in the garden shed. The cat was the same cat — the female — that had been there the day before. She was a frisky little thing, and though Jazz was much more a dog person than a cat lady, she enjoyed a few minutes of whisking a string back and forth along the floor and watching the cat make a grab for it.

Until she heard a noise outside the shed.

One finger to her lips — maybe she was a cat lady after all, because she actually expected the cat to know what she wanted her to do — Jazz moved into the shadows beside an old wooden workbench and waited.

"It's not locked," she heard a whisper outside the door, a girl's voice.

"Perfect," another girl answered.

"Can we just get this over with!" A third voice, tight and panicked, wavered on the edge of tears. "I can't hold this thing much longer."

The door swung open and Jazz stood still and waited until all three girls stepped into the shed. She recognized them instantly.

Eighth graders.

Cammi Markham.

Juliette Briggs.

Taryn Campbell.

Taryn was the owner of the quivering voice. There were tears on the girl's cheeks and there was something wrapped in a towel in her outstretched hands.

Like a gift.

Or a sacrifice.

Cammi made a move to scoop up the cat, but it clearly had no intention of being caught and darted behind the open door. "Don't let it get away," Cammi hissed to Juliette. "Grab the stupid thing."

"I'm not getting scratched," Juliette shot back. "Taryn, you —"

"And what am I supposed to do with this thing?" Taryn was a redhead with pale skin, and in the dim light her eyes were big and dark and round. "I can't catch the cat."

"The real question is why you want to catch the cat."

When Jazz stepped out of the shadows, the three girls froze.

"Ladies." Jazz nodded a greeting. "You want to tell me what's going on?"

"Ms. Ramsey . . . we're just . . ." Cammi swallowed hard. "We're just checking on Titus," she said, forcing a laugh. "We've been praying for him, you know, and we were worried about him. We brought him some treats."

"Treats are a great idea. Go ahead." Jazz waved toward the cat, who at the sound of her voice had come out from behind the door and jumped on top of the workbench. "Get the treats out. I bet she'll come to you once you do."

Cammi looked at Juliette. Juliette looked at Taryn. Taryn burst into tears.

Jazz crossed her arms over her chest. "Who wants to explain?"

"It wasn't my idea," Taryn blurted out at the same time Cammi warned, "Shut up!"

Jazz wasn't one for threats, but she hated being treated like a fool. "We can do it here or we can do it in Sister Eileen's office," she told the girls.

Juliette started crying, too.

Cammi clicked her tongue.

Taryn, her nose wrinkled and her hands still out like she wanted to keep as far as possible from whatever was wrapped in that towel, seemed like the most likely choice to cave, so Jazz turned to her. "You want to unwrap what's in that towel?"

Taryn shook her head.

"Then you want to tell me what it is?"

"We were j-j-just trying to be nice," Juliette stammered. "You know, to make Ms. Quinn think her prayers were really working. We were being kind. At least that's what we thought. But then . . ." Her gaze flickered to the towel. "Then Cammi said —"

"It was just sort of a game." Now that she'd had time to collect herself, Cammi sounded more like the girl Jazz had heard in the cafeteria, ordering her friends around, telling them where to sit and who not to talk to. "It's not like we hurt him or anything."

In that moment, Jazz knew exactly what was in the towel.

"Over there." She ordered Taryn to set the towel on the workbench and the girl did and stepped back, putting as much distance between herself and the bundle as she could.

Jazz flipped back the towel. Just as she expected, Titus — the real Titus — was inside it. Dead.

She squeezed her eyes shut for a moment, wishing him peace, before she turned to the girls, her fists on her hips. "You better not have had anything to do with that."

"We didn't, Ms. Ramsey, I swear!" Taryn

hiccupped around her tears. "He died all on his own, right after we —"

"Shut up, Taryn," Cammi warned her, but she really didn't have to.

"You took Titus and replaced him with a cat that looked enough like him that you knew it would fool Ms. Quinn." When nobody objected, Jazz knew she was on the right track. "You hung on to Titus over the weekend and he died."

"In my garage." To try to get rid of the memory, Taryn shook her shoulders.

"And then you brought the dead cat back here because —" The logic of the thing eluded Jazz.

"Because Mrs. Popovich is coming home today," Juliette explained, even though it wasn't much of an explanation. She added, "And we figured it would teach Ms. Quinn another lesson, you know? Like if prayers can work, well, then sometimes they don't work, too."

"Cammi thought it was funny," Taryn said.

Cammi rolled her eyes. "Ms. Quinn, you know how much she likes to use games and puzzles in class. Well, we were just following her example, giving her a puzzle to follow. We were going to show her —"

"A dead cat?" Jazz flipped the towel, covering Titus's body. "And what were you

90

going to do with the live one?" she wondered.

"We w-w-weren't going to hurt her," Juliette stammered. "She belongs to the lady next door and my family is watching her 'cause Mrs. Popovich, the lady next door, on account of how she was on vacation. And Cammi and Juliette were over this weekend and they saw the cat and they said how much she looked like Titus and . . ." Taryn's shoulder's drooped. "Cammi said it would be funny."

"You all thought it was funny, too," Cammi shot back. "Ms. Quinn, she would have come out here to check on the bouncy little cat she found yesterday and —"

"And her heart would have been broken." Jazz pinned the girl with a look. "Really, Cammi, you think there's something clever or funny about that?"

"I . . ." Cammi shrugged. "Okay, maybe not. But Ms. Ramsey, you don't know what she's like! Ms. Quinn is always talking about God this and God that."

"She is a religion teacher," Jazz reminded them. "And this is a Catholic school."

"Okay, sure. But it's like she's from another planet. Can you blame us for —"

"Making fun of Ms. Quinn?" Jazz shot a look from one girl to the next. "I hope you're learning to be better people than that here at St. Catherine's."

"So what . . ." Juliette was so afraid of the answer, she could barely get out the words of her question. "What are you going to do?"

"Me?" Jazz left Titus right where he was and picked up the other cat. "I'm going to take this cat back to Juliette's where she belongs. Then I'm going to come back here to school, and when I get here I better find the three of you talking to Sister Eileen and Ms. Quinn, explaining what you did and why you did it."

"But —"

Jazz cut off Cammi with a glare. "And you know what else you're going to do? After the last bell rings today, you three are going to meet me right here. I'll have Frank get some gloves and some shovels. You three are going to bury Titus."

CHAPTER 6

The day Gus and Jazz found Bernadette's body, the girls who had rides or permission from their parents were dismissed early. The rest of them stayed in the gym where Eileen had delivered the news of Bernadette's death and led the girls in prayer. While Eileen went back to her office and gave a flawless statement to the media, Tracy Durn, the phys ed teacher, organized a volleyball game for the girls who felt like playing. Carly Tanner, the school librarian, gathered up any of the girls who preferred peace and quiet and spirited them to the library. Jazz's friend Sarah Carrington took charge of the rest of them and gave them free rein in the art room. By the time the school day officially ended and everyone was gone and Eileen was in her office behind closed doors with St. Catherine's board members, Jazz felt stretched tight, antsy, exhausted.

Eager for a distraction, she went out into the first-floor hallway. The school was deathly quiet, as if the building itself was holding its breath, waiting to see what shock waves would result from the day's horrible discovery. And yet . . .

Jazz glanced down the hallway and couldn't help but smile. Leave it to Sarah — bubbly, artistic Sarah — to know exactly what the girls needed to see when they came back to school on Monday. Before she left for the day, she hung the pictures the girls had painted in the hours after they learned of Bernadette's death. The hallway outside Jazz's office was a rainbow of paintings.

Flowers, sunshine, clear summer skies. If nothing else, the girls' drawings proved the young were resilient.

Comforted by the thought, Jazz strolled down the first-floor hallway, examining picture after picture, feeling better at the sight of the bright colors and the sweet sentiments scrawled alongside the drawings.

Good-bye, Ms. Quinn.

God bless you.

Rest in Peace.

It was the drawing closest to the doorway of Bernadette's former classroom that stopped Jazz cold.

This painting wasn't hung with the rest of

the pictures. It was taped below the neat row of drawings Sarah had hung at eye level.

An afterthought.

The sheet of drawing paper was a study in monochrome, black and gray. Except for the lower right corner — the spot where the other girls had signed their names — where there was one fat drop of red.

Jazz had no intention of insulting the artist, whoever she was. But she clearly remembered the looks on the faces of the girls as they'd filed out of school a few hours earlier. Dazed. Shocked. Afraid. Teetering between two worlds as the young always did, trying so hard to act like adults at the same time all they wanted to do was melt down in tears. There was no way Jazz was going to let them feel any worse. Carefully, she untaped the picture from the wall and took it into her office. She'd just tucked the grim painting into the top drawer of her desk when Marilyn Massey walked in.

Though Eileen wouldn't in a million years use the word, Marilyn was what some of the staff called one of the principal's *projects*. Eileen had met Marilyn — middle-aged, down on her luck, and a recovering addict — at a local food pantry and after talking to her for thirty minutes hired her on the spot to clean at St. Catherine's. That was fifteen years earlier, just as the school was about to open, and Marilyn was the first to admit those thirty minutes changed her life. She'd been clean and sober since; she'd gotten her GED. Marilyn was meticulous and so hardworking a few of the teachers hired her to clean their homes on weekends.

She had a bucket in one hand, and in spite of the fact that it was empty, Marilyn's shoulders were stooped as if she carried the weight of the world.

"Tough day." It was an understatement, but Jazz didn't know how else to ease into the conversation. "I thought Eileen told everyone on staff they could go home early if they wanted to."

Marilyn's shrug spoke volumes. "Going to be plenty to do next week. Figured I might as well get a jump on it," she said. She set down the bucket and swiped one hand through her bleached shoulder-length hair. "Funeral is Tuesday. Up in the chapel. But I guess you know that."

Jazz did and told her, "Bernadette's parents are long dead, but the cops contacted one of her cousins and Eileen talked to him. He said that's what Bernadette would have wanted, a funeral here. He said she always talked about how much she loved the chapel." It brought up an interesting thought. "I didn't realize Bernadette had any relatives; did you?"

Marilyn pulled a rag and a can of Pledge out of the wide pocket on the front of her apron. She excused herself around Jazz so she could clean Jazz's chair and her desk. "I never talked to her much. She was . . ." Jazz didn't want to put words in Marilyn's mouth, so she kept quiet. "It wasn't like she was unfriendly. That's what I told that cop. Those cops who were here today, they talked to everyone, you know. And the one who talked to me, I told him it wasn't like that Ms. Quinn was unfriendly. It was more like her head was always off somewhere . . ." — Marilyn made a waving motion with one hand and the rag in it — "and none of us was in the same place."

"So she never mentioned a cousin?"

"Not to me." Marilyn moved away from the desk and brought out a bottle of Windex and a paper towel to wipe down the leaded-glass doors on the bookcases on the other side of the room. "She tried to save me once, you know."

"You mean like you stepped in front of a moving car and she jumped into the street and dragged you to safety? Or like she tried to save your soul?"

Marilyn made a face. "My soul, of course.

97

That Ms. Quinn, that was all she cared about. Souls and salvation. I'm not saying that's not important, but these girls, they'll find out soon enough that real life is all about redemption and forgiveness. They're still kids; they don't need it pushed down their throats every day. I didn't need it pushed down my throat."

No, Jazz was pretty sure she didn't. She offered Marilyn a smile. "Your soul didn't need saving."

Marilyn grunted a laugh. "Didn't think so. Still don't. But that Ms. Quinn, she was plenty religious." She shook her head as if even after all this time, it didn't make much sense. Marilyn turned and propped one hand on her hip. "There were times I had to kick her out of the chapel. You know, when I was closing up the building for the night."

Jazz didn't know. "You should have said something," she told Marilyn.

It was inconsequential, and Marilyn's one-sided grimace told Jazz as much. "It's not that she ever argued with me about it or anything. Or like she ever refused to leave. If she did, I would have told Eileen. Or you. You know, the big guns."

Jazz laughed. She'd never considered herself a big gun.

Marilyn shook her head. "More evenings than not when I got up to the chapel to give it a quick once-over, that Ms. Quinn, she'd be up there on her knees, praying like there was no tomorrow, mumbling to herself. Or talking to God."

Remembering what Eileen had said earlier — the truth but not the whole truth — Jazz weighed her words. "Bernadette obviously hung around after the rest of us left. I guess that was her quiet time."

Marilyn nodded. "I always cleaned the chapel last so she knew she'd have it to herself until I got up there. How she could be up there all by herself . . ." She shivered.

"You don't like the chapel?"

Maybe because she was embarrassed, or maybe because she needed to dispel the shudder that crawled along her shoulders, Marilyn got back to work. She crossed the room and cleaned up the table where the refreshments had been set up for their Assembly Day speakers, stacking plates and cups, gathering up the last of the napkins.

"It sure is pretty up there." Marilyn brought the vases of flowers over to Jazz's desk and set them down. "But the way the sound plays tricks on you . . ." She shook her slim shoulders.

"It's just because of the whispering walls,"

Jazz said, even though she was sure Marilyn knew the story. The curved walls of the chapel played tricks with sound, causing unsettling echoes and even enabling a whisper from one side of the chapel to be heard on the other. A cutting-edge sound system had pretty much taken care of the problem when the girls were in the chapel for Mass. But yeah, Jazz imagined that when the sound system was off, when the school was empty, when Marilyn was up there alone and each of her footsteps was amplified and banged back at her, it could get unnerving. It was the main reason staff and teachers never talked about the acoustical acrobatics up in the chapel with students. Early on, Eileen had decided it would only cause problems if the girls thought of the chapel as a fun house attraction.

By way of telling Jazz she knew it and she knew it was silly to let it bother her, Marilyn lifted a shoulder. She finished with the coffee machine and Jazz asked, "What about the fourth floor?"

Marilyn froze. "They found her up there."

"I found her up there," Jazz said, though she was sure Marilyn had heard the story. St. Catherine's was a small community and word traveled fast, especially when the word was all about a dead teacher and the handler

100

and dog that had found her. "Have you ever been up on the fourth floor?" she asked Marilyn.

Her top lip curled. "Early on. Before the school ever opened. Me and Eileen was up there to see what needed to be done. I cleaned it. I cleaned it real good. But then Eileen and the board members, they decided it would cost too much to make the space usable. You know, on account of that narrow stairway and the fact that the heating and cooling ducts don't run up there."

"And you haven't been up there since?"

Marilyn thought about it. "Once," she said. "I don't know, maybe two, three years ago. Diedre McColm, her classroom is right under that space and she said something about how there must have been a dead animal up there because . . ." Marilyn's mouth fell open. "I sent Eddie up there and he found a dead squirrel and we figured that was that. And I sprayed some air freshener and we went back downstairs and we locked up and . . ." She gulped. "It was more than just a dead squirrel, wasn't it?"

"Did you tell the cops?"

"Do you think it's important?"

Jazz had to admit she didn't know. "They need all the information they can get. I have no doubt Detective Lindsey will be back.

101

I'll mention it to him. He might want to talk to you again."

This time when Marilyn shivered, it had nothing to do with the weird sound effects in the chapel. "I don't like talking to cops."

"I can be there with you if you want. Or Eileen."

Satisfied with the plan, Marilyn moved across the room to wipe down the sills of the windows that looked out over Lincoln Park across the street.

"The way I figure it," Marilyn said, "I can do most of the cleaning up in the chapel on Monday when it's light out and the school is buzzing. It never bothers me then. Not when I know there are other people around and —"

As if they'd been snipped with scissors, Marilyn's words cut off. Her mouth fell open.

"What?" Instinctively, Jazz hurried to her side. "What is it?"

"It's . . ." Marilyn leaned forward for a better look out the window. "It's that man."

Jazz looked where Marilyn was looking. In the hours since word went out about the discovery of the skeleton in the school, local news crews had set up across the street. There were three vans parked there, each with a satellite dish on its roof, and since there was nothing going on at the moment and there wouldn't be until the journalists saw the board members or Eileen leave the school, the crews were socializing, sipping coffee, smoking. To their right, a couple of young girls from the neighborhood jumped rope. To the left of the TV vans, a man stood alone on the sidewalk.

"Him?" Jazz asked, and when Marilyn nodded Jazz did a quick assessment. The guy was in his thirties. He had shaggy, dark hair, a wisp of a beard. He was short and squat, and he was wearing brown pants and a navy-blue windbreaker. "Who is he?"

"That's the man . . ." Marilyn didn't need to point, but she did anyway. "He was here. In the school."

He wasn't a parent; Jazz was sure of that. He wasn't a vendor, because all of them worked through her. He wasn't someone who'd come to do maintenance or grounds work, either. "For what?"

Marilyn inched closer to the window just as the man turned and paced down the sidewalk, then spun around and walked back in the direction of the school. "Back when Ms. Quinn was here. Yeah, it's him, all right. See the way he walks? He sort of rolls from side to side. Like maybe he's used to being on a boat. He doesn't look like a sailor, though, does he? I remember him, all right. I remember that walk."

"Why was he coming around here when Bernadette was here?" Jazz wanted to know.

Marilyn slid her a look. "To see her, of course."

"Bernadette?"

Marilyn bobbed her head. "A time or two. At least as far as I know. I saw him with her. Always late. Always after school was done for the day and there wasn't anyone around. Like I said, she used to go up to the chapel and sit there for hours. And sometimes, I think he went up there with her."

It was absolutely against the rules. Bernadette should have known that. Without a pass, visitors weren't allowed in the school. That fact may or may not have been important. For now, Jazz wanted to know, "Were they friends?"

Marilyn had to think about it. "Well, once I saw them sitting in the chapel talking. Just talking. But one time when I was cleaning on the second floor, I saw them going up to the third. They were holding hands."

"Then friends for sure. Or maybe more?"

Marilyn's lips puckered. "Not the last time I saw them together. That's for sure. I just finished up for the night and I was heading

home. It was cold; I had my winter coat on."
As if she was wearing it then, she bunched
one hand against her chest, holding an
imaginary coat closed against the icy chill.
"They were out in the parking lot. Over by
Ms. Quinn's car."

"Doing what?" Jazz wanted to know.

Color shot through Marilyn's cheeks. "It
wasn't like I was putting my nose where it
didn't belong or anything. But it was
strange. That's what I thought at the time.
Ms. Quinn, I'd just seen her up in the
chapel and told her it was time to get a
move on. And he wasn't up there with her
then. He must have been waiting outside
for her. And I thought it was strange on account of how it was so cold. You'd think
when it's like that outside, you could find a
better place to talk."

"About?"

She tried to come up with the words and
failed, shrugged. "It was a while ago. And I
couldn't hear real good. I remember that
whatever it was, his voice was really mellow.
Like he was trying to be sweet. You know
how men can be." She gave Jazz the sort of
conspiratorial look that said there wasn't a
woman in the world who didn't know what
she was talking about. "Like he wanted
something from her."

"And Bernadette?"

"Stood just like that." Marilyn pulled back her shoulders and clutched her hands together at her waist, her head high, her chin up. "You know, like she was a statue or something. Or like she was trying to show him that no matter what he said, she wasn't listening."

Jazz took a moment to study the man in the park. He looked harmless enough, a plain guy in unremarkable clothes. A little overweight. He looked left and right up and down the street. He glanced at the school. He stepped forward, then back. Like he wasn't sure what he was supposed to do next.

"Were they yelling?" Jazz wanted to know. "Arguing?"

Marilyn thought about it. "No. If they started to tussle, well, I would have done something. I mean, it's not like I could have fought him or anything." Marilyn glanced down at her own scrawny body and chuckled. "But I've stood up to some guys. I know I don't look up to it, but it's true. I would have made a scene. I would have called the cops. I would have done something if I thought she was in some sort of danger. But there was nothing physical. None of that. It was just sort of awkward. Pathetic. Then whatever he said, well, Ms. Quinn, she started to cry and she turned away from him and he . . ." She cocked her head, picturing the scene. "It was like he was a balloon and somebody poked him with a pin. That's how it looked to me. That's what I thought. Like I was watching all the air leak out of him. It wasn't until he backed away from her that whatever she said must have registered. Because that's when he talked louder, like the words were all bunched up inside him, straining at his heart, and he couldn't control how they came out."

"What did he say?"

Trying to remember, Marilyn squeezed her eyes shut. "How she'd be sorry. How she'd regret it." She lifted her hands, then let them flop back to her sides. "That was it. He turned around and walked away. And that Ms. Quinn, she stood there crying and shaking, and then she got in her car, and she drove away."

"Do you have any idea who he is?" Jazz asked.

Marilyn shook her head.

"How about when this all happened? I don't suppose you remember that?"

"Well, I do. See, that's the thing. I never thought anything of it. Because when we got back from vacation, everyone said Ms. Quinn quit and we wouldn't see her again, except none of us knew . . ." She looked up at the ceiling. Up to the fourth floor where Bernadette had lain wrapped in plastic sheeting for three years.

Jazz imagined Marilyn was thinking just what she was thinking. About the skeleton. About the cross around its neck.

She cleared her throat and Marilyn flinched. "When was it, Marilyn?"

"I was just heading home and I was so relieved because we were going to be on vacation soon."

Jazz sucked in a breath. "Not the day before Christmas break started?" The last time anyone saw Bernadette alive.

"No." Marilyn sucked on her bottom lip. "A couple days before, maybe. I remember I saw Ms. Quinn the next day in the hallway and I thought about saying something to her, about asking how she was. But you know how she could be, she walked right by me like I was invisible, and I thought if that's the way she wanted to be, I wasn't even going to ask." She slid Jazz a look. "She was alive and well. I can tell you that."

"That doesn't mean this guy, whoever he is, that doesn't mean he didn't come back another day." Jazz spun away from the windows and went to the desk where she'd left her phone.

"You going to call that detective guy?" Marilyn wanted to know.

She was, but not the detective guy Marilyn thought she was going to call. "I know someone . . ." When she got Nick's voice-mail, Jazz made a face at the phone and disconnected the call. "I'll try him again in a few minutes," she assured Marilyn. "I'm going to have him drive by and talk to this guy. Until then, we'll keep an eye on him and —"

Jazz went back to the windows and her voice sagged along with her spirits.

Whoever he was, however he knew Berna-dette, whatever they'd been fighting about in the days before Bernadette disappeared, he was gone.

CHAPTER 7

She was in the backyard working on *come* and *stay* with Wally when Nick's unmarked police car pulled into the driveway. It was Saturday evening, and she wasn't surprised he was on the clock. Nick was always working. Then again, he was something of a superhero, what with finding and collaring bad guys. After the shock of finding Bernadette's skeleton, after the grim realization that Bernadette had been killed in a place that should have been solely about learning and nurturing, one look at Nick and Jazz felt a sudden rush of warmth. Back in the day when they were a couple, it was all about sex. Right then, right there, it was deeper than that. Stronger. She felt safe when Nick was around.

She gave him a big smile that was totally wasted since he ignored her completely and headed right for Wally. Aside from gnawing on shoelaces, the puppy liked nothing better than making new friends and seeing old ones, and he jumped up on Nick and yipped a greeting. "He's getting so big!"

"Bigger and feistier every day." Jazz told Wally that jumping was not acceptable behavior, and while she was at it, she reminded Nick, too. "Don't let him do that."

Nick rubbed a hand over Wally's woolly head. "Why not? He's cute."

"It's not going to be so cute when he weighs sixty pounds and he's knocking people over."

"Point taken." When Wally jumped up again, Nick told him no and backed away. "He's doing well?" he asked Jazz.

"As happy as a clam and as smart as an Airedale is supposed to be. And that's plenty smart."

"And plenty stubborn, right?"

"He has his moments." Since Wally insisted on proving this by jumping up again and again, she hooked his lead to his collar and reeled it in nice and short so he couldn't get near enough to Nick to hop onto the legs of his khaki pants. Wally tugged, tried again, grumbled, and finally gave up and sat down at Jazz's side. "All in all, he's a great dog."

"I'm glad." Nick smiled down at the dog, then up at Jazz. It was seven in the evening, but it was nearly summer and the light was still strong, and the sun glinted against his sandy hair and sparked in his blue eyes. "I'm on dinner break. Thought you might want to get something to eat."

It wasn't the first time in the weeks since they'd reconnected that he'd offered the gift of his time — and a meal. All those other times, Jazz had been reluctant. What they'd had, her and Nick, had been so good that when it fell apart thanks to the pathetic but undeniable fact that they both forgot they were supposed to be the most important thing in each other's lives, it made her ache in ways she never knew were possible.

She refused to think about letting herself fall under the spell of his kindness and his intelligence and his darned sexy self again because she hated the thought of getting hurt again.

But not nearly as much as she hated not having Nick in her life.

She looked down at her black running shorts. "Do I need to change?"

"I was thinking of La Bodega."

One of her favorites, and she didn't need to change.

"I'll put Wally in his crate," she told Nick. "And lock up. We can walk."

"We'd be crazy not to. You don't think

112

there's anywhere to park around here on a Saturday, do you?"

He was right and Jazz knew it. More than one hundred years earlier when the neighborhood was settled by immigrants who built its working-class houses, its churches and schools, no one had imagined modern traffic. Streets were narrow. Parking was at a premium, and Jazz always thanked her lucky stars that her Kurcz grandparents, who had once owned her house, had the foresight to buy the lot next door and put in a driveway.

Jazz got the puppy into the house, and while she was inside she checked her hair (presentable), changed her shirt (the T-shirt she'd been wearing was a little threadbare even for La Bodega), and changed out of her crummy house sneakers into ones that were a little more decent.

She stepped out onto the back porch, locked the door, and turned to find Nick at the bottom of the stairs, grinning up at her.

"You look terrific."

"I look like a woman who's been cleaning the house all day and just spent the evening outside with her dog."

"Yeah, like I said" — when she descended the steps, Nick wound an arm through hers — "terrific."

It was good to walk side by side with him, great to feel the warmth of his body so close to hers, distracting (in a good way) to breathe in the woodsy scent of his after-shave.

All of which didn't mean she'd completely lost her mind.

"What do you want?" she asked him.

"I was thinking of the roast beef sub. You know, the one with the caramelized onions and mushrooms."

When they stopped to wait for traffic to go by so they could cross the street, she slid him a look. "Not what I meant and you know it."

"Or maybe the Greek sub with the arti-choke hearts and —"

She untangled herself from him and crossed to the restaurant, where she pushed open the door and stepped up to the counter to order. She decided on a salad with chicken and walnuts, and while Nick or-dered — who knew if it would be the Greek or the roast beef sub — she snagged a table outside near the sidewalk.

He joined her in a minute and set down two bottles of iced tea. "They'll bring our dinners out when they're ready." He sat next to her, opened his iced tea, and took a drink. "So . . ." He set the bottle on the table. "Tell me about it."

Of course she knew exactly what he was talking about, but she took her time, collecting her thoughts, her emotions. Washing the kitchen floor, scrubbing the bathroom, and doing three loads of laundry had pretty much helped to push thoughts of yesterday's discovery at the school out of Jazz's head all day.

Now she was forced to face them again.

She opened her iced tea and took a long drink. "It?"

He leaned forward. "No way you're not thinking about the skeleton at school."

A chill scraped her shoulders. "That would be pretty impossible."

"Then tell me about it."

"You're not working the case."

"That doesn't mean I don't care."

"About the case?"

"Maybe about the woman who found the skeleton in the first place."

It was on the tip of her tongue to tell him she was fine and, while she was at it, to ask him why he cared, but she never had the chance. Tony, a man who'd worked at the restaurant forever, came out of the restaurant with a plate in each hand, took one look at the two of them, and grinned.

"Hey, Detective Nick!" Tony set down

115

both plates so he could shake Nick's hand. "And Jazz! I haven't seen you two in here together in forever. What, you decided you didn't like the food?"

"The food is always good," Jazz said at the same time Nick mumbled something about being busy.

"Well, this one . . ." Tony glanced her way. "She's in here once a week, I bet. Always by herself. I asked her a couple months ago . . . remember, Jazz? I asked you a couple months ago where Supercop was."

"And Jazz said?" The question was meant for Tony, but Nick looked at her when he asked it.

"Just like you said, told me you were busy!" Tony answered before Jazz could, and it was just as well, since she wasn't sure what she would have said. "I told her I don't care how busy you are, you gotta eat. Isn't that right, Detective Nick? You gotta eat. I'm glad you're here eating now." He put one hand on Jazz's back, the other on Nick's. "You two enjoy!"

Once Tony was gone, Jazz thought about the other times he'd been to their table to chat, all the times she and Nick had sat just like this — at ease and at peace, not wanting anything more than to enjoy each other's company.

116

Nick was a good man. No matter their differences, she'd never forgotten that. No matter how hard she tried not to get too close, not to get too involved, not to get so wrapped up in him and in their relationship, she could never deny that. Nick was honest and he was loyal. He could be funny and he was a great dancer. For weddings on her mother's side of the family, he'd learned to polka. On her dad's side . . . well, none of them could really do an Irish jig, not properly, but at least Nick was game enough to try.

And he could slow dance.

Oh, how Nick could slow dance.

The memory caused a rush of heat and she sat back and smiled.

"What?" Nick wanted to know, basically proving with that one word what she already knew about him — he was suspicious of everyone and everything, even the smile that lit her face and the color that touched her cheeks.

"Nothing. I'm just enjoying the moment, that's all. This is good."

"How do you know? You haven't touched your salad yet."

She could have played along with his misconception, but there was something about the evening air and the delicious

117

promise of summer and the fact that he'd come to see her on his dinner hour that made her brave, reckless.

"I wasn't talking about the salad. I was talking about this." As if it would somehow demonstrate what she was saying, she tapped the table. "Being here. Now. With you. This is good."

A slow smile lit his expression. "Like the old days."

"I hope not," she said, and then so he didn't get the wrong impression, she added quickly, "It would be nice if we could work around the things that went wrong back then."

"Like me working too much."

"And me devoting all my free times to the dogs."

"And then there's your family, of course."

Seeing her spine straighten and her fingers tighten over the fork she held in one hand, Nick made a face. "You are pretty devoted to them."

"That's how families are supposed to be with each other."

"Yeah, I get that. I guess." She couldn't blame him for being confused. Nick's family consisted of just his mother, Kim, an alcoholic with rotten social skills and a talent for ripping out her only child's heart and stomping on it every chance she got. "I think sometimes it's hard for me to understand all that warm and fuzzy stuff."

"How is Kim?" she asked, and she could have spoken the answer along with him, because it was the one she always got when she asked.

"Fine."

"And how are you with handling Kim?"

He lifted one shoulder. "Same as always. She won't listen to advice. She refuses to go to rehab. She keeps reminding me that she's an adult."

"Then I hope you're telling her to start acting like one."

His smile was soft. "She's not going to listen."

She reached across the table long enough to squeeze his hand. "None of it is your fault."

"No, but it is my problem."

"Not if you just walk away."

"Like you'd do that if it was someone in your family?"

It was his turn to bristle, and she couldn't blame him. "I know you'd never do that," she jumped in and told him. "You're too kind a person."

"Or maybe I just always want to be in charge of everything and everyone." As if he could so easily get rid of the problem that was Kim, he jiggled his shoulders. "Speaking of which . . ."

Nick slathered his roast beef sandwich with horseradish and mustard. "Skeleton?"

"Yeah, Bernadette Quinn." Jazz pushed her fork through her salad. As long as she had the attention of an expert, she figured it didn't hurt to ask. "It is her, isn't it?"

"Sure looks that way." Nick took a bite of his sandwich and chewed. "Skeleton's the right size, right age. Her hyoid bone . . ." Nick pointed to a spot on his neck under his chin. "It was fractured. She was strangled. I hear Lindsey hasn't had any luck tracking down dental records so far, so that's not going to help with final identification, but there's DNA, of course. For now, we're going with what we know. Or at least what we're pretty sure of."

"It's her, all right," Jazz told him. "The clothes, the cross. Still, it just seems . . . I don't know . . . wrong."

"Wrong that it's her?"

"Wrong that she's dead. That her skeleton has been up in the attic all those years and no one knew. Why would anyone want to kill Bernadette?"

"I'm sure that's what Gary Lindsey's asking himself."

"And if it was you, what would you be asking yourself?"

He took another bite of his sandwich, chewed, considered. "Enemies?"

"None we knew about, and though she was admired for her teaching skills, she didn't really have fans, either. She was odd. And she was seen around school with a man." Jazz filled him in on the details she'd learned from Marilyn Massey.

This time when he bit and chewed, he raised his eyebrows, too, waiting for her to tell him more.

"There really isn't any more. We don't know who the man is, but if I see him around again I'll let you know. The only other thing about Bernadette . . . well, she was really holy."

"That's a good thing at a Catholic school, isn't it?"

Jazz thought about what Eileen had said. The truth but not the whole truth. She understood Eileen's reasoning. If the media got ahold of the entire story, they'd make a mockery of Bernadette, and of St. Catherine's, too. She couldn't let that happen.

"You won't tell?" she asked Nick.

He didn't have to think about it. "If it affects the case —"

"It doesn't. But if the press gets hold of

the details, it could get ugly."

"If it points to any suspects —"

"Definitely not."

He gave her that old, familiar smile. "Spill the beans!"

Jazz took a bite of chicken, added a bit more dressing. "She . . . Bernadette . . ." She pulled in a breath and let it out slowly. "She said she talked to angels."

Nick wiped mustard off his mouth, then pursed his lips. "Isn't that what prayer is? Talking to God? Talking to saints and angels?"

"Well, yeah. Except Bernadette believed the angels talked back."

He wasn't expecting this, and for a minute Nick simply stared at her. At least until he found his voice. "To her?"

"I know, I know!" She set down her fork, the better to put out both her hands, palms toward him as if to signal that he needed to stay quiet, to hear the rest of the story. "It sounds crazy."

"Amen to that!"

"It *is* crazy. She was crazy. Nick, it's not something Eileen wants the world to know."

"Because she doesn't want the blowback. Yeah, I get that. It's bad enough the remains were found in the school; if the public knew this teacher was some sort of nutcase —"

"Exactly."

He took another bite of his sandwich, and while he was at it, he poked a finger at her salad, urging her to eat, and for a few minutes they concentrated on their food.

Finally, Nick took a drink of tea and sat back. "What did they tell her?"

"Who?"

"The angels, of course. What did the angels tell Bernadette?"

"You don't really believe that stuff about how they talked to her, do you?"

"Ah, see, that's the whole point." A satisfied smile lighting his face, Nick opened the bag of potato chips that came with his sandwich and offered the bag to Jazz. He knew her well. She was a sucker for potato chips.

Jazz grabbed a handful of chips and pushed the bag across the table at him, and after Nick chomped on a couple he leaned his elbows on the table.

"If Bernadette made up the fact that the angels were talking to her, then what they told her was really just the workings of Bernadette's mind, and that's interesting in one way," he said. "But if the angels really were talking to her —"

"Nick, are you listening to yourself?" Jazz actually might have laughed if they weren't

123

discussing something so weird. If there wasn't a murder involved. "How could angels talk to her? Why would they?"

He wrinkled his nose. "Why wouldn't they? Don't Catholics believe in miracles?"

"Bernadette did," Jazz admitted, and in spite of the warmth of the sun, she felt the icy pain of remembrance, of telling Bernadette that Titus the cat had really never been cured, that he was dead. "I guess in her world, it was perfectly normal to expect to hear from angels. The rest of us . . . well, it's not like everyone in school knew about it, thank goodness, but Eileen and I did."

"And Eileen . . . ?"

"Offered her the name of a good therapist and told Bernadette not to say anything to anyone. We couldn't let people think we had a crazy teacher!"

"Could someone have found out?"

"And killed Bernadette because of it? Why? They were jealous that Bernadette was hearing from angels and they weren't? They were afraid Bernadette would talk about it too loud, too long, that people would hear, the news would spread?"

"There had to be some reason."

"Maybe, but —" Jazz was about to stab a dried cranberry with the tine of her fork and she shot Nick a look. "You're thinking

124

about Eileen. You're thinking that if she was afraid Bernadette was going to embarrass the school —"

"Was she?"

"Yes, of course she was. We both were. We still are. If word of this gets out . . . It's not the Middle Ages, Nick. People aren't going to flock to St. Catherine's on pilgrimage. They're going to talk psychosis. And personality disorders. They're going to question Eileen's judgment and say that Bernadette never should have been allowed through the front door of St. Catherine's."

"Do you think that's true?"

Jazz shook her head. "We didn't know about it. Not when she was hired. She never said a word. But then, that's not exactly something you just start talking about with people you hardly know, is it? Early in the semester, she said something to me about angels, but heck, I thought it was just a figure of speech. It wasn't until about the middle of the term that she mentioned it again. That she told me they were talking to her."

"And you told Eileen."

"Of course I did. Bernadette was a teacher; she was responsible for our students. If there was something wrong with her —"

"Was there?"

Jazz felt as helpless as she did the day she'd informed Eileen of what Bernadette told her and Eileen asked her the same question. "I'm not a psychiatrist. I don't know."

"And that's when you two — you and Eileen — decided to keep things under wraps."

Jazz wasn't cold, but she wrapped herself in a hug. "You make it sound like a cover-up."

"Was it?"

She drew in a long breath and let it out slowly. "I told you, Eileen told Bernadette she wanted her to get counseling."

"And she wanted her to keep quiet. So did you."

"That doesn't mean I killed Bernadette!" When Jazz realized how loudly she'd spoken, she cringed and looked around. Except for two people sitting nearby who stopped their conversation and gave her funny looks, no one else there seemed to notice. She lowered her voice. "That doesn't mean I killed Bernadette. And it doesn't mean Eileen did, either."

"I hear she's the only one who has a key to the room where the skeleton was found."

Suddenly Jazz wasn't so hungry anymore.

She pushed her plate away. "That doesn't mean anything, either."

"No, it probably doesn't. But I guarantee you it's what Lindsey's thinking."

"Then his thinking's as bad as his fashion sense."

Nick laughed. "The man's just doing his job. He's got to follow where the facts lead him."

"Then we've got to find the right facts."

"Oh, no! Don't even think about doing that again." He might have gotten away with the warning if he didn't add a finger wag. One little gesture and Jazz's anger shot through the roof.

She kept her voice calm, innocent. "Doing what?"

"Investigating."

"I was never investigating. Last time, all I did was ask some questions."

"Yeah, and it could have gotten you killed."

"But it didn't, did it?" She pushed back her chair. "I'm not going to sit back and watch Eileen get railroaded."

"And I'm not going to, either. Look . . ." Nick stood when Jazz did. "I'll see what I can find out, okay? I'll ask around. I'll talk to Lindsey and see what he knows and what he's thinking."

She looked up into his eyes. "Really?"

"But only if you promise to stay out of it."

She had no choice but to agree. That, or lose his support.

It was a good thing he grabbed her right hand and held it when they crossed the street and headed back toward Jazz's house.

That way, he never knew the fingers of her left hand were crossed.

CHAPTER 8

It was Monday morning, and Jazz had just opened her desk and pulled out the grim painting she'd found hung outside Bernadette's classroom on Friday when Sarah Carrington sashayed into the office. That day she was decked out in black pants, a black T-shirt, and a filmy kimono top in shades of pink and blue and an earthy green that matched the stripe of color in her blond hair. She plopped into Jazz's guest chair and blew an errant curl out of her eyes.

"What do you think?" she asked Jazz.

"About . . . ?"

"About how today is going to go, of course. Friday went too well. The girls were . . ." As if she could snatch the right word out of the air, Sarah fluttered her hands. "They were calm. Accepting. Almost as if they knew Bernadette was dead and it was no big deal."

In an attempt to get rid of the chill that

crawled along her skin, Jazz rubbed her hands up and down her arms. "Don't say that. They were stunned, that's all. They were shocked. We all were."

"And now they've had all weekend to think about it."

"It's going to be a long day." Jazz said what they both were thinking. "There will be counselors available all week for the girls." She darted a look at Sarah. "And for the teachers, too."

Sarah didn't miss the subtle inference. "How about for the staff?"

Jazz dropped into the chair behind her desk. "I don't need counseling. I need answers."

"You mean, who killed her?"

"And why. Maybe that's what we all need. Maybe that's the only way things will get back to normal around here. We can't act like nothing happened. We can't pretend life just goes on. That wouldn't be fair. To the girls or to Bernadette."

"Bernadette." When Sarah shook her head, her pink beaded earrings swayed. "Doesn't it figure she'd be the one to go and get herself killed here at school?" As if she expected Jazz to lecture her, she instantly added, "You know what I'm talking about, Jazz. She was . . ."

"Strange?"

If only Sarah knew!

Jazz tucked away the thought. This was not the time for gossip. And Sarah was certainly not the person to tell. Not about the mystery man who'd been visiting Bernadette here at school. And certainly not about the angels. Until Jazz knew more — and was certain of every bit of it — she'd keep her mouth shut. Sarah had a tendency to say too much to too many people about things she knew too little about. It didn't make her any less lovable. It just meant Jazz knew she had to be careful.

"Speaking of strange . . ." Jazz handed the gloomy painting across the desk to Sarah. "Did you happen to see who painted that on Friday?"

Sarah took one look at the painting and let out a long, low whistle. "This I would have noticed," she said. "Though I have to tell you, there were so many girls up in the art room, I couldn't keep a close eye on them all. Besides . . ." Her mouth thinned, she slid the picture back in Jazz's direction. "You don't really need to ask, do you?"

"I was thinking. . . ." No, that wasn't really true. Jazz wasn't just thinking about the situation. She was hoping. Praying. She would have liked nothing better than to find out she was wrong. "I just want to make sure before I say anything. Was Maddie Parker up in the art room with the other girls?"

Sarah's gaze flickered to the painting. "If I told you no —"

"I wouldn't believe you." Jazz ran her hands through her hair. "You know Maddie's not going to be here next year. Well, not after summer school."

"I heard." Sarah pulled her gaze away from the grim painting. "Right about now, that's sounding like a good thing, isn't it?"

"They were close." Jazz wasn't sure that fully explained the Bernadette/Maddie relationship, but it was a start, and Eileen had said the truth, but not the whole truth. "Of course Maddie's upset. It will be good for her to get away next year."

"Sunny Honduras!" Sarah smiled. "A year abroad while her parents work at some clinic down there. Couldn't come at a better time for Maddie. The sooner she's away from here, the sooner she'll forget Bernadette."

"You know it's not that easy." Jazz shouldn't have had to remind her. "Bernadette tutored her. Bernadette had a problem with dyslexia, too. I think that's one of the things that brought them together. They both had challenges and it was kind of Bernadette to help Maddie. They were . . . friends." Did that explain their relationship any more than saying they were close? Jazz didn't think so, but maybe now it didn't matter. "Maddie's taking Spanish in summer school."

"I'm glad it's not art." Sarah's attempt at humor fell flat, and her shoulders rose and fell. She leaned forward and grabbed the painting. "Truth is, I can only tell you she was in my art room on Friday. I can't tell you if she painted that picture. Or even how long she hung around. I had thirty girls in a space designed to hold twenty and I knew they were hurting so I let them mess with my iPod and play some music and I dug out the snacks I keep in my bottom desk drawer for emergencies."

Above all else except for her children, Sarah loved the candies she got from a vegan-friendly chocolatier, and her stash was hidden and secret. "You shared your peanut butter cups?"

Sarah fluffed off the thought. "The girls needed a distraction. And to my way of thinking, chocolate and peanut butter cures just about anything."

"Did it help them?"

"It hyped them up." A smile flitted across Sarah's face. "And hey, if it helped them

133

forget, even for a little while, it was worth it."

Jazz made a mental note to pick up more chocolates for Sarah at the same time Sarah said, "I couldn't keep track of every one of the girls, what with them singing and washing brushes and digging out every jar of acrylic paint I had in the art cabinet. Early on I saw Maddie in the back of the room sitting by herself. But sitting by herself, that's not unusual for Maddie, is it?"

It wasn't. Maddie, a junior, was a quiet kid with a learning disability that made her self-conscious. She was middle-sized, with straight dark hair and a splotchy complexion, one of those girls Jazz knew would grow up to be a poised, confident adult — if only she could get through the awkward teenage years intact.

"Maddie and Della Robinson are pretty friendly, but I know Della's mom came and picked her up early after word about Bernadette went out on Friday," Jazz told Sarah. "Maddie probably didn't know too many of the other girls who were in your room."

"Probably," Sarah conceded. "Or maybe Maddie didn't want to sit with anyone who would see her drawing." She reached for the painting and slipped it closer. She made a face. "She's upset."

"You think?"

Sarah laughed. "Well, at least give me credit for making a stab at a little psychology! Honest, Jazz" — with a sigh, she set down the picture — "I hate the thought of Maddie being in such a dark place."

Jazz nodded. "I'll talk to Maddie and strongly suggest counseling."

She put the picture away. "I'm surprised I didn't hear from you over the weekend," she told Sarah. "I called."

"And I should have returned your call." Sarah's cheeks flushed. "I was kind of busy."

The blush, the smile, could only mean one thing. "Let me guess, Matt had the weekend off." Matt Duffey was a firefighter like Jazz's two brothers, and he'd been a friend of the Ramsey family forever. He and Sarah had just started dating, and Sarah was still feeling the first rush of love. That would explain why at the mention of Matt's name, she practically melted into a puddle of mush.

"He's so terrific." Sarah might be closing in on middle age, but she giggled like a St. Catherine's girl. "Honest to gosh, Jazz, I can't even believe it myself. He's so sweet and he's so romantic. He cooked Saturday night. Can you even imagine it? The guy actually cooked dinner for me."

For a woman who'd grown up with a dad

who frequently offered to make dinner so he could use his family as guinea pigs for the recipes he'd make for his fellow firefighters, it came as no surprise to Jazz. But for Sarah, divorced, devoted to her job, and the mother of two young sons, Jazz could only think it must have been a luxury.

"What do the boys think of him?" Jazz wanted to know.

"They met Matt for the first time on Saturday. Before they went over to Loser's." Sarah's face twisted the way it always did when she talked about her ex. "I think they were a little confused about seeing a man in the house. Lord knows, they shouldn't be. Loser's had a string of women in and out of his house since we split up. You'd think the boys would be used to it by now."

"Except then it didn't involve their mother."

"They'll be fine with the whole thing once they get used to Matt. They'd better!" She smoothed a hand over her kimono top. "I think it's safe to say he's going to be around for a long time."

Jazz was glad. Or at least she would have liked to be. She loved Matt like another brother, but he did not have a good reputation when it came to women. He had a tendency to love 'em and leave 'em, and when it came to men Sarah tended to lose interest sooner rather than later. When what they had of a relationship fell apart —

With a twitch of her shoulders, Jazz set the thought aside. It wasn't her problem. It wasn't her responsibility.

"I'm thrilled everything's going well," she told Sarah, and didn't add *for the moment.* "Now if we could figure out what went on around here when Bernadette died . . ." The thought dissolved on the end of her sigh.

"Where are you going to start?" Sarah wanted to know.

Jazz logged on to her computer and checked Maddie Parker's schedule. "I think I'll just pop up to the library," she told Sarah, who slapped a hand over her heart, pretending to be astonished.

"You're not actually going to read a book?"

Jazz grinned. "Not a chance!"

Still smiling, Jazz left the office and stepped into the hallway and dodged a couple sleepy-eyed teachers so she could make her way to the third floor. There, the chapel dominated one end of the building. The other was taken up by the school's library.

"A hidden Cleveland treasure."

That's what Sarah called the library, but

since Jazz hardly ever went up there, she couldn't say if Sarah was right or wrong. She did know that when she pushed through the wooden swinging doors that led into the library and they swished shut behind her, she felt as if she was in a different world. The room smelled like knowledge and history, like plans and dreams.

Jazz was not the fanciful type, and she grinned at her own crazy runaway imagination and concentrated on what she was best at, what was real. The library was paneled in rich wood, just like Jazz's office, but here one wall of the room was dominated by three stained-glass windows that had been in place since the building was a seminary. The center window featured the resurrected Christ, his robes blindingly white and his right hand raised in a blessing. The windows that flanked it showed Saint Theodosius on the right and Saint Sergius on the left (or was it the other way around? Jazz could never remember), with their bristling beards and in their priestly robes.

The morning light hit the window and color spilled over the floor at Jazz's feet. Green and blue and red.

Like blood.

Her smile dissolved and she shook off the thought and the shivers that crawled along her spine and looked around, from the floor-to-ceiling bookshelves to the computers at stations throughout the room, the 3-D printers, cloud computing, virtual reality. The girls of St. Catherine's had advantages students in other schools never dreamed of.

There was no sign of Maddie Parker and that was unusual. Three years earlier, Bernadette had convinced Maddie to volunteer at the library. She told the girl that reading the titles on the spines as she reshelved books would help with her dyslexia, and from what Jazz had heard from Maddie's mom, Bernadette was right. Maddie's disability wasn't serious, but it was enough of an inconvenience to cause problems for Maddie when it came to getting her homework done and finishing tests on time. Since she'd started at the library, both test times and homework had improved, and Maddie never missed a morning of work.

Jazz grumbled under her breath. Maddie's mother hadn't called her in sick. She had to be around somewhere.

A choking cry took Jazz to the other side of the room. She followed the sound between two long rows of bookshelves. At the end of them, in a dark corner she found Maddie crumpled behind a book cart, her butt on the floor, her knees pulled up to her chin, the sleeves of her blue cotton blouse pulled down around shaking hands.

"Hey, Maddie."

The girl's head came up and she scrambled to her feet.

"You okay?" Jazz asked her.

Maddie scrubbed the cuffs of her blouse over her face. It got rid of the tears that glimmered on her cheeks, but it did nothing at all for her swollen eyes or a bottom lip that trembled.

"I'm . . . I'm . . ." Maddie sucked in a breath.

Jazz stepped back and motioned toward the nearest table. "If you want to sit and talk . . ."

Maddie's voice bumped over a sob. "I . . . I've got work to do, Ms. Ramsey. I need to get these books back on the shelf." She spun toward the book cart and grabbed up a handful of books, and she would have taken off down the nearest aisleway if Jazz didn't step in front of her.

"It's all right, Maddie," she told the girl. "We all know you and Ms. Quinn were close. The news of what happened, of what we found upstairs on Friday, that must have hit you very hard."

Maddie's shoulders shot back. "Not really. I'm . . . I'm fine."

140

Jazz dared a step nearer. "We've got counselors here all day and —"

Maddie sniffled. "Why would I need them?"

"Because you're upset. We all are. Not just the students, but the teachers and the staff, too. We all feel bad about what happened to Ms. Quinn."

"Bad? I don't . . ." Maddie choked over a sob. "I don't feel bad at all." She lifted her chin and her voice was suddenly flint. "Why should I? Why should I?" She shoved past so fast, Jazz's head snapped back, her feet tangled, and she banged into the nearest bookshelf. Before she could right herself, Maddie was running down the aisleway, heading for the door. Her voice echoed back at Jazz from the high ceiling.

"Why would I care? I hated Bernadette Quinn! I'm glad she's dead!"

Jazz knew going after Maddie would upset her even more. On the way back to her office, she talked to Maddie's homeroom teacher and to Jessica Shore, St. Catherine's guidance counselor. Their concern and advice would mean more to Maddie than Jazz's ever could and she left Maddie in their hands.

If only it was so easy to get rid of the questions that pounded through her after the encounter.

"Maddie and Bernadette were close," she said when Eileen arrived for the day and she finished telling her what happened in the library. "You know."

"Only too well." Eileen poured a cup of coffee from the machine in Jazz's office. "I hope to God there wasn't more going on than we were aware of."

Jazz had thought the same thing. She just wasn't brave enough to put it into words. "Maddie never complained about anything inappropriate."

"No, and none of the digging we did at the time uncovered anything. Still . . ." Coffee in hand, Eileen hurried into her office. "I'll make sure Jessica has a long talk with Maddie."

Jazz took the dark painting out of her desk and gave it to Eileen. "She might want to mention this."

Eileen studied the picture. "We'll get Maddie's parents involved, too. They're good people and they love her to the moon and back. They'll want to know what's going on." Eileen added, "I'll call them."

For the next couple of hours, Jazz kept busy with morning announcements, the details of the day, and putting the final touches on the next day's church service in Bernadette's honor. By the time she was done with that — and the three cups of coffee that fueled her while she worked — it was lunch hour. She knew exactly how she'd spend it.

Jazz hurried to the cafeteria, the better to be there when the girls started to arrive. She wasn't surprised when Cammi Markham breezed into the cafeteria ahead of the crowd. Now a junior, Cammie knew her way around the school, its rules, and its invisible power structure. There were girls who were more popular than Cammi. There were plenty who were brighter and more talented.

But not many of them had as much chutzpah.

Unfortunately, Cammi didn't always know how to use it wisely.

Jazz stepped back, waiting patiently until Cammie found where she wanted to sit, looped her purse over the back of her chair to mark it as saved, and went up to the serving counter for chicken stir-fry. When Juliette Briggs joined Cammie with the identical lunch, Jazz made her move.

"Hello, ladies." She slipped into the chair across from the girls and was gratified when Cammi winced. "I didn't want to pull you

143

away from your classes. This is perfect. We'll have plenty of time to talk."

The girls exchanged looks. Juliette, a tiny girl with short blond hair and big blue eyes, was the weaker link and Jazz knew it. While Cammi dug into her stir-fry, Juliette fumbled with her silverware.

"I was just thinking about the good old days," Jazz told them. "You remember Titus the cat."

Juliette gulped.

Cammi had long dark hair streaked with gold and she tossed it over her shoulder. "Let me guess, because of the stupid cat, you think we killed Ms. Quinn?"

"Did you?" Jazz wanted to know, and even Cammi was shocked by her nerve. She choked, coughed, washed away her surprise with a drink of water.

By the time she collected herself, the bored look she wore like a second skin was back in place on Cammie's face. "Why would we do that?"

Jazz shrugged, the better to make it look like she really didn't know and maybe she didn't care, either. "I'm just trying to figure out what happened," she admitted. "And I was thinking about how the two of you —"

"And Taryn," Juliette reminded her. "Taryn Campbell —"

"Juliette!" Cammi elbowed her friend in the ribs to get her to shut up, and when she did Cammi turned a smile on Jazz. "Everybody liked Ms. Quinn's classes, but nobody liked her," she said. "It wasn't just the three of us. She dressed funny. I mean, all those long plaid skirts." Cammie rolled her eyes. "She never wore makeup. I mean, come on! She wasn't cool, not like you, Ms. Ramsey, or Ms. Carrington." Jazz suspected she was supposed to be thrilled at the compliment, but instead, she just sat and listened, and waited for more. "Ms. Quinn, she told us she never listened to music. I mean, not music that anybody cared about. One day she said we could have music on in class while we read and we got all excited. Then she played something that sounded like angels singing. Really? And you know, she never watched TV, either. She told us that. Said it was a waste of time and we'd ruin our brains. She said the same thing about social media, too. And shit . . ." She waited a heartbeat for Jazz to criticize her language, and because it was exactly what Cammi was expecting her to do Jazz didn't.

When she didn't get the rise out of Jazz that she wanted, Cammi went right on, "We were just eighth graders back then. I'm pretty sure eighth graders couldn't kill anybody."

"Why not?" Jazz wondered, and realized that like it or not, it was a legitimate question. "If you dislike somebody enough —"

Juliette swallowed a mouthful of food. "We might have disliked her, but —" On a look from Cammi, her words dissolved.

"It's not like we were ever really mean to her." Cammi thought better of the statement and added, "I mean, except about the stupid cat."

"But you got into plenty of trouble for that," Jazz reminded them. All three girls had been suspended, had plenty of work to make up, and were required to do volunteer time at the Animal Protective League. "I know you blamed Ms. Quinn for it, and I imagine both your parents had their own way of letting you know how displeased they were." She didn't have to imagine very hard. At the time, she remembered how Cammi's parents grounded her and Juliette's took away internet privileges.

"To teach us a lesson." Cammi had the nerve to pull back her shoulders and clutch her hands together on the table in front of her. "It worked. It made us change our ways."

"It obviously didn't work for Taryn," Jazz

pointed out, though she was sure she didn't have to. Not long after the Titus incident, Taryn had been expelled for plagiarism.

"Taryn's a loser," Cammi said. "Maybe you should be talking to her."

It was something Jazz had already thought of, but she didn't bother to mention it. Instead, she opened the file folder she'd brought along with her and flipped it open. Automatically, both girls leaned forward, eager to see what was in it.

"Your schedules from back then," Jazz told them, and turned the folder so they could see she was telling the truth. "All three of you . . ." She glanced at Cammi. "You and Juliette and Taryn, too, all three of you were in Drama Club that year."

"Oh, that was so lame!" Cammi said. "We tried it out because we thought it would be fun, but honestly —"

"Honesty would be appreciated," Jazz told them.

Cammi bit her lower lip. "Hanging around after school so we could help paint sets wasn't exactly what we had in mind," she said, and shrugged. "So after that, we didn't join again."

"But you did hang around after school." Jazz leafed through the papers in the folder, checking dates. "At least until after Christ-

147

mas break. It says here that after break, that's when you dropped out of Drama Club."

"Like I said . . ." Though she wasn't done with her lunch, Cammi set her silverware across her dish, wadded up her napkin. "It wasn't as much fun as we thought it would be."

"That's not what Ms. McGuinness said." Mary McGuinness was the Drama Club moderator. "When I asked her, she said she's pretty sure the three of you had no idea what goes on in Drama Club. That when she needed you to paint scenery or move props, you three were never around."

"And what, you think that means we killed Ms. Quinn?"

Cammi's look was as fiery as her question, but Jazz met it with perfect poise.

"Actually, I think it means you might not have been where you were supposed to have been the day she was killed. Did you stay late that day? Did you see anything?"

Cammi looked at Juliette. Juliette looked at the ceiling.

Cammie grabbed her tray and stood. "If you're trying to prove we killed her, you're way off base. You ought to talk to Taryn Campbell's father. Don't you remember

Taryn's last day here? Mr. Campbell, he was the one who threatened to kill Ms. Quinn."

CHAPTER 9

The crowd was hushed. The music was appropriately solemn. The chapel of St. Catherine's was packed to the rafters. Because there was no way it could hold all the girls, lower-level classes were kept in their homerooms. The older girls — the ones who were at St. Catherine's when Bernadette taught there — were seated all around Jazz.

Bernadette's death and the discovery of her body was a lot for them to process, and Eileen told them so in her short but moving eulogy. She told them to remember that though Ms. Quinn was a member of the St. Catherine's family for only a short time, her history and theirs was forever entwined. Though she didn't initially think it was a good idea, she finally caved to Jazz's suggestion and told the girls that if they remembered anything that might help the police in finding out what had happened to Bernadette, they should come forward with the information.

Or maybe the angels could just solve the whole mystery.

It was a ridiculous notion, of course, but it popped into Jazz's head and she couldn't silence the cynical voice that whispered the suggestion.

Bernadette was so devoted. She was so sure that God's messengers spoke directly to her and heard her every word, the least they could do was speak up and help out with the investigation.

Except Jazz knew that wasn't the way things worked.

The choir started in on "On Eagle's Wings," their high, clear voices soaring up to the dome above the chapel and wrapping around Jazz. It was a beautiful song that had been sung at her dad's funeral and listening to it never failed to make her heart clutch. Rather than think about it — and the role angels might play in finding out what happened to Bernadette — Jazz slipped out of her aisle seat in a pew toward the back of the chapel. Maybe she could get rid of crazy thoughts about angels by standing at the back of the chapel and scanning the crowd, just to make sure all the girls were behaving. While she was at it, she made a special effort to look for Maddie Parker.

Jazz found Maddie seated with the other girls from her homeroom, her arms wrapped around herself in a hug that did nothing to hide the fact that she was shaking so violently, it was a wonder she didn't fall over.

Jazz positioned herself at the end of the row, caught Maddie's eye, and with a crooked finger beckoned her over. They were in the chapel. Maddie was surrounded by her schoolmates. Her homeroom teacher was watching.

She had no choice but to do as she was told.

She stepped around the other girls and out into the aisle and Jazz led the way out of the chapel and into the hallway, all the way to the stairwell just to be sure no one would overhear and they wouldn't disturb anyone.

"It looks like you could use a little fresh air," Jazz told the girl.

"Not really, I'm —"

"Fine? Yeah. That's what I always said when people asked me how I was doing after my dad was killed."

Maddie gulped. "It's not the same, I don't think."

"Because . . ."

"It's not like Ms. Quinn was anything to me," Maddie said. Jazz might have actually believed her if a tear didn't slip down the girl's cheek. "I mean, not like your dad must have been to you. I didn't feel . . ." Maddie looked at her shoes. "I didn't feel anything for Ms. Quinn."

"Except yesterday, you told me you hated her."

Maddie sniffled. "I felt guilty about saying that yesterday."

"Because it was something you shouldn't have told me?"

"Because . . ." Her words caught behind a sob. "Because it isn't true. I was just so . . ."

"Angry?" Jazz ventured.

Maddie shrugged. "I guess. Maybe angry. All this time . . ." Her words stuttered over a long breath. "I thought she left me. Just like that. I thought she left and never said good-bye."

"And of course that made you angry."

Maddie glanced up at Jazz. "You mean I'm not a bad person for feeling that way?"

"We're all feeling that way."

Maddie scrubbed a finger under her nose. "Really? I know Ms. Quinn . . . I know she wasn't exactly a favorite around here."

As if Jazz couldn't have guessed, she asked, "Who told you that?"

"She did." It was obviously a confidence, and already feeling bad about for betraying it, Maddie blushed. "She didn't want to seem like she was whining. She didn't want to say anything about it to anyone else. But she told me. She told me —"

"What?"

Maddie's cheeks were streaked with tears. "I know she was going to get fired."

"If that's what Ms. Quinn told you, she was wrong. That wasn't official. In fact, we were trying to work with Ms. Quinn to help her settle in here at St. Catherine's. We even offered her a different job if it would make her more comfortable, a job in the library. Did she tell you that?"

The girl nodded. "She said that would have been the easy way out, and because it wasn't what God wanted, she couldn't do it. She had to keep going, no matter what it cost her. You know, like the early martyrs. She had to bring girls into Christ's light by teaching religion. She said it was her mission."

"Did she say who told her so?"

"You mean the angels?" Maddie wrinkled her nose. "I didn't believe her. Not at first. I mean, I was just an eighth grader and there was this teacher, telling me she talked to angels, that they talked to her. And I was . . ." When she shook her head, Maddie's long dark hair twitched around her

154

shoulders. "I guess I was confused. At least until she proved it to me."

"She proved that she talked to angels? Maddie, you might have believed that when you were in the eighth grade, but now —"

"No! It's true, Ms. Ramsey. You were there the day it happened. Don't you remember?"

It was a Friday, late. Except for the Drama Club going over their lines for *The Crucible* in the media room and the girls on the cross-country team who, along with Jazz, had just returned from a meet, the school was quiet, empty. If Jazz hadn't been careless and left her phone somewhere before they headed out to the meet, she'd be home by now. The way she remembered it, she had the phone at lunchtime. She'd called her dad about dog training that weekend. After that . . .

With a sigh and a grumble, Jazz took the steps two at a time, hurrying up to the third floor.

They'd had a florist in that afternoon to look over the chapel and give them an estimate on the cost of flowers for the celebration of Saint Catherine's feast day on November 25, and Jazz wondered if she'd left the phone up there. She hoped so. She knew exactly where she'd sat as the

155

florist went over flower suggestions, pricing, and his vision of having palms — a symbol of the saint — in clusters at every pew. If the phone was in the chapel, she'd have it in a jiffy and be back downstairs in a flash.

She'd better be. It was already after six, and she had a date at seven thirty.

On the steps that led up to the school's third floor, Jazz paused, caught her breath, and smiled. She'd met Nick Kolesov at a friend's wedding the weekend before. At the time they'd shared a table and a dance, exchanged smiles and phone numbers, and the next thing she knew, though Jazz swore she'd never date a guy whose job was public service like her firefighter brothers, she had agreed to go out with a cop.

A cute cop.

She didn't need to remind herself about that. Just thinking about Nick — tall, honey haired, blue-eyed, and as sexy as they came — made her tingle with anticipation. He was the total package, and normally Jazz would know better than to surrender to the craziness that seeped into her brain and made her blood whoosh inside her ears.

But this was different.

Nick was different.

They'd agreed to meet for pizza at Edison's, a place right in the neighborhood.

Not exactly formal, but still, Jazz wanted to get home in plenty of time to get ready. She didn't know many cops and she'd never dated one, but she knew if they were anything like firefighters, Nick's time off was precious. She wanted to make the most of every minute they had together.

Still smiling, she got to the third floor, pushed through the chapel door, and stopped cold.

Bernadette Quinn was already in the chapel.

And Maddie Parker was with her.

They were sitting side by side in a pew on the far side of the chapel, and at the sounds of Jazz's footsteps and her rough breathing they both whirled toward the door.

At the same time Jazz moved toward the pew where she'd sat earlier in the day — her phone was there and she scooped it up and tucked it in the pocket of her windbreaker with the St. Catherine's Panther on it — she pasted a smile on her face and closed in on Bernadette and Maddie.

"It's late. What are you two still doing here?"

"Ms. Quinn, she's telling me about the —"

"Maddie's been having a little trouble with testing." Bernadette cut the girl off.

"We're coming up with a plan for her to work on her reading."

"That's . . . great." By now, Jazz was closer to them and she saw that whatever they were talking about, Maddie didn't look upset or tense. In fact, she was grinning.

"You must have come up with a good plan," Jazz said. "You look happy about it, Maddie."

"It's just . . ." Maddie shrugged. But then, what did Jazz expect? Maddie was in eighth grade, a conscientious kid who was eager to please but sometimes, thanks to her dyslexia, was on the wrong end of her classmates' not-so-funny jokes. Maddie got to her feet and she and Bernadette exchanged looks. And smiles.

"And you're right, Ms. Ramsey," Maddie said. "It *is* late. My mom had to work a few extra hours at the hospital. She should be here soon." She gathered up the pile of books on the pew next to her. "I'll see you on Monday, Ms. Quinn."

Once Maddie left the chapel, Jazz braced her hands on the front of the pew and leaned forward. "You're spending a lot of time with Maddie."

Bernadette slipped into the black sweater that was on the seat next to her. "She's trying very hard and I know her parents have arranged for tutoring to help with her reading, but it never hurts to give her a little extra reinforcement. I developed some study strategies in college that really helped me, and I'm just passing them on to her. She's . . ." Bernadette's chest rose and fell. "Maddie's a great kid."

Jazz stepped back to indicate that she'd let Bernadette walk out of the chapel ahead of her. "Do you really think it's a good idea to meet with her privately?"

Bernadette was already out of the pew. She genuflected, bowed her head toward the altar, and popped up again. "Are you suggesting something's going on between me and Maddie that's improper?"

Jazz knew better than to fight that battle. At least here in the chapel where there were no witnesses and no one to back up what either of them might — or might not — say to each other.

"I'm saying that's exactly what we don't want anyone to say," she told Bernadette. "We can make sure of that if you'd have your tutoring and counseling sessions in your classroom like Sister Eileen asked you to do."

Halfway to the door, Bernadette stopped and turned to face Jazz, her hands clutched at her waist. "You're right. Of course you're

159

right, and so is Sister Eileen. But Maddie's a shy kid and she hates it when the other girls see us working together."

"If any of them are giving Maddie a hard time —"

"You can be sure I won't let that happen." Even Bernadette was surprised to hear the sharpness of her own words when they echoed back from the dome above their heads. She winced, drew in a long breath, forced a smile. "What I mean, of course, is that I'm keeping close tabs on how the other girls treat Maddie."

"If there's a problem —"

"If there's a problem . . . ." Bernadette steadied her shoulders and raised her chin before she turned and marched away. "You can be sure I'll deal with it."

There in the stairwell with the last strains of the last prayer of the service for Bernadette filling the air, Maddie lifted her chin and clutched her hands at her waist, the gesture so like what Jazz had seen Bernadette do a dozen times, it made her feel as if she saw a vision from the grave.

"Don't you see, Ms. Ramsey, Ms. Quinn proved it to me that day you found us in the chapel together. About talking to the angels, I mean. Back before she . . ." Her

160

voice and her breath wobbled. "Back before she died. She proved to me that she talked to angels. And you know how? Because that day you came up to the chapel and saw me there with Ms. Quinn, she told you a little white lie. She told you we were talking about my reading, and that is usually what we did. We worked on reading exercises, and she really helped me. You know that, too. She really helped me with my reading and with my oral presentation skills. But that's not what we were really talking about that day. Because see, that was the day Ms. Quinn told me about the angels. She told me the angels told her about Alanda Myers and that guy she was dating. Seth . . . Seth Somebody."

It had happened three years earlier and all Jazz could say for sure was that she remembered Alanda was a senior at the time, a kid with decent grades and a good head on her shoulders. Why she and her boyfriend would be of any interest to angels was anybody's guess.

"What about them?" Jazz asked.

Too excited to keep still, Maddie rolled up on the balls of her feet. "They broke up!"

Apparently, Jazz's blank expression wasn't what Maddie was expecting.

"Don't you get it?" the girl asked Jazz.

161

"One day, the angels told Ms. Quinn that Alanda and Seth broke up. And Ms. Quinn, she told me about it. Then the next morning . . . well, that's when the story went all around the school. Alanda told her friends what was going on. She really did break up with Seth. Don't you see that this proves everything? Ms. Quinn, she knew all about it before anyone else did. She knew because the angels told her."

Maybe it was a good thing the memorial service ended and the doors of the chapel swung open. Jazz wasn't sure how to deal with the rush of exhilaration that made Maddie's eyes spark. When the crowd started for the stairwell, Jazz and Maddie descended to the next landing and stood back as a long line of girls, many of them with swollen eyes and tears on their cheeks, headed back downstairs.

Jazz turned to Maddie. "You can wait here for your homeroom," she told the girl. "And I'll —"

Jazz's words dissolved. She'd been looking at Maddie. She couldn't be sure. She stood on tiptoe and scanned the crowd, searching for the man she swore had just walked past.

A man who rolled from side to side as he walked. Like he was used to being on a boat.

CHAPTER 10

It was nearly impossible to break into the steady stream of girls and teachers coming down the steps. Jazz stood back and waited for just the right moment and managed to wedge her way between one junior home-room group and another, inching through the crowd with them, step by step, trying to catch a glimpse ahead. Even when she stood on tiptoe, she didn't see the man with the funny gait, and she wondered if her eyes had been playing tricks on her.

Most of the girls left the stairway at the second floor to return to the upper-class homerooms, and by the time Jazz got back to the first floor the hallway was empty except for Frank and Eddie from Mainte-nance and Loretta Hardinger, chatting outside her office.

They told her they hadn't seen the man she described and Jazz ducked out the front door of the building and glanced up and down the street.

If the man Marilyn had pointed out as the one who visited Bernadette — and argued with her — had been at the memorial, he was gone now.

Or maybe he'd never been there at all.

Wondering if it mattered, she dragged back inside, and since Frank and Eddie and Loretta were still there, she offered them coffee from her state-of-the-art (and donated) machine, and while she was at it she poured one for herself, too. Loretta declined. The coffee she made in the old percolator she kept in the cafeteria was better by far than anything Jazz's fancy machine could produce and they both knew it. Frank and Eddie weren't so picky. They grabbed cups of coffee, and before they had a chance to walk out of the office Eileen walked in with a man at her side.

"I was hoping we'd catch you." Eileen set down the stack of prayer cards she'd brought down from the chapel with her. The cards featured a picture of Saint Francis of Assisi (Eileen and Jazz had decided it was what Bernadette would have liked) on one side and information about Bernadette, including her birthday date and where her ashes would be interred, on the other. Done with that, she got a cup of coffee for her

164

guest and poured one for herself, too.

"Jazz Ramsey," Eileen said, "Sam Tillner, Bernadette Quinn's cousin."

They shook hands, and Jazz took a moment to think how much Sam didn't look like Bernadette. He was tall, thin, and his hair was a color that reminded her of oak leaves in autumn. It fell around his shoulders in luxurious waves and brushed the black-and-white-striped silk scarf he had looped at his throat. He was arty, flamboyant. He didn't have to say a word; she just knew it. By the way he walked, relaxed and easy. By the way he stood, shoulder slightly forward, chin up. Tillner was thirty-five or so. He had a small nose, full lips, a scar shaped like a half-moon on his left cheek. He wore khaki pants that were a little too baggy for his slim frame and a white cotton dress shirt.

He wasn't used to formal occasions like funerals, Jazz decided. He didn't own a suit.

Or maybe he didn't think enough of his cousin to wear one in her honor.

Jazz pushed the thought away. "I'm very sorry about your cousin," she told him. "Thank you for coming today."

"I wanted to be here." When Jazz waved toward the guest chair in front of her desk, he sat down. "I'm not a religious person.

but Bernadette sure was. She's going to be cremated and her ashes will be buried at Calvary Cemetery next to her parents' grave. This was her only chance to get the kind of church send-off I know she would have liked."

Send-off.

Jazz thought it was a flippant way to think of a memorial service, but at the same time, she wondered something else.

"What did you do three years ago?" she asked Tillner.

He shifted his coffee cup from one hand to the other, waiting for her to explain.

"I mean . . ." Jazz sipped her coffee. It gave her time to think. Time to line up her questions. "Bernadette never came back to school after Christmas break."

Tillner nodded.

"And we never thought anything of it . . ." Eileen was standing over by the windows and Jazz glanced her way, "because her resignation letter was waiting here for us when we came back to school after the first of the year."

Another nod. Tillner had, no doubt, heard all of this from Detective Lindsey.

"But by the first of the year when we got that letter," Jazz explained, "she must have already been dead. So what did you do?"

she asked him. "When she didn't show up for Christmas dinner? When she wasn't at a New Year's Eve party or some holiday brunch? When you called and she didn't answer?"

He leaned forward so he could set his coffee cup on Jazz's desk. "The police have already asked me," he said. "And I'll tell you what I told them. Bernadette and I are all that's left of the family and it was never very big to begin with. My mother and her father were brother and sister. My mom was years younger than Uncle Ben; they didn't have much in common. Mom was a trained opera singer. Uncle Ben worked at a gas station. They didn't exactly travel in the same circles." He fingered one end of his scarf. "Consequently, Bernadette and I were never close. So you see, it didn't matter about Christmas dinner or New Year's Eve, or anything else. Bernadette and I . . . we never saw each other."

In Jazz's world, not spending the holidays with family was a mortal sin. When she realized Tillner was watching her, trying to make sense of her confused expression, she smiled. "Big family," she explained, and pointed a finger at herself. "Brothers, cousins, aunts, and uncles. Very close. Sometimes too close. It's great to have them

167

around. And it can be crazy making, too. But . . ." She wrinkled her nose. "I can't even begin to imagine what it would be like to not have them in my life."

Tillner laughed. He had slim hands and long fingers and he wore four heavy gold rings on each hand. There was a garnet at the center of one of them, and it winked at Jazz and reminded her of the fake gemstones in Bernadette's cross. "The way our family was . . . well, that's why it was so strange . . ." As if he'd thought through the problem before and wasn't any closer to finding an answer to it now than he had been then, he frowned. "Well, that's why I thought it was weird when Bernadette asked me to take care of her cat."

It was such a surprise, Jazz flinched. "Like she knew she was going away?"

He shrugged. "Well, I can't say for sure. I mean, at the time, it struck me as odd that she would call me at all, but —"

"She called you? When? Can you remember exactly?"

Another shrug did not fill Jazz with confidence. "Would it make a difference?"

"Sure." This was important news and it made Jazz feel as if she was finally getting somewhere with her inquiry into Bernadette's death. Rather than pace the room and let Tillner know how his words stirred her hopes and shot her through with adrenaline, she dropped into her desk chair. "If it was after break started then my whole theory —" She caught herself and felt her cheeks get hot. "What I mean, of course, is that the police think Bernadette was killed the last day of school before break. That's what they've told us, anyway. But if there's any chance she called you after that, well, that changes everything."

Tillner shifted in his chair. "It's hard to remember exactly. I'm sure . . . I'm pretty sure it was before Christmas. I mean . . ." His laugh was light and nervous. "It must have been, right? Because like you said, by Christmas, Bernadette was already . . . uh . . . She must have already been . . . uh . . . d-dead." He tripped over the word and Jazz understood. One of the things she'd learned from working with cadaver dogs was that people were not comfortable with the idea of death. It wasn't just overwhelming. It was too much of a reminder of their own mortality.

"I wish I could be more accurate." Tillner sighed. "But hey, it was three years ago, and at the time it's not like I thought it was all that important."

"Except like you said, you never talked to

her. And all of a sudden, she called and asked for your help." Jazz considered the implications and would have gone on considering them if Frank and Eddie hadn't distracted her by stepping back into the office to refill their coffee cups. Once they were gone, she asked Tillner, "What did she say when you talked to her?"

"Oh, I didn't talk to her. She left a message. On my voicemail. She asked me to look in on her cat."

"And you did."

He nodded. "Bernadette gave a house key to my mother years ago. You know, in case of an emergency. Mother was getting old and forgetful and she was afraid she was going to lose it so she gave the key to me. I found it and went over there and . . ." He gave his shoulders a twitch. "It was obvious the poor cat hadn't eaten in a few days. I took care of him, checked again in another few days, and —" He threw his hands in the air and they slapped back down against the arms of the chair. "After a while I stopped questioning it. I'd go check on the cat; Bernadette would be nowhere around; I'd feed the cat, clean the litter box, and leave."

"How long did you do that?"

"Months."

170

"And you didn't think to call the police?"

"Why?" Tillner's shrug spoke volumes. "Bernadette told me to stop by. She told me to watch the cat. And it wasn't the first time she dropped off the face of the earth."

This was news.

Jazz and Eileen exchanged looks before Eileen stepped forward. "What do you mean?"

"Well, it's not like I know any of the details," Tillner admitted. "Like I said, we weren't anywhere near close. But Bernadette and I both went to Rocky River High School. And I remember . . ." Thinking, he closed his eyes. "It was a year or so after we graduated, I think. One of our older distant cousins got married and everyone from the family was there. Everyone but Bernadette. When I asked where she was, Uncle Ben and Aunt Agnes, they just blew me off, like they never heard me. And everyone else . . . well, no one kept in touch with the family so everyone else was just as much in the dark as I was. So you see, when I thought she went away, I didn't think anything of it. It was no big deal."

"No big deal that you got a voicemail message from a woman who disappeared?" Jazz countered.

"Only I didn't know she disappeared, did

171

I?" Tillner snapped. The next second, he dipped his head and pulled one corner of his mouth tight by way of apology. "All I knew was that she called and asked for a favor. Yeah, it seemed odd, but there was a lot about my cousin that was odd. I figured she needed help and I knew she didn't have friends. I thought it must have been pretty important if she actually picked up the phone and —"

"Did she?" Something about the story struck Jazz as odd. "Was it Bernadette who picked up the phone and left a message? Did you recognize her voice?"

He huffed out a breath. "It was a long time ago."

"Yeah, but it seems to me that's the kind of detail you'd remember. When you listened to the message about watching the cat, are you sure it was from Bernadette?"

The tips of his ears got red. "Like I said . . ." He put out his hands, palms up, as if that would explain the lack of words, the lack of a real explanation. "We weren't very close."

"Which means it didn't sound like her."

"Which means I can't say if it was or it wasn't her. I was on my way somewhere when I picked up the voicemail. I do remember that. I was in my car, in a hurry, I listened to the message; I grumbled because . . . well, who could blame me? My holy roller cousin who never had a nice thing to say about me or my friends, or anyone else for that matter, calls out of the blue and suddenly needs me to look after her cat? Honestly, I don't know if it was Bernadette. I just assumed it was. You think . . ." He was pale to begin with and his face turned ashen. "You think it was the killer?"

"There's no way we can know that for sure." Jazz didn't know if this was as reassuring as she wanted it to be. Tillner's hands beat out a nervous rhythm against the arms of the chair. "You didn't save that voicemail, did you?"

"All this time? Obviously not. I probably didn't keep it after I listened to it once. I took care of the cat and that was that."

Jazz was almost afraid to ask. "Is he still alive? Is he being cared for?"

"Pumpkin? Sure." Tillner pushed out of the chair. "Look, I really appreciate your concern about my cousin, but I have to get going. Thank you. . . ." He stepped forward and shook Eileen's hand, then did the same with Jazz. "Thank you both for putting together that wonderful service. Bernadette would have loved it."

173

Jazz managed to wait until he'd walked out of the office to tell Eileen, "I wonder how he knows she would have loved it. Bernadette was pretty much a stranger to him."

"He's the one who called here and asked about having the memorial in the chapel," Eileen said. "He obviously knew she taught here."

"And if they were never in touch, how could he possibly know that?" Jazz asked.

Eileen finished her coffee and took her cup across the room to deposit it on the table with the coffeemaker. "I suppose the police told him."

"I suppose," Jazz conceded. Which didn't mean she was satisfied. She unlocked the file cabinet where staff records were kept and took out Bernadette's folder and flipped through it.

"He's not listed as next of kin," she told Eileen, and held the page out to her so she could see it for herself. "Bernadette left that line blank."

It was just as well the school year was winding down.

The end of the school year usually meant the girls were so antsy, they couldn't sit still. They were anxious for vacation, eager to move up a grade, looking forward to summer jobs and summer adventures.

At least that's the way it had always been. Before Bernadette was found.

The day after the memorial service when Jazz walked through the hallways, she realized there was no buzz of excitement in the air, not like usual. There was no chatter, no laughter. Just an errant breeze that fluttered the paintings the girls had done the day Bernadette's remains were found, as if an invisible hand was rustling the pages, telling them not to forget.

The girls needed the summer to recover.

They all needed some closure.

That thought in mind, Jazz finished up her work as quickly as she could and headed out early and with Eileen's blessing.

Jazz didn't warn Taryn Campbell's dad she was coming. If she had, she knew he would have told her to get lost, go to hell. Instead, she drove to a neighborhood on the west side of Cleveland where the lawns were well-groomed, the beds were bursting with springtime flowers, and the houses were modest but sturdy, like the city itself. She arrived on the front porch of the trim white house with blue shutters, rang the bell, and took a deep breath.

Leon Campbell answered the door, took one look at her, and his mouth fell open. At least for the space of one heartbeat. Then his top lip curled and he growled, "Go to hell."

"Mr. Campbell —" Before he could close the door in her face, Jazz put a hand on it. "If I could just talk to you for one minute."

"What, like you and the rest of those rich snobs talked to me and my girl three years ago?" Campbell, a bus driver, was a big man with wide shoulders and a square jaw. His face twisted, his eyes sparked. "I'm done talking to you. I was done talking to you back then. If you had an ounce of sense, you'd know that."

Jazz had promised herself she wouldn't be goaded into an argument. That she wouldn't get defensive. That she wouldn't lose her cool.

So much for promises.

"It isn't my fault Taryn plagiarized her scholarship essay," she snapped. "That was Taryn's doing. Mr. Campbell, I know you were angry then and I can understand that you don't want to see me now. But I need to talk to you."

He'd seen the news; he didn't need to ask what she wanted to talk about.

"Bernadette Quinn was a nutcase," he said.

It wasn't Jazz's place to agree or disagree.

176

"She had high expectations for her students."

"Is that what you call 'em? Ex-pec-ta-tions?" There was no humor in his laugh. "She piled homework on those girls until they barely had time to breathe. Made them read and read and read some more. And praying!" A shake of his head told Jazz exactly what he thought. "I expect some praying at a religious school, sure I do. But do you know, on Monday mornings, she actually had the nerve to ask the girls how much prayin' they'd done over the weekend."

Jazz did know it. So did Eileen. It was one of the things that had first alerted them to the fact that Bernadette might have been too zealous.

"You argued with her," she said.

Campbell's eyes bulged. "You bet I did! I didn't like the way the woman was always pickin' on my girl. No father is going to let a teacher get away with that. No father worth calling himself a father, anyway."

"You can understand how Ms. Quinn might have been sensitive. Taryn was one of the girls who brought the cat to school and —"

"Okay, all right. That was harebrained and me and Taryn's stepmother, you can believe we told her so. Grounded her for months after. But that one stupid decision about the cat didn't give that Ms. Quinn the right to watch Taryn like a hawk, to eavesdrop on her conversations and go behind her back when she turned in that essay and —"

"Verify that it was really her work? That was exactly what Ms. Quinn was supposed to do, and you know it. What Taryn did was wrong."

"And you expelled her."

He didn't mean Jazz personally, but she got the drift. "There are rules," she said, "and —"

"And nothing."

She had meant to be more polite, to be slicker and bring it up more carefully, but there was only so much Jazz could take. "You threatened Bernadette."

Campbell froze. Right before his hand tightened on the door. "Are you accusing me of something?"

"No." She wanted to make that perfectly clear, even if it wasn't completely true. "But I am trying to find some answers. When we had the meeting about what Taryn had done, when Ms. Quinn explained everything to Sister Eileen and the board, you were there, and you weren't happy."

"Did you expect me to be?"

"I expected you'd be upset. But we all heard you after the meeting, Mr. Campbell. Out in the hallway. We heard you tell Ms. Quinn —"

"That I was going to wring her neck and toss her on the garbage heap, just like you all tossed my girl out."

Jazz let the words settle. "Ms. Quinn was killed soon after that."

"Yeah, she was. And you know what? I think the world's a better place without that crazy bitch in it."

His words still hung in the air when he slammed the door in Jazz's face.

There was no use knocking again and trying to learn more. Three years and Leon Campbell was still as mad as hell.

Mad enough to kill?

Jazz wondered. She was still considering it when she got back to where she'd parked her car at the curb, three doors down from the Campbells'. Before she could open the door, she heard someone call out, "Hey, Ms. Ramsey! Wait up."

Taryn Campbell dashed out of the backyard. At the front of the house, she glanced over her shoulder at the door. There was no sign of her dad, and she joined Jazz near the SUV. "I thought that was you talking to

my dad," she said. "I just wanted to tell you
—"

The front door opened and Leon stepped onto the porch, fists on hips.

Taryn told her dad she'd be right there, then turned back to Jazz. "I just wanted you to know, that's all. I just wanted you to know that what happened to me back at St. Catherine's, I'm not mad about it anymore. I'm good with all of it now."

It was a remarkably mature thing for Taryn to say. "You like your new school then?" Jazz asked her.

"I'm getting college credits for the classes I take. And it's public school, so no tuition. My stepmom and dad don't have to work so hard all the time. And the good news is, leaving St. Catherine's got me away from Cammi and Juliette."

"Taryn, you get over here!" Campbell's voice boomed through the neighborhood.

"Gotta go," Taryn told Jazz. "Only I know what you came to talk to Dad about, Ms. Ramsey. We heard all about Ms. Quinn on the news. My dad . . ." Just when she said it, he took a couple steps down the stairs and Taryn backed away. "He makes a lot of noise, but he wouldn't hurt anybody. But, Ms. Ramsey, you need to talk to Juliette and Cammi. Ask them about the angels."

CHAPTER 11

Thursday.

Just one more day.

One more day and the school year would be finally — blessedly — over.

Jazz had just finished logging the last batch of summer school applications into her computer and she sat back, sighed, and hoped the way she felt was more a reflection of everything that had happened over the last months and not a result of major job burnout.

She had always liked working at St. Catherine's. Her job was challenging, fulfilling. It was different every day. The school was second to none, the girls were (usually) great, and the teachers were professional and believed in what they were doing. She adored Sarah and was glad they saw each other just about every day. She liked and admired Eileen and she worked hard to live up to the principal's high expectations.

But right then and there, on that Thursday afternoon in early June, even with the sun streaming into her office windows and the sound of birdsong floating in from the park, she hated the way she felt. First there was the murder of Florie Allen, who'd once been a St. Catherine's girl. Then there was Bernadette. It was enough to make her feel as if she was being crushed under a pile of rocks. As if the life had been sucked out of her. As if there was nothing left of her but bones.

Just like Bernadette.

Jazz rubbed her hands up and down her arms.

"No way you're cold." Eileen sailed out of her office. "It's sweltering in here. I was just going to go find Eddie and ask him to check the AC. You need a sweater?"

"I need a . . ." Jazz hated herself for sighing, but sigh she did. "I need answers," she admitted.

Halfway to the door, Eileen stopped, turned around, and came to stand at Jazz's desk. "I know you're looking for them."

"I'm at a dead end."

The principal cocked her head. "You sure?"

"You know about something I've missed?"

"I didn't say that. Believe me, if I knew

something you didn't know, I'd be only too happy to share. I just got off the phone with Detective Lindsey."

Jazz popped out of her chair. "The guy's a jackass."

"A jackass with a badge," Eileen reminded her. "And a bug up his ass. He actually thinks I killed Bernadette. He's just waiting for the pieces to fall into place and then . . ."

Jazz refused to even consider the *and then*. "We're not going to let that happen," she told her boss. "I swear to you, I'm going to do everything I possibly can to —"

"I know that." The warmth of Eileen's smile was enough to melt the spurt of anger that coursed through Jazz. "I'm not worried. Not exactly. At least not too much." Her smile faded. "Lindsey can't find any evidence if there isn't any, right?"

"That's how it's supposed to work." Jazz didn't want to upset her, so she didn't add that she wasn't sure justice always prevailed. Sure, she'd brought Florie Allen's killer to justice. But then there was her dad. Michael Patrick Ramsey had been killed in an arson fire more than a year earlier and no one had ever been held accountable for that. Justice? She wanted desperately to believe in it, but these days all she believed was that justice was a slippery thing.

She was almost afraid to ask. "What did you tell Lindsey?"

Eileen's shrug spoke volumes. "I told him he was barking up the wrong tree."

"Did he believe you?"

"He . . ." She twitched away the memory. "He reminded me . . . like I needed the reminder . . . that at the time of her death, I was on the verge of firing Bernadette and that she'd threatened to sue. He said I had plenty of motive since Bernadette might have ended up with a big settlement and the school couldn't afford it. A court case would have been bad for our bottom line and it would have made me look like the captain of a sinking ship. He mentioned in passing . . ." Eileen's expression twisted. "He just so happened to mention that I'm the only one with a key to the fourth floor."

"But are you?" It was a thought that hadn't occurred to Jazz until that moment, and from the look of surprise on Eileen's face she hadn't thought of it, either. "There must have been other keys, right?" Jazz warmed to the thought. "Back in the day. There must have been all kinds of keys to all the rooms in the building. How do you know you have the only one to the fourth floor?"

Eileen's shoulders rose and fell. "I guess I

always thought . . ."

"And while we're questioning that, let's take a look at some of the other facts we've always assumed. Like, how do we know some of the other people who had a beef with Bernadette might not have been here in school that day?" Jazz dropped back into her chair and tapped her keyboard.

Eileen came around the desk so she could lean over her shoulder.

"What are you looking for?"

"Records."

"Lindsey asked for a copy," Eileen told her. "I sent over all of December of that year."

"Except we know we don't need to look through all of December. Bernadette was alive and kicking most of December. We know that for a fact because she was here every day. We saw her. The real question is, what about that last day of school before break?" Jazz found the date she was looking for and glanced over the screen. "Look!" She didn't need to point it out since Eileen could see the screen, but Jazz did anyway. Her finger tapped on a name. "Leon Campbell signed in that day. So did his wife. They were helping clean out Taryn's locker."

"My goodness!" Taking in the news, Eileen stood up straight. "I'd forgotten all about that."

"And I can check their personal records, but my guess is that Cammi and Juliette were both here in school that day, too."

Eileen's face went pale. "You don't think —"

"I don't know what to think. I know the girls weren't crazy about Bernadette, but something tells me Cammi and Juliette took it to a whole new level. And I'm not just talking about that poor cat."

"Maybe I never should have given them all a second chance after that cat incident." Eileen never second-guessed her decisions, but before Jazz could remind her she went right on. "Look at what happened with Taryn. I've been keeping an eye on Cammi and Juliette, but —"

"But it all went down at the same time," Jazz reminded her. "You tried to intervene with Bernadette; you offered her a different job. She threatened to sue. We found out what Taryn was up to with that scholarship essay of hers. The way I remember it, it was a mess!"

"And not the best Christmas ever," Eileen admitted. "It would have been even worse if we knew." She cleared the emotion from her throat with a cough. "About Bernadette."

"There was nothing we could do about it then, but we can do something about it now."

Jazz kept reading her computer screen and the listing of key card swipes and sign-ins for that last day before Christmas break.

Like most days before breaks, that Wednesday had been a busy one. The school choir was in and out, according to the log-in. They'd gone to a nearby nursing home to visit the residents and sing Christmas carols. There was the usual coming and going of lower-class parents because both the seventh and eighth grades hosted parties for kids at a nearby Head Start preschool and volunteer parents went along to help. As a special treat for the kids, Jazz had taken Manny and the two of them passed out candy canes. A rep from a limo company came by to arrange transportation for a group of seniors in AP Lit who would be going to a Shakespeare performance in downtown Cleveland right after break.

"And there was a pizza delivery," Jazz said, reading the words on the screen.

Eileen bent nearer. "Look who ordered it," she said, and pointed. "Bernadette. That's odd. Didn't she always bring her lunch to school?"

"Except the pizza didn't come at lunchtime; it came after school. And look who delivered it while I was still out at the Head Start party." Stunned, Jazz stared at the screen that showed a scan of the form the pizza delivery guy had signed when he showed up. "Sam Tillner."

With more than three hundred thousand burials, Calvary was the largest Catholic cemetery in the Cleveland area.

Jazz wasn't intimidated by its size or by the neighborhood that was far from her Tremont home and, so, unfamiliar. She'd done her homework. She'd talked to Eddie Simpson, who lived not too far from the cemetery, and found out the easiest and quickest way to get there. She'd checked the cemetery's online records, too, before she left school that afternoon. She knew exactly where to find Ben and Agnes Quinn.

Finding her way around the massive cemetery with its twisting roads and endless lines of tombstones, angels, and crosses was another thing altogether and she got turned around a few times before she finally came across the marker for section eighty-five, the section listed on the prayer cards they'd passed out at Bernadette's memorial service. She parked and double-checked the map of the cemetery they'd given her at the office near the front gate. When she got out of the car, she looked toward where she thought the grave of Bernadette's parents should be, and caught her breath.

She was in luck!

There was a man standing over one of the graves in that direction and yeah, he could have been visiting anybody. But this man was short and squat and his dark hair, blown up and around his head by a late-spring breeze, was just as shaggy as it had been the day Bernadette's body was found and Jazz saw him pacing the sidewalk that circled the park across the street from St. Catherine's. In spite of the fact that it was a warm evening, he was wearing the same navy-blue windbreaker.

She was grateful that she'd caught a break. But not nearly as grateful as she was curious.

She took her time walking over to where he stood with his head down and his shoulders rolled forward. She didn't want to spook him. She didn't want him to turn and run toward a blue Chevy pickup, the only other vehicle parked nearby. Instead, she glanced at the headstones that dotted the ground all around her like autumn leaves, quietly reading over name after name while she prepared herself for what she was about to do, all she was about to say.

She started with "Hello" when she was still a couple rows away from where Bernadette's cremains had been interred next to the graves of her parents, and when the man looked up, startled because he thought he was alone, there were tears on his cheeks.

"You're here to visit Bernadette."

He scrubbed his knuckles over his face, sniffled. "You . . ." Collecting himself, he looked away and cleared his throat. "You knew her?"

"We worked together." Jazz closed in on the grave. The gray granite tombstone that marked Ben and Agnes's final resting place was undisturbed, but the ground next to it had been recently turned over. She offered the man a smile. "Were you a friend?"

He didn't seem to know the answer. He poked his hands into the pockets of his jacket. "They say she's been dead three years. Three years! Why didn't anyone know?"

"You were at the memorial service."

He nodded. "They wouldn't let the public in. Except for the people on a special list. They knew there would be gawkers. There are always gawkers, aren't there?"

"But you got in."

Another nod. "I talked to some guy named

Eddie. I told him . . ." He looked down at the mound of freshly turned earth. "I told him I knew Bernadette and I wasn't on the list, but I wanted to pay my respects. I slipped him a few bucks, and I pointed out that one more person . . . well, I told him how it would hardly make a difference."

He was right, but that didn't mean Eddie hadn't broken the rules and risked school security. Jazz wondered if she'd mention it to Eileen, and while she wondered it she played the only card in her hand.

"It wasn't the first time you were in the school, up in the chapel."

He'd been absorbed in his grief, but now his head came up, his eyes narrowed. "Why would you say that?"

"Because it's true. Because you were seen up there. With Bernadette."

"We were . . . I was . . ." He pulled his hands from his pockets so he could run them through his hair. It left him looking more disheveled than ever. "I'm Mark Mercer," he said. "Forestall, Clemons, and Stout. I was helping Bernadette with some legal issues."

"You're an attorney."

"No." He shook his head. "I'm a paralegal. We met the first time she came to the office to talk to Odessa Harper about taking her case. Bernadette . . ." As if waiting for permission, he looked down at the mound of lumpy earth. "I suppose keeping her confidence doesn't matter anymore."

"I know what was going on. There was talk about Bernadette's contract being terminated." It was as much as Jazz was willing to reveal. Let him think the information came directly from Bernadette and not because she took notes at the meetings Eileen had with the board and the school's attorney.

"It was totally wrong. They weren't the least bit justified. At least . . ." He kicked one foot through the grass.

"At least . . . ?" Jazz waited for more.

"Well, if Bernadette told you about the dismissal, then I'm sure she told you what the so-called problem was. That principal, she wanted Bernadette to get counseling."

"Did she tell you why?" Jazz asked him.

He stuffed his hands back in his pockets. Brought them out again. "They didn't appreciate everything Bernadette did for those girls," Mercer insisted. "She was kind and caring. She wanted what was best for them."

"Did she tell you why they wanted to terminate her contract?"

He blew out a breath. "If you're talking about the angels . . . well, that was supposed to be confidential. Nobody was supposed to know about that."

"Except Bernadette told me." That was true at least, so Jazz didn't feel guilty saying it.

"That doesn't mean she was crazy."

"Nobody said she was."

"I know . . . I know it sounds a little weird." He walked a circular path around the grave and ended up back where he'd started. "The first time Bernadette told me about it, I'll admit I thought it was a little crazy, too."

"Did Odessa Harper think it was crazy?"

Mercer studied Jazz closely. "You know I can't tell you that. That would violate attorney-client privilege."

"Except your client is dead. And you're not her attorney."

"And it's not my place . . ." Like he was cold, he shivered. "It's not my place to talk about what Ms. Harper might or might not have thought. I can only speak for myself."

"And you thought it was crazy. That's what you said."

"I said at first I thought it was crazy. But who are any of us to judge? You were a friend of Bernadette's; you know how she could be. She was so zealous, so filled with certainty. If anyone could talk to angels, it would be Bernadette. She was devoted to her beliefs. Maybe too much so."

"The two of you argued."

He pulled in a long breath and let it out slowly. "I wondered if anyone saw us, and how long it would be until someone remembered. It doesn't mean anything. We had a difference of opinion, that's all. It doesn't mean I killed her."

"No, it doesn't." Because he was looking at the ground again, Jazz tipped her head to try to catch his eye. "What was your difference of opinion about?"

"Why does it matter? It was three years ago, and that night we argued, that was the last time . . ." He choked over the words. "That was the last time I saw Bernadette. It must have been just a couple days after that she . . ." His words trailed off.

"It sounds like you knew her pretty well. Did she ever talk about anyone who she thought might want to hurt her?" Jazz wondered.

"Did she ever mention that to you?" he countered.

It was another opportunity to be honest and Jazz took it. "No."

"Not even that Sister Eileen? The one in charge of that school?"

"Bernadette was . . ." She chose her words

194

carefully. Now that she thought about it, she did remember a time when Bernadette swore Eileen was out to get her. But that wasn't the same as hurting her, was it? It wasn't the same as murder.

"Bernadette was understandably upset by all that was happening. She loved teaching."

Mercer nodded. "She did. It's all she ever wanted in her life. But that Sister Eileen, she wasn't going to let that happen. She wanted Bernadette out of there. She would have done anything to make that happen."

"Anything legal," Jazz reminded him. "That's why we —" She swallowed down the word. "The way I understand it, that's why the school was looking into legal action. You can't believe that a nun would actually —"

"Why not? From what I heard, Eileen Flannery was jealous of Bernadette." When he saw astonishment flash across Jazz's face, he smiled. "Surprised? You shouldn't be. Jealousy, that would explain why Sister Eileen didn't like it that Bernadette heard the angels."

"Because Eileen wanted to talk to angels?" The theory was so preposterous, Jazz couldn't help but laugh. "You don't know Sister Eileen. And the whole problem the school had with Bernadette, it wasn't just

195

about the angels. She wasn't comfortable meeting with parents. She didn't like it when the girls didn't toe the line as far as her way of thinking and her beliefs. And when she consulted the law firm, did she happen to mention Maddie Parker?"

Mercer's jaw tightened. He stepped back. "Parker? No, no." Another couple rolling, lopsided steps back and he trampled the bouquet of carnations on a grave in the next row. He didn't stop to fix the flowers; he just kept walking backwards.

"Whatever you're talking about," he told Jazz, "Bernadette never mentioned that person to me. If she had . . . If she had . . ." He spun around and hurried toward his truck and his words floated back at her. "I absolutely would have remembered it."

Jazz stood there long enough to watch him hoist himself into the pickup and drive away before she looked at the mashed flowers. They were on the grave of a woman named Martha Watkins. Jazz bent down to pick them up and did her best to stick them back into the vase where they'd been before Mercer took his unceremonious leave.

It was no use. The stems were snapped.

"Sorry, Martha." Jazz broke off the stems and tucked them in her pocket, then put what was left of the flowers back into the vase, and it wasn't until she was standing again, staring at the place where Mercer's truck had been, that she realized she was still talking. Maybe to Martha. Maybe to herself.

"Seems a little strange, don't you think? One mention of Maddie and he took off like his shoes were on fire."

CHAPTER 12

Five. Four. Three. Two. One.

The bell rang.

The school year was officially over.

Jazz collapsed in her chair and the air rushed out of her on the end of a long sigh.

"Hey, it can't be all that bad. Smile!" Eddie Simpson, broom in hand, ducked into the office from the hallway. It was that or get trampled by the stampede of girls headed for the school doors. "You all right, Jazz?"

She sat up. "I'm fine, Eddie. Just tired. The last week has been —"

"Yeah." He bent forward to peek into Eileen's office. She wasn't there, but he lowered his voice anyway. "That cop was back today."

Jazz knew. She'd signed Detective Lindsey in when he arrived. "It doesn't mean anything," she told Eddie, and she hoped she was right. "He's just nosing around. That's what they do."

"Like you, huh?"

Eddie had an infectious smile, all teeth and good humor, but Jazz couldn't make herself smile back. "I talked to Mark Mercer," she told him, then realized he might not know the paralegal's name. "You know, the man you let into Bernadette's memorial service even when you weren't supposed to."

Eddie had the decency to turn as red as a beet. "He seemed like such a nice guy!"

"Maybe he is, but he wasn't on the guest list."

"He was so . . . you know . . . sincere."

"And he paid you to let him in."

Eddie shuffled his feet. "You gonna tell . . ." He looked at Eileen's office again. "Her?"

"What do you think I should do?"

Eddie leaned against his broom. "You should tell. Only . . ." He had the nerve to slide her a smile. "You're not going to, are you?"

Until that moment, she wasn't really sure.

"No, Eddie. I'm not going to tell. But if I ever find out you've let someone else into the school —"

"Not going to happen, Jazz. Cross my heart." Eddie did.

Jazz was glad when Gwen Moran, a sophomore — well, now officially a junior — showed up because she'd lost her bus fare and didn't know how she was going to get home. Talking to Gwen meant Jazz didn't have to wonder if she'd just made a mistake with Eddie.

While she took care of Gwen, Eddie pushed the broom around her office, checked to see if the coast was clear, then headed back into the hallway.

"What are your plans for the summer?" Jazz asked Gwen at the same time she dug one dollar and three quarters out of her purse for the girl. "Vacation?"

"Helping my grandpa at his stand at the West Side Market." Gwen didn't look especially happy about spending the summer at the city's historic market and she made a face. And an excuse. "It's great getting paid, but we have to be down there at like five every morning." She rolled her eyes. "I'd love to have a real vacation like you have and just sit in the sun all day."

Jazz laughed. "Is that what you think happens once the school year is over?" She put the bills and coins into Gwen's hand and told her to "forget it" when Gwen swore she would pay her back at the beginning of the next school year. "I'll take a few days off next week before summer school starts," she told the girl. "And another two weeks at the end of July. But aside from that, I'll be right here. No sitting in the sun for me!"

"That sucks," Gwen decided. "You think there's anybody who really gets summer vacation?"

"Not me!" Sarah breezed into the office. Gwen was one of Sarah's art students, a talented graphic designer, and Sarah sidled up to her. "I'll be here teaching oil painting one session of summer school and computer animation another. And you . . ." She gave Gwen a look. "Remember, you promised you'd do some design work over the summer. I'd love to see what you come up with. Scan it and email it to me."

Gwen promised she would and headed out.

"Another year bites the dust!" Sarah plopped into Jazz's guest chair. "I don't know about you, but I'm glad to see this one gone. You celebrating tonight?"

"Wally and I are working on long stays."

Sarah's eyes widened. "That does sound like celebrating!"

"I just want some quiet time." Jazz shuffled the papers on her desk. She was off Monday, Tuesday, and Wednesday of the next week, and she wanted everything to be in order when she got back. "What are you doing to celebrate?"

Instead of answering, Sarah smiled.

"Matt." Jazz didn't need her to confirm or deny; the way Sarah sparkled spoke volumes. And who was Jazz to put a kibosh on that kind of exhilaration? Still, she couldn't help herself. Sarah was a friend, a good friend. And good friends always deserved honesty.

"Are you two moving too fast?" Jazz asked.

"Look who's talking!" It was a completely justified criticism, and to prove it Sarah laughed. "You and Nick jumped into bed practically the moment you met."

"Practically," Jazz admitted. "But it didn't work out, did it?"

"This is different." Sarah's chin came up. "Matt and I are different. Jazz, I'm telling you, this feels like the real thing!"

"And you know I'm thrilled for you. As for me and Nick —"

"As for you and Nick, hey, he brought you that puppy of yours, didn't he? The guy knows the way to your heart." A smile playing around her lips, Sarah got up and sauntered to the door. "Maybe this time things will work out for you, too."

"Maybe," Jazz admitted to herself once Sarah was gone. "Or maybe . . ." Maybe she didn't want to think about maybes.

Instead, Jazz finished her work, gathered her things, and headed out. Long stays with Wally would have to wait.

She had a stop to make before she went home.

Jazz's Tremont neighborhood abutted a part of town known as Ohio City, a neighborhood that was just as trendy as Tremont, just as lively, and just as busy thanks to restaurants, bars, and boutiques. From the day Bernadette was hired at St. Catherine's, Jazz had known she lived in Ohio City, but it wasn't like they'd ever been sociable outside of school.

At the thought, Jazz made a face.

Heck, she and Bernadette were hardly sociable even in school!

Bernadette never joined the staff on those rare occasions when they went out for a drink after school. She didn't go to Sarah's that weekend Sarah's divorce was final and they all met to commiserate, watch chick flicks, and eat junk food.

Bernadette didn't come to any of the cross-country meets. She missed the staff Halloween party and used the excuse that she couldn't come up with a costume idea. The Sunday before Thanksgiving when they all got together for brunch, she told them she was so sorry, but she had other plans.

Naturally, Jazz had never visited Bernadette at home.

That Friday after she left St. Catherine's she drove to Franklin Boulevard, got out of the car, and double-checked the paper in her hand, the one that listed Bernadette's last known address. She was in the correct place, all right, and at the same time she closed in on the house she wondered how a woman like Bernadette — plain and modest to a fault — could have lived in a house so downright . . .

Astonished, Jazz pulled in a breath and studied the house, from the two turrets that loomed three stories above the street to the wraparound front porch, from the gables with their mustard-yellow gingerbread trim to the fanlight stained-glass window above the double front doors. The gardens surrounding the house were lush with early-summer blooms — tulips and pansies in a muted purple that matched the color of the house, white geraniums, riotous pink roses, vibrant orange daylilies that added more than just a pop of color; they added charm and panache.

The house wasn't just amazing, it was spectacular, and so unlike Bernadette, she couldn't help but wonder if they'd ever known Bernadette — really known her — at all.

She rang the bell.

There was no answer.

Then again, what did she expect? She had no idea what Sam Tillner's schedule was like and stopping by in the hopes that he just might be there checking the house or feeding the cat had been a crapshoot from the beginning.

She'd just turned to start down the front porch steps when she heard a noise behind her and the front door opened. She turned back just in time to see a sleepy-eyed Sam Tillner tighten the belt on this green satin smoking jacket.

"Ms. Ramsey?"

At least he remembered who she was.

Jazz stepped to the door. "I wasn't sure you'd be here," she told him. "I knew I was taking a chance. It's lucky that you just happened to be —"

It took a moment for the details to register, and when they did Jazz did a second mental inventory of Sam Tillner's appearance.

His feet were bare. So were his legs. His hair tumbled over his shoulders. His eyelids were heavy.

"You're not here feeding the cat. You live here!"

Suddenly he didn't look so sleepy anymore. He opened his mouth to respond. Snapped it shut again. Before he could get any words out, the front door of the house next door popped open and a middle-aged woman walked outside carrying a watering can. She waved. Tillner waved back. After he rolled his eyes.

He pushed the door open wider and stepped back. "Why don't you come in and we can talk about it," he said.

The entryway had a polished marble floor and a crystal chandelier that hung beside a spiral staircase. The walls were painted a delicious soft caramel color. The rug on the floor was an old Persian in shades of red and tobacco and deep green.

Ahead of her was a dining room and beyond that was the kitchen, where stainless appliances gleamed alongside sleek black cupboards.

As long as she was gaping, Jazz figured she might as well go all out. She turned to take a look at the fanlight window above the front doors. The sun gleamed through the riot of flowers depicted on the window, gold and red and green and a vibrant blue that the way she remembered it — and she remembered it all too well — was the exact color of Nick's eyes.

"I never knew . . ." Jazz wondered how to say it and not insult Tillner's late cousin. "I never imagined Bernadette had such a wonderful home. Or such fabulous taste."

"Bernadette?" Tillner snorted. "Bernadette had as much taste as a bowl of cold oatmeal. Why don't you . . ." He stepped back and waved to his right. "Why don't you go sit down, Ms. Ramsey. I'm going out late tonight and I was just trying to catch a few winks. I'll go upstairs and get some clothes on and then I'll bring in some iced tea." Before she could agree on either staying or having iced tea, he bounded up the stairway and Jazz went where she was told.

Back when the house was built — it must have been well over one hundred years old — the room had once been a formal front parlor and Jazz imagined it hadn't looked much different then than it did now. There was a stiff and uncomfortable-looking red velvet fainting couch along one wall, and another couch across from it. That one was maroon, with fat cushions and piles of brightly colored pillows tossed onto it. An antique secretary desk filled one corner of the room, an old red English phone booth another. The tables were chockablock with porcelain figurines, there was a player piano nearby, and the lamp on the table in the front window had a stained-glass shade in colors that reminded her of the peacocks at the zoo.

There was a faux tiger skin rug on the floor.

Carefully, Jazz stepped over it and sat down on the maroon couch. She sank so far down into the overstuffed cushions, she had to squirm and reposition herself so her knees weren't up around her chin. By the time she was settled, Tillner was back wearing jeans and an "I Love Cleveland" T-shirt. He carried a silver tray with two glasses of iced tea on it, and he set it down on the low table between the two couches and sat down in a wing chair upholstered in fabric that reminded Jazz of a medieval tapestry.

"It's not what you think," he said, and he handed her one of the glasses of tea.

"This isn't what I think?" She looked at the glass in her hand. "Or this . . ." She glanced all around, from the tin ceiling to the stuffed swordfish that hung above the wide doorway that led into a library. "This whole incredible house isn't what I think?"

"Well, I guess the house actually is what you think it is since you think it's incredible." Tillner's laugh was as uncomfortable as his couch. "What you said before, though, you were right. I do live here." He picked up his own glass of tea, set it back down. "But I'm not a squatter or anything. I'm Bernadette's only living relative, after all. If anyone deserves to live in the house, it's me."

"You may have known you were her only relative, but for all you knew, she could have come waltzing in here anytime." Her gaze pinned him. "Unless you knew all this time that she was dead."

"What I knew . . ." Pumpkin jumped into Tillner's lap and he ran a hand through the cat's orange fur. "What I know is that I came over here to feed Pumpkin. Just like I promised Bernadette I'd do. And I came again, and again, and again, and again. And she was never here. Pumpkin needed companionship."

"And you needed . . . ?"

He scooped up the cat and set Pumpkin on the floor so he could cross his legs. "Just to help. I just wanted to help. I lived in Chicago for a while, and sure, it's not like Bernadette and I were close, but we were family. And I was back in town, craving a little family time, looking for full-time work, and —"

"And delivering pizzas."

209

He went perfectly still. Except for his chest, rising and falling suddenly as if he was running a marathon.

While she still had it, Jazz used the element of surprise to her advantage. "It was the last day of school before Christmas break. Bernadette ordered the pizza right before the last bell rang. You arrived at St. Catherine's with it at exactly four o'clock in the afternoon."

"All right. I get it." Like a traffic cop at a corner, he held out a hand. "You did your homework. You're right. Of course you're right." His shoulders folded into the high back of the chair. "It's like this. I've got a master's degree in art history. As you can imagine, it's not easy to find work in the field. At the time . . . three years ago . . . my options were pretty limited. These days I work at an auction gallery and I get to surround myself with beautiful artwork and find some amazing deals." His hand slipped to the table beside him and the porcelain figurine of a shepherdess in flowing skirts. "But back then . . ." He wasn't happy about it then. He wasn't happy about talking about it now. He frowned. "I took the only work I could get and the only work I could get was delivering pizzas."

"And you delivered one to Bernadette.

That's how you knew where she worked."

He tried for a smile that dissolved instantly. "I know when I saw you after the memorial service I told you I hadn't seen Bernadette in years, but obviously that's not true. I did see her that day. I'm sorry I lied. I just didn't want to get into the whole thing right there in your office with Sister Eileen standing there and those maintenance guys coming in and out."

Jazz could only imagine. "That day before Christmas break, you were surprised to see Bernadette?"

"Of course."

"And was she just as surprised to see you?"

Tillner cleared his throat. "Bernadette could be quite judgmental. You knew her, so I'm sure you know that. She wasn't rude to me. Not exactly. But she was stunned to see me walk into her classroom with that pizza box in my hands, and she did make it clear that if I was a different person — if I followed the rules more closely, if I lived what she liked to call a cleaner life, if only I would find my way back to the religion I was raised with . . ." He let out a long breath. "Well, she told me if I was a better person, I could turn my life around. That I wouldn't have to live with the humiliation of delivering pizzas."

Jazz knew Bernadette could be sanctimonious, harsh. She leaned forward. "I'm sorry."

"Thank you for that. Unless you mean you're sorry I was delivering pizzas. I'll tell you what, that was one of the best experiences of my life. I met some really nice people, learned my way around town, came to appreciate the value of working hard. After years in school, I needed that dose of reality to bring me out of the ivory tower of academia and back to my senses."

"And let me guess, Bernadette didn't get it."

"I don't think that friend of hers did, either, because while Bernadette was criticizing me inside and out . . . well, that other woman, she never said a word."

Jazz sat up. "Other woman?"

"Is that important?" Tillner wanted to know.

Jazz had to admit she wasn't sure. "It's just that Bernadette . . ." She thought about trying to be politically correct, then decided with the way Tillner felt about his cousin, it really didn't matter. "By the last day of school before Christmas break, Bernadette really didn't have any friends at school." Anyone but Maddie, she reminded herself.

"Any chance the person with her was a student?"

He didn't have to think about it. "Definitely not. Nicely dressed, as far as I remember. About the same age as Bernadette." Tillner shrugged. "That's all I can tell you except for the fact that when my cousin came at me like the self-righteous little bitch she was, that other woman sat there and didn't say a word."

"And Bernadette didn't introduce you."

Tillner grinned. "Bernadette didn't care much for niceties. And by the way, she tipped me seventy-five cents."

"But that day you took her the pizza, the day she criticized your life and your religious beliefs, and ran down your job and your lifestyle . . . as far as we know, that could be the day Bernadette was killed."

"And you think I killed her because she only tipped me a lousy seventy-five cents?" His laugh was harsh.

"But the house . . ." Once again, Jazz looked around the room. "Having a house like this —"

"It didn't look like this then. Not when Bernadette lived here. The house had been in her mother's family for years. That's how Bernadette ended up with it. And in all those years, no one ever bothered to restore

it to its original beauty. Beauty was *not . . .*"
He emphasized this last word. "It was not
something Bernadette cared about. Oh, she
took care of general maintenance, but the
walls were painted white. The carpet was
beige. The whole place was unoriginal and
unimaginative."

Since Jazz's walls were white and she
didn't even have carpeting, she was not one
to criticize. Rather than think about how
that made her unoriginal and unimaginative, she asked him, "So you were saying,
about how you ended up moving in and
redecorating and making the place your
own?"

His cheeks flushed. "Things were a little
iffy for me back then in the way of finances.
Even after I delivered the pizza to Bernadette that day and she treated me like crap,
I still came over to check on the cat. It was
the most natural thing in the world. Anyone
would have done it! I started visiting more
often, staying longer. Someone had to keep
poor Pumpkin company. And it's a good
thing I did. Back when I first started coming here, I let him outside one day and
someone tried to kidnap the poor baby!
Nearly snatched him right out of the backyard. That's the last time I let him out, I'll

tell you that much. Besides, the way I see it . . ."

Tillner sat up, his elbows on his knees, his fingers twined together so tightly, all those gold rings he wore sat one next to the other and looked like brass knuckles. "I thought I was actually doing Bernadette a favor by staying here and looking after the house. A year later when there was still no sign of her, I couldn't stand the drab place anymore, so I painted and decorated. The gardens were a holy mess, and I redid them and put in a patio in the backyard. What you said earlier, you were right. For all I knew, Bernadette could have come walking in the front door any day. I was looking after the house for her and I did a hell of a lot for her property value."

"Didn't you wonder where she was?"

"No." It was as simple as that. At least to Tillner. "I figured she'd come home eventually and when she did and saw how I'd taken care of everything, even the cat, I hoped she'd let me stay. I've developed quite a love for this house. And if she said no to that, well, I inherited some money when my mother passed; I was willing to make her an offer, a generous offer, to buy the house."

"And now . . . ?" Jazz wanted to know.

215

"Now? You mean, what's going to happen to the house now that Bernadette is dead?" He massaged his right hand with his left. "Her attorney called. She had a will. Believe it or not, the house is mine."

Jazz didn't bother to point out it made one heck of a good motive for murder.

She didn't have to.

One second, Tillner's cheeks flushed with color. The next, the blood drained from his face. "You don't think that means I could have —"

It wasn't her place to say. Instead, Jazz asked him, "What happened to her things?"

Tillner was so busy considering how he suddenly looked like a suspect, it took him a moment to collect himself. "Bernadette's things? I never touched them. Not for months, anyway. But I'll tell you what, there's only so long you can live with pictures of Jesus staring back at you from every wall. And the candles and the statues!" He shivered. "Don't get me wrong. I'm not against religion. But Bernadette was a little over the top. I put up with it all for a while; then one day, I finally couldn't stand it anymore. I scooped it all into boxes and dragged everything up to the attic."

"Can I look?"

"Look?" He popped out of his seat and

headed for the stairway. "There are a few boxes. If you can help me carry them down, you can have them all."

CHAPTER 13

She had just finished unloading the boxes from Bernadette's and stacking them in one corner of her living room, and Jazz stepped back and wondered which one to start on first. There were two shoe boxes, four archive boxes, a battered box with an ill-fitting cover and the name of some long-gone department store printed on its side.

She'd just decided to go with the archive boxes, one by one, when her doorbell rang. She caught a glimpse of her mom out the front window, so the boxes would have to wait. She was already smiling when she opened the door.

At least until she saw there was a man standing to Claire Ramsey's right.

Six weeks before, when she announced the news to Jazz, Claire had been up front about dating a man she'd met at church, Peter Nestico. But Jazz had never met him. Aside from the usual "Where did you go?"

218

"What did you have for dinner?" "Did you have a nice time?" she'd never asked much about him in the subsequent weeks when her mom called her to update her on how things were going with Peter.

It wasn't that she didn't want to know.

And it wasn't like she didn't care.

Her mom meant the world to her.

It was just that . . .

The familiar pang of heartache stabbed Jazz's insides.

This Peter Nestico character wasn't her dad. He never could be.

But there he was, standing on her front porch, and now she gave him a quick once-over.

Peter was tall — but not as tall as Michael Patrick Ramsey had been.

Peter had blue eyes — but the color wasn't nearly as deep or as gorgeous as her dad's.

Peter was a man close to sixty, she guessed, and he had a trim figure and wide shoulders. But he was nowhere near as muscular as Michael Ramsey.

Peter had iron-gray hair.

Ha!

Though her dad's dark hair was shot through with gray, he was years away from going totally silver. Jazz couldn't say why it was important to her, but it was. Maybe it was because when she dreamed about her dad he was forever fifty.

"Honey?" Her mother's voice penetrated her thoughts and Jazz shook herself back to reality. "Jasmine, I'd like you to meet —"

"Peter Nestico." He stepped forward, stuck out his hand, and offered a smile. There was a gap between his two front teeth. "Your mom talks about you a lot. I'm glad to finally meet you, Jasmine."

No one called her Jasmine.

Except her mom.

And her dad.

A quick, fierce shot of resentment marched across Jazz's shoulder blades before it dug down deep. Her spine went stiff. Her chin came up. Somehow, she managed a smile. She wondered if it looked as tight around the edges as it felt. "Come on in," she told her mom and Peter.

Naturally, the sounds of activity and the voices of visitors roused Wally from the nap he'd been taking in the kitchen and a scramble of claws against the hardwood floor announced his arrival. He knew Claire. He gave her a tail wag and a lick. Peter was new. Before Jazz could stop him, Wally jumped up on Peter.

"Off!" Jazz commanded.

Wally didn't even acknowledge her. But

then, he was too busy enjoying the attention when Peter rippled a hand over his woolly head and said, "Oh, he's all right. I don't mind."

"I mind," Jazz told him. She hardened her voice. "Off, Wally. Sit."

Wally had heard the iron in her voice before. The time he got into the garbage. The time he'd chewed her newest pair of running shoes.

He sat.

"He's going to be big," she told Peter, mad at herself for feeling she had to make excuses, that she had to apologize. This man was dating her mother. He was trying to take her dad's place. He's the one who owed the apologies. "I don't want him to develop any bad habits."

"I get it." Peter sent one smile to Jazz and another to Wally, who ate up the admiration with a slurp and a butt wiggle. He stroked Wally's back. "We had Labs when the kids were young, so I'm used to big dogs. I'm used to crazy puppies, too." He rubbed a hand over Wally's head and Wally let out a whimper of approval. "I know you need to be firm. This little guy is just so adorable, I wasn't thinking straight."

Okay. All right.

Some of the starch went out of Jazz's

shoulders.

So Peter Nestico liked dogs and he knew a little about training them. He had good taste; he thought Wally was adorable.

One point in Peter's favor.

Still, Jazz couldn't stop herself; she glanced at the photograph on a shelf nearby. Jazz and Manny, her first HRD dog. Her dad and Big George, his search and rescue dog. In the picture, Dad was smiling.

Jazz turned toward her mom and saw that looking at Peter, Claire was smiling, too.

It hit her then. Somewhere between her heart and her stomach. In the fourteen months since her husband's death, Claire had been chipping away at her grief and Jazz and her brothers had been doing all they could to help, hoping that someday their mom would rise above the crippling agony of remembrance and live again.

It looked like Claire had. It looked like she would.

It was time for Jazz to watch, to learn, and to do the same thing. She'd never get over the sadness. She'd never forget. But here and now, it was time to move on.

Jazz's eyes welled, and before either Peter or her mom could notice, she turned away and swiped at them with her fists.

Peter had done what she and her brothers

still struggled with. He made her mom happy. Damn! She had no choice but to give Peter another point.

"Why don't you . . ." She turned back around, cleared the emotion from her throat, and her smile was genuine when she waved toward the couch. But before she had a chance to tell them to settle in and she'd get drinks, Claire wound her arm through Jazz's.

"We're not here to stay," her mother told her. "We're taking you out to dinner. You know, to celebrate the end of the school year."

Jazz looked over the pile of boxes she'd brought from Bernadette's. She was itching to look through them, anxious to uncover their secrets. "That's really nice, Mom, but —"

"But nothing." Peter grinned. "Your mother has made up her mind, and if there's one thing I've learned, once that happens, not much is going to change it."

He knew her mother well. "But I have plans," she told them both.

"Plans with Nick?" her mother wanted to know.

"No, not with Nick. With —"

"Maybe another guy?" Claire wondered.

"No, not with a guy."

223

"Well, I know you're not going anywhere with Sarah tonight because Matt and Sarah have a date." Jazz didn't even bother to wonder how her mother knew. Matt and her brothers, Hal and Owen, were great friends. Hal and Owen told her mother everything. And even if they didn't bring up the subject of Matt's dating, Claire would somehow manage to worm the information out of them. She was talented like that. "Who exactly are you going out with?"

"I'm not going out with anybody. Wally and I are going to work on long stays and —"

"See." Claire leaned in close to Peter and spoke in a stage whisper clearly meant for Jazz's ears. "I told you that's exactly what she was going to say."

"You two were talking about me?" Jazz threw her hands in the air, exasperated. Her mother could be nosy, interfering —

And totally loving and wonderful. It was so good to see her happy and joking again.

"I'll grab a jacket," Jazz said. "Where are we going?"

"Thought we'd try Bourbon Street Barrel Room." Jazz had already started up the stairs to her bedroom and Peter called up to her, "I hear they've got a kick-ass jambalaya!"

224

When she got to her bedroom, Jazz made a face at herself in the mirror that hung above her dresser.

She knew this day would come sooner or later. She knew she was bound to meet Peter. And she'd promised herself that when she did, she'd stay strong. There was no way she was going to like him.

And here she was, going to dinner with him.

And giving him another point.

After all, the man loved kick-ass jambalaya.

Peter Nestico was not as good a storyteller as her dad. He wasn't as funny or as irreverent. He wasn't as handsome and he didn't know every second person they passed on the way to the restaurant, which was close to Jazz's home. No matter where they went, her dad always knew someone, to the point that there was a running joke in the family — he ought to run for mayor.

What Nestico was, however, was attentive to her mother. A good conversationalist. Proud of his three kids and the seven grandchildren they produced. He had loving memories of his late wife and he wasn't embarrassed about sharing them. Peter knew enough about wine to order a bottle that suited the jambalaya perfectly. As promised, it was kick-ass.

In the course of dinner conversation, he brought up the subject of the skeleton at St. Catherine's. Of course he did. If he hadn't, Jazz would have known he was trying to shield her from the emotional upheaval that followed the discovery, and talking about it meant that he trusted her enough to know she could handle the subject. But thank goodness, he didn't beat it to death. He didn't pry. He wondered what she knew. He asked how she was feeling and promised the next time he saw her he would bring along some of his favorite chamomile-based herbal tea, just in case she had trouble sleeping. He hoped the police would find the killer soon and bring the monster to justice.

Peter paid for dinner and he insisted that since he and Claire had driven Jazz to the restaurant, it was only right that they drive her back home. Either he was the perfect gentleman or he'd heard stories about the crime rate in Tremont — he didn't pull his car out of her driveway until Jazz was safely inside her house.

"I tried not to like him," she told Wally when she got him out of his crate and snapped his leash to his collar. "But he did think you were adorable!"

Wally barked his agreement, and together they headed out on their nightly walk.

Weeknights, the neighborhood had a different feel. Laidback, quiet. There were nights when Jazz swore she could feel the history of the place vibrating from the slate sidewalks and catch a glimpse in the shadows of the ghosts of residents long gone.

Weekends . . .

Ready to cross a street, Jazz stopped to let a line of traffic by and was happy to see Wally sit right down beside her without a command. "You're a good boy," she told him before they crossed.

It was a warm night, and Wally had been patient while she went out with her mom and Peter. They did their usual sweep around the school across the street from Jazz's house; then to reward him — and to work off some of that kick-ass jambalaya — they headed up to Lincoln Park.

More traffic, more crowds. Conversations floated in the air. Music vibrated through the neighborhood. Techno dance music from one bar. Mellow standards from another. Much to Jazz's delight, Wally didn't mind any of it. He wasn't skittish or antsy, not even when a waiter on a nearby patio dropped the tray he was carrying and silverware clattered and clanked. Wally greeted — politely — the people they passed. He obeyed commands without too much sass. By the time they spent a few minutes in the park, then turned around to go back home, Jazz was feeling pretty darned proud of her dog training skills, and more positive about life in general.

They crossed Starkweather and Jazz breathed in the scent of the petunias someone had planted nearby and the honeysuckle that twined around the fence of a house that was being renovated. She only hoped that the yellow paint on the front of the house looked less garish in the daylight than it did in the dark.

It was, she decided right then and there, a perfect night in a perfect place.

The thought had just had time to settle when a punch landed between Jazz's shoulder blades and the air rushed out of her lungs on the end of a gasp of surprise. Before she had time to recover, while her head was still banging forward and her shoulders were still instinctively hunched, another jab slammed into her, this one at the small of her back.

She crumpled and her knees hit the pavement. So did her forehead.

Wally barked. He growled. But she

couldn't find her voice to tell him to sit and stay. Her breath was gone. Stars exploded behind her eyes. Right before someone grabbed her hair and yanked her head back and held a knife, cold and shiny, to her throat. He nicked her neck with the blade of the knife and a hot trickle of blood snaked down her throat.

"Mind your own business," he said, the whispered warning rough against her ear.

He shoved her forward and her elbows slammed the pavement.

Stunned for a second or two, Jazz listened to her own rough breaths. She winced from the pain in her back and wiped a trickle of blood out of her eye. But she'd be damned if she was going to give up. To hell with the pain. Her right hand already balled into a fist, her arm cocked, she jumped to her feet and spun around just in time to see a shadow slip into the backyard of the nearest house.

Her attacker was gone and Jazz let go a breath that stuttered around a cry.

It was good. She was good. She was safe and so was —

It wasn't until she looked down and saw the sidewalk beside her was empty that panic overwhelmed her.

Yeah, her attacker was gone.

But so was Wally.

It was nothing but adrenaline. Pure and simple.

She was an experienced dog trainer, an expert handler. She knew exactly what she was supposed to do. Keep her head. Make sure her voice rang with assurance and command.

But Jazz couldn't help herself. Her head pounded. Blood streamed from the scrapes on her knees. Her legs were rubber. It felt as if a hand had reached down into her insides, clawing her stomach, tightening around her heart.

When she called out, "Wally, *come!*" her voice was sharp and desperate.

If he was on Starkweather, on the sidewalk or even in the street, she would see him. But there was no sign of the puppy either in front of or behind her, and realizing that he was frightened and on the run made Jazz's blood whoosh in her ears. Her heart balled into a tight wad and jumped into her throat and her eyes filled with tears, and she called to him again and again, and when she didn't get a response she took off for the park.

She tried to run, but her knees hurt too much. Her breaths were too shallow; her back ached. She limped back the way she'd come, calling out to Wally the whole time, and she was nearly to the park when she heard an unmistakable bark and saw him in the pool of light thrown by the fixture above the front door of the building that housed the Polish Legion of American Vets.

By the time she got to where two seniors, a man and a woman, had ahold of Wally's leash and were doing their best to keep him from breaking free and bounding toward her, Jazz was weeping with relief.

"His leash slipped out of my hand!" she wailed, and when Wally jumped up on her she didn't correct him. Her knees screamed with pain when she stooped down to give him a hug.

"Thank you. Thank you!" When he offered it, she took the leash out of the man's hand and held on tight. "He's usually better behaved, but he got spooked and —"

"His leash got tangled around that bush," the man said, and pointed. "Lucky thing he was caught. There's too much traffic around here for a dog to be out running around at night. Especially a dark-colored dog like him."

Jazz dashed the tears from her cheeks and stood up and the woman leaned forward to peer into her face. "Honey, you're bleeding. What happened?" She didn't wait for Jazz to provide an explanation, just dug in her purse and pulled out a tissue and handed it to Jazz. "Your forehead and your knees." She looked Jazz over. "Your elbows. And your neck, too." She got another tissue.

"You want us to call the cops?" the man asked.

"No. Really." Jazz hung on to Wally's leash — and what little composure she had left — for all she was worth. The last thing she wanted to do was talk to some cop she didn't know and explain about Bernadette and why some guy with a rough voice and a knife wanted her to mind her own business. "I'm fine."

"You don't look fine." The woman was short and had chubby cheeks. A grandmother from a Norman Rockwell painting. But there was flint in her eyes. "We've got to get you taken care of. We can drive you to the hospital."

"No. Honest." Jazz stepped back, farther into the shadows, farther from the light. "I was out walking Wally and I tripped and fell and —"

"You sure about that?" When the man looked at her, his salt-and-pepper eyebrows were low over his eyes. "There's bound to be a police car around here somewhere. We can just —"

"No. Really." She stepped back and away from them. "I live close by. I'm going to get Wally home and —"

"Well, you're not walking by yourself." The way the woman's voice reverberated against the redbrick building told Jazz she was clearly not going to listen to an argument. "David . . ." She shot the man a look. "You get the car. I'll walk with her and you can ride along beside us. I can understand you don't want to get into a car with strangers," she told Jazz. "David, he'll be in the car, right there where he can jump out and help if we need him. We'll get you home safe and sound."

They did, and when they got there they refused to acknowledge that they'd done anything special. They wished her well and made her promise she'd call someone to come look after her.

Jazz promised, even if she had no intention of following through. She was a big girl and she could take care of herself.

But once she was in the house and the door was locked behind her and she was on the couch giving Wally a hug and crying, the adrenaline drained out of her and left her shaking and bleeding. Her back hurt like hell.

She thought about calling her mom, but

Mom would only panic, and she was with Peter, anyway, and Jazz didn't want to spoil their evening.

She considered giving Sarah a call, but she knew Sarah was spending the evening with Matt.

And who was she kidding anyway?

Jazz grabbed her phone.

She needed someone to talk to. Someone to take care of her and make her feel safe again.

There was only one person who fit the bill.

CHAPTER 14

Exactly fifteen minutes after she called, Nick showed up on her front porch, and once she limped to the door to let him in he didn't hesitate for one second. He scooped her into his arms and hugged her close.

"You were crying so hard when you called, I couldn't understand you when you told me what happened." It wasn't until he held her at arm's length and took a good look at her that the concern that had settled into the creases next to his eyes smoothed out. That his jaw went rigid. That his worry turned to anger.

"What the hell?"

"It's . . . I . . ." Jazz sniffled, and since Wally was being a pest, jumping on Nick and demanding attention, she bent to grab his collar. Before she could get hold of him, Nick called to him, led him into the kitchen, got him a treat, and put him in his crate. By the time Nick got back, she was slumped on the couch. She took one look at him with a crumb of Milk-Bones biscuit on the front of his black T-shirt and burst into tears.

"I couldn't find Wally!" she wailed.

Nick sat down and slipped an arm around her shoulders. "But you did find him. He's here. He's fine. But you're hurt. And something tells me there's more going on than just Wally running away."

She nodded. Shrugged. She blubbered. And hated herself for it.

"I was walking Wally and he came up behind me and —"

When her words dissolved in tears, Nick planted a gentle kiss on top of her head. Was it nothing more than a sign of concern from an old friend? She actually might have believed it if she didn't feel the quiver of anger that tingled through him like electricity. It took every ounce of self-control he had, but Nick played it cool, buying time to understand exactly what had happened — and who was responsible — before he marched out the door and raised holy hell.

She had never loved him more than she did in that one moment.

Maybe he knew it, because he cupped her chin in one hand and smiled. "You go upstairs and get changed. And bring your first-aid kit down with you. We'll talk once we get you taken care of."

She was too tired to insist she was fine, and since she was the one who called him it was too late to say she didn't need his help, so Jazz did as she was told. She was back downstairs in a few minutes, wearing soft cotton drawstring shorts and an oversized T-shirt. She found Nick pacing the living room, his hands balled into fists.

"I called the local station." As if to prove it, he lifted his phone to show it to her. "I figured you didn't want to make a statement now. They'll send an officer over in the morning."

"You really didn't have to."

"Yes, I did." It was as simple as that and she wasn't about to argue, not when blue fire flashed in his eyes. The next moment, the fire settled to a comfortable warmth. "Come on. Let's take care of you."

He took her hand and led her to the couch, then took the first-aid kit she carried, set it on the coffee table, and opened it up. She'd brought down a washcloth, too, because she'd tried to clean the blood off her knees and her elbows when she was upstairs and the water hitting her raw skin stung so much, she didn't have the guts to finish the job herself. Nick took the washcloth into the kitchen to run warm water on it, and when he was in there and when she heard Wally's treat jar rattle and the puppy give a yip of approval the pain didn't feel so bad any more.

Nick came back and brandished the washcloth. "This is not going to feel good."

Jazz had taken an inventory of her injuries when she was upstairs changing. She'd seen the blood and the scraped skin. She'd noted the tiny cut on her throat and the red marks on her back. She braced herself and winced when he touched the washcloth to her left knee.

"I'm going to be as gentle as I can," he promised.

"I know." She made herself sit stock-still. "Just get it over with."

He finished with one knee and left to rinse out the cloth in the kitchen, and when he came back again he had a can of beer with him.

"Thirsty?" she asked.

"It's for you. I thought wine would be classier. Or brandy. Isn't that what they always drink in movies after something traumatic happens? Beer is all you've got in the fridge in the way of alcohol." He handed the beer to her and with a motion urged her to drink up. "It will help you relax."

She sipped while he washed the other knee, took care of her elbows, got the blood off her forehead. When he came back yet another time with the washcloth rinsed and cleaned, he touched it to her throat.

"That's a knife wound."

She didn't confirm or deny. She didn't want to think about it. While Nick dabbed antibiotic lotion on the cut, she held her breath and waited for the burning to subside.

He got bandages out of the first-aid kit. "Want to start at the beginning?" he asked.

She stalled with another sip of beer. "We were just walking, me and Wally, like we always do. Someone came up from behind me and —"

"Damn it." When he smoothed a bandage over the damage on her knee, his touch was gentle enough, but his voice simmered with rage. "I'm going to go over to the park and run in every low-life derelict I find over there."

"It wasn't random, Nick."

She watched the news register on his expression. Confusion. Comprehension. Denial. His mouth thinned. "Of course it was random. There have been other muggings in the neighborhood recently. You don't think —"

"He told me to mind my own business."

Nick had opened his mouth to say something and now he snapped it shut again and gathered the wrappings from the bandages he'd already opened and wadded them in a fist. "Are you telling me you've been nosing around about that skeleton at school? That the person who killed that teacher had something to do with this?"

"I'm telling you . . ." He messed up the bandage on her right knee and had to loosen the tape so he could readjust it and she sucked in a breath. "I guess I've made somebody mad asking about Bernadette," she said.

"I guess you have. And whoever it is, I'm going to . . ." He didn't need to elaborate. He reached for another bandage. "What else hurts?" he asked.

"My back," she admitted. "He punched me."

"That's it." He was off the couch in a flash. "We're going to the ER."

"No. Please, Nick. I'd have to find someone to stay with Wally." She wound her fingers through his and tugged him back to the couch. "If I'm not better in the morning, we'll go then. I swear."

"Promise?"

"Do I promise to swear?"

"Well, yeah. Do you swear and do you promise?"

"Yes."

He never actually surrendered. It wasn't something Nick did. But he did sit back down, and in the great scheme of things she considered that a victory. "You could have been killed."

"If he wanted to kill me, I'd already be dead."

Nick grumbled a curse. "It's not funny, Jazz."

"I'm not trying to be funny. It's true, and you know it. He didn't want to kill me; he just wanted to scare me. And you know what. . . ." She snuggled close to him. "He did."

His arm went around her. "Can you describe him?"

"I never saw his face. He hit me from behind, warned me to mind my own business, and by the time I jumped up all set to smash him in the —"

The last thing she expected from Nick was a chuckle. She pulled far enough away to look at him. "I wasn't trying to be funny about that, either."

"I know. You're just being Jazz. That's why I'm laughing. I'm surprised Wally didn't join in the fun and bite the guy in the keister."

"I think he would have if his leash didn't slip out of my hand. By that time, Wally was scared and he took off. It was awful, Nick. All I could think about was how heavy the traffic is around here on weekends, about how he's black and brown and he'd be hard to see at night and . . ." Just thinking about what might have happened made her stomach bunch.

Or maybe it was the beer.

She set the can on the coffee table. "Maybe I can add some attack skills to Wally's training."

"Something tells me it just might be easier for you to stay out of trouble."

"You mean mind my own business?"

He wasn't looking for a fight, but he wasn't going to back down, either. He ran a hand over his face. "Yeah, that would be the idea. But I've got a confession to make, I haven't been minding my own business tonight, either. I was at the baseball game."

The stadium where the Cleveland Indians played wasn't far away. "That explains how you got here so quickly."

He nodded. "I wasn't by myself. I was at the game with Gary Lindsey."

"What, you two are BFFs now?"

Nick laughed. "Hardly. But I figured if anyone knew about the case, it was him."

"And you wanted to know about the case because . . . ?"

"I've got a sort of vested interest." He took her hand in his. "I was curious because I figured you were curious. Looks like I was right."

"And what did you find out?"

He gave her a lopsided smile. "You mean other than the fact that Lindsey's something of a pinhead?"

"He thinks Eileen killed Bernadette."

Nick nodded. It was not the response Jazz hoped for. "According to Lindsey, Eileen did have a motive. There were tensions between Bernadette and Eileen, and Bernadette talked about suing the school."

"Maybe but . . ." Too antsy to sit still, she grabbed the beer and took another drink. "I can pretty much guarantee you Eileen isn't the one who jumped me tonight."

"Who do you think did?"

She slanted him a look. "Did Lindsey say he had any suspects who were men?"

"Do you?"

"Bernadette's cousin, Sam, has taken over her house lock, stock, and barrel. And it's a fabulous place, by the way. So he sure has motive. And then there's that paralegal at the firm Bernadette was going to retain to sue the school." She thought about Mark

Mercer. "He and Bernadette were seen at school after hours. And they were arguing."

"Interesting," Nick admitted. "Anyone else?"

"Taryn Campbell's father for one," Jazz told him. "He was mad at Bernadette for reporting Taryn when she found out Taryn plagiarized a scholarship essay. Taryn got expelled because of it. Leon Campbell is still mad, which tells you how much madder he was three years ago. And then there's the girls, of course." Jazz thought about it. It was a man's voice that had whispered his rough warning in her ear. It was a man's fist that had slammed her back.

"Cammi and Juliette are nasty little critters," she said. "And they took great joy in harassing Bernadette. But Cammi and Juliette sure didn't jump me tonight."

"That doesn't mean someone they know didn't do it."

Jazz hated to admit that was true.

"So . . ." Nick motioned for her to turn around. "Let's get a look at your back."

"You really don't have to —"

"It's me or the doc in the ER."

She turned around.

He gave her a gentle tap. "Shirt up."

She had never been embarrassed with Nick. Never self-conscious or shy. But that

244

was back in the old days. Back when they were a couple. He was more of a stranger now, a stranger who was asking her to lift her shirt so he could check out her back.

And she was acting like some teenaged virgin.

Jazz turned around and lifted her shirt.

"Red in a couple spots," he said, taking a look. "And you might end up with some bruising. There could be internal bleeding and —"

"He didn't hit me that hard."

"Maybe not, but right here . . . ." He touched a hand to her back, and this time when Jazz winced it had nothing to do with pain except the pain of remembrance.

He skimmed a finger along her skin, tracing the outline of the red mark she'd seen when she changed, and Jazz held her memories of Nick's touch at bay at the same time she held her breath.

"This one's not as red." He brushed a thumb over the small of her back and his fingers swept over her ribs. "Does it hurt?"

"I've got an ice pack in the freezer," she told him, because it was the wrong time to say what she wanted to say — that when he was touching her, nothing could possibly hurt. "If you could get it . . ." She glanced over her shoulder, into his eyes.

His pupils were wide and dark. His eyes were warm, mellow, and the look he gave her said everything neither of them could.

One moment melted into two before he pulled himself away and smoothed her shirt back into place. "Yeah. Sure. One ice pack coming up."

He went into the kitchen, and when he came back he had the ice pack, another beer for her, and one for himself.

"I'm staying here tonight," he announced.

Somewhere deep inside her, it was what she hoped he'd say. Except the way he fluffed the pillows at one end of the couch told her she was jumping the gun. And he was being the voice of reason.

"You don't have to."

"Sure I do." He plopped down. "You're not going to sleep if you don't feel safe, and you're not going to feel safe here by yourself."

She sighed. "I'm not going to sleep, anyway. I'm way too jittery. Maybe we could . . ." She knew she'd have the upper hand only as long as he was trying to comfort her. After she was better, calmer, less terrified of the memory of all that had happened, he'd be back to reminding her that she needed to leave the investigating to the professionals.

"Maybe we could go over everything we know about the case."

"You mean Gary Lindsey's case."

"That's the one." Jazz spun around so she could pile up some pillows and position herself so the ice pack was wedged between the couch and her back. The cold felt heavenly. "Let's go over my list of suspects again."

Before they did, Nick went into the kitchen for a pad of paper, and since Jazz said she didn't want another beer he made her a cup of peppermint tea. He came back with the tea — loaded with sugar — and took notes while they talked, and when they were done he sat back and tapped a finger against the paper.

"This Mercer guy, the paralegal, you don't know why he suddenly looked antsy when you mentioned Maddie, the girl from school?" Nick asked.

"Not a clue." Jazz sipped the tea. "Maybe it doesn't mean anything," she admitted. "Here he was, trying to mourn a friend's death, and there I was, this complete stranger asking him questions that were none of my business. Maybe I just imagined his reaction."

"Or maybe there's something you're not telling me?" His voice was gentle enough, but his look was penetrating. When she didn't answer, he leaned forward. "Jazz?"

It was exactly what Eileen had warned her against — telling too much of the truth.

She squeezed her eyes shut. "Eileen doesn't want to drag the details out into the light."

"Maybe that's the problem."

"Maybe," Jazz admitted.

"You gonna tell me what happened?"

She drew in a breath. Took another drink of tea. "It's hard to know where to start."

"I know the basics. But what happened right before Christmas break?"

Jazz pulled in a breath, then was sorry she did. Her ribs ached. Her back was sore. She finished her tea.

"Bernadette was tutoring Maddie and things were going really well. But right after Halloween, that's when Maddie's parents showed up at school. They told us Bernadette was following Maddie."

Nick sat up. "Stalking?"

A shrug didn't seem nearly adequate enough to explain. "They didn't have any proof, Nick. You know if they did, Eileen would have been the first one to call the cops."

"Or taken care of the problem herself."

If she had the energy, Jazz would have

jumped off the couch, the better to tower over him when she read him the riot act. The way it was, she tried to keep her cool, just as she had the day Scott and Kate Parker showed up at school with fire in their eyes and mayhem in their hearts.

"They said they'd run into Bernadette a time or two when they were out. At a movie, shopping, that sort of thing. Come on, Nick, you know that doesn't prove anything."

"No. But it is curious. What did Bernadette say about it?"

"That it was completely accidental and wasn't it lovely that she had a chance to see one of her students outside of school."

Nick slanted her a look. "Did you believe it?"

"We couldn't say otherwise."

"And Maddie?"

"Eileen talked to her. The school counselor talked to her. I know her parents talked to her. She never said a word against Bernadette. Still, Eileen wasn't taking any chances. She stopped the tutoring sessions. She put Maddie in another homeroom. We juggled schedules to make sure Bernadette and Maddie didn't eat lunch at the same time or even come and go in the same hallways at the same time."

"And how did Maddie react to it all?"

"I think she missed the extra attention she got from Bernadette, but other than that, life went on and things settled down. At least with Maddie and her parents."

"But not with Bernadette."

Jazz sighed. "She seemed to accept the changes well enough. But then something happened. I don't know what. Whatever it was, Bernadette was a mess. She looked terrible. Like she wasn't eating, like she wasn't sleeping. She even missed teaching a couple classes. Eileen tried to intervene, and when Bernadette refused to cooperate, well, that's when Eileen told her about being put on probation, and that's when Bernadette threatened to sue. As far as Eileen was concerned, she was welcome to try. In the meantime, we tried to work with her, and Eileen suggested counseling. We hoped she'd relax and recover over Christmas break, but after break . . ." Jazz remembered arriving at school after the first of the year, and Bernadette's resignation letter waiting for her.

"Lindsey didn't say anything about fingerprints on that letter from Bernadette, did he?" she asked Nick.

"None," he told her. "That means we can't say if the victim did, or didn't, write the letter."

Jazz ran her hands through her hair. "It's crazy making!"

"And it's not going to make sense. Not tonight. Not when you're tired." He tugged her to her feet and turned her toward the stairway. "Get to bed. I'll see you in the morning."

Sleep was exactly what she needed, and the thought of Nick waiting for her in the morning actually made Jazz smile. Still, in the small hours after she promised Nick she'd get some rest and climbed the stairs sleep refused to come. Her head was filled with questions, and when there were no answers to go along with them she got more and more antsy. She sat up and read through her email for a bit, but it didn't make any difference. Thinking about what had happened to Bernadette made her think about her dad.

About the dead.

Jazz finally gave up and crept to the stairway. If she was quick and she was quiet, she could grab a couple of the boxes she'd brought home earlier that day — well, the day before now — and get back upstairs to look through them before Nick ever knew.

Except he wasn't asleep on the couch.

At the bottom of the steps, Jazz leaned

forward, certain the dark and her eyes were playing tricks on her. A second later, she realized why. Nick was wide awake, too, standing at the front window, silhouetted against the glow of the security light from the school across the street.

"You okay?" she wanted to know.

"Are you?" He met her halfway, their shadows mingling in the space that separated them.

"My brain won't shut off," she admitted.

"You're thinking about Bernadette?"

Jazz glanced at the pile of the boxes in the corner. "About her. About the things people leave behind."

Since there was no use pretending either one of them was going to get any sleep, Jazz flicked on the light next to the couch and crossed the room. A couple of months earlier when her brothers gave her the framed photo of her and Manny with her dad and Big George that they'd taken out of her dad's locker down at the softball field, she'd put the picture in a place of honor. Now she took it off the shelf and handed it to Nick.

"I saw it earlier," he told her. "Great picture."

"Hal and Owen found it. And it's not the only thing they gave me." There was a desk in the dining room and she went to it and took out a box where she'd stashed the rest of the things her brothers had collected from the locker — recipes, shopping lists, notes. Among them was a business card from a real estate developer named Sean Innis, and she found the card and handed it to Nick.

He looked it over. "What does it mean?"

"I wish I knew. Maybe Dad had plans to build, or maybe he was going to invest in some project. Except . . ." She turned over the card and showed him the message written on the other side. *Ask Darren Marsh.* Her dad's no-nonsense handwriting.

"Darren Marsh. The name's familiar," he admitted.

"He's the firefighter who committed suicide at the station where Matt Duffey works. It happened right before my dad died."

Nick handed the card back to her. "And . . . ?"

"And it's been bothering me, that's all. And thinking about all this stuff I got from Bernadette's house just made me think about the card. I feel like it's . . ." As always happened when she looked through the box of softball locker items, a shiver cascaded over her shoulders. "Why would he keep a card like that?"

"Because he knew this Darren guy had dealings with Sean Innis and he wanted a recommendation?"

"Possible."

"Or he'd heard something bad about Innis and wanted to confirm that."

"Also a possibility."

Nick put a hand on her shoulder. "The most obvious possibility is the most logical one. There was no way your dad knew he was going to die in that fire. He had the card because it was something he was going to deal with. But he never had a chance."

She knew it was true. Which didn't mean she had to like it.

Jazz didn't so much twitch Nick's hand away as she shook off the uneasiness that wrapped around her every time she thought about the card, about her dad's death.

"You can tell me I'm nuts, Nick, but I think it's more like Dad was leaving some sort of message. I think he was trying to tell us something. Only I don't know what it is."

"Something about . . . ?"

"I have no idea. But remembering that card, it got me to thinking, that's all. Thinking about Bernadette. Those boxes are hers, Nick; I helped Sam Tillner take them out of her attic. Maybe she left some sort of message, too."

Nick considered the suggestion, but only for a moment before he headed into the kitchen. "I'll put on the coffee."

CHAPTER 15

"I don't suppose there's any rhyme or reason to any of this." Coffee steamed in two mugs nearby and Nick lifted the first box and put it on the dining room table. "Does Tillner seem like the type who would have taken his time? Arranged things?"

"There's only one way to find out." Jazz popped the lid off the first box, looked inside, and made a face. "File folders." She ruffled her fingers through the alphabetically arranged manila folders. "Cable bills, electric bills, gas bills. Charge statements, church collection envelopes waiting to be filled."

"There might be something interesting there." Nick must have been expecting her to give him exactly the look she did — mouth screwed up, eyes squinted — because he laughed. "Hey, being a detective isn't all about car chases and excitement. Sometimes clues are in the most boring places."

"Let's save these boring clues for when we're more awake." Jazz put the lid back on the box and set it on the floor and Nick lifted the second box to the table.

Jazz opened it and looked at the mess of papers and old photographs heaped inside. "Looks like Tillner scooped up whatever he could find and shoved it in here to get it out of the way."

"And my guess . . ." Nick's eyes glowed at the prospect of what might be hidden in the mound of junk. "There might be some treasures here."

They sat down and got to work. The idea was to sort the items in the box — pictures in one pile, any correspondence in another, magazines and newspaper clippings over on the other side — but they'd just started when Jazz took out a small scrap of paper printed in color on one side, in black and white on the other. She found a second scrap, then another, then a fourth.

"What's all that?" Nick wanted to know.

He hadn't been raised Catholic like Jazz. Nick didn't know about prayer cards.

While Jazz explained, she dug through the rest of the box and came up with dozens of more pieces. To give herself room, she pushed the box to one side and got to work, setting out the pieces, color-side up, and sorting them as best she could.

"Brown monk's robe." She set that piece to her left and looked over the other scraps. "Aha! Another piece of brown monk's robe." That piece went with the first. She made a pile of light blue pieces, another of golden ones, and when she was all done she started fitting the pieces together like little jigsaw puzzles.

"Pictures of angels and saints," she told Nick, and showed him a scrap of paper with a halo on it to prove it. "People give out prayer cards at funerals as mementos of the person who died and with information about them printed on the back. That's how I knew where Bernadette's ashes were interred, from the prayer cards at her memorial service. Or sometimes, teachers give them to the kids at school. You use them to mark your place in a prayer book, or if you're my grandmother you hang them on the refrigerator and think about all your dead friends."

"Okay." He didn't look or sound convinced of the advantages of any of this. "So why would Bernadette have ripped ones?"

"Good question." Jazz fit the Virgin Mary's face under a particularly showy golden halo. "Bernadette was so . . ." She found the face of a male saint, tried it on one, two, three bodies before she realized it fit perfectly above a green clerical robe. "Knowing Bernadette, she would have treasured these, not ripped them in a million pieces."

"Here's a couple that aren't ripped." Nick plucked them out of the box. "They're just mangled."

They were crushed the way Nick had wadded the bandage wrappers. "When you were angry," she mumbled.

To which Nick had every right to respond, "Huh?"

Jazz took the crumpled cards from his hand and smoothed them out on the table. One showed Saint Joseph with the Christ child. The other was an image of an angel in a long white robe.

"When I was telling you what happened to me tonight," she reminded Nick. "You were holding the bandage wrappings and you crushed them in your hand."

To demonstrate, she grabbed the two prayer cards and squeezed them in a fist.

"That's what she did," Jazz said, looking down at the cards wadded in her hand. "Bernadette mashed these two cards, and I bet she's the one who tore up the others."

"But you said she was so religious, such a believer. Why would she?"

Jazz thought back to the last weeks Bernadette was alive. "I have no idea why it happened," she admitted. "But I bet I know when."

It wasn't a cry; it was a high, tight keening. A sound that crept through the hallways of St. Catherine's like a bone-chilling mist. It bounced off the ceilings like the echoes of a bad dream.

The wail of a lost soul.

Jazz paused at the top of the third-floor stairway and looked around. It was late and except for the Drama Club students practicing for the Christmas program and the staff catching up on their work, most everyone had left St. Catherine's hours before. She'd volunteered to stick around so she could get Eileen's Christmas gifts to teachers and staff wrapped and she'd come upstairs because she knew Sarah kept ribbon in the art studio and she wanted to add some to the presents.

There was no one in the hallway, no one in any of the classrooms Jazz passed, and for a moment, she wondered if the ghost stories the girls told about the unused fourth-floor space really were true.

Was St. Catherine's haunted?

A door bumping closed and the high-pitched titter of girls giggling snapped Jazz out of her fantasies. Ghosts, she imagined, didn't need to open and close doors to come and go.

Students were another story.

The sounds of scrambling footsteps confirmed her theory, but wherever the noises came from — whoever ran from the direction of the chapel — she didn't see a soul. And the high-pitched wailing? It never stopped.

Jazz pushed through the chapel door and the sound washed over her, amplified by the whispering walls until it rang in her ears and vibrated in her breastbone. This time of the year, it was already dark, and with none of the overhead lights on in the chapel, she stood with her back to the door, searching the shadows for the source of the pathetic sound, letting her eyes adjust. A little light seeped from the neighborhood outside and through the chapel's stained-glass windows threw muted pools of color on the floor and over near the altar, the sanctuary lamp with its red shade was lit, and its glow spilled over a shape crumpled on the floor.

Jazz's heart bumped, and she raced to the front of the chapel, tallying the details as she went.

White blouse.

Plaid skirt.

She had her phone out and the flashlight app on before she dropped to the floor next to where Bernadette Quinn was on her knees, her shoulders crumpled, her chest heaving, her head bent until it nearly rested on the floor.

"Bernadette!" Jazz touched a hand to the teacher's shoulder. "What's wrong? What's happened?"

Like a wild animal, Bernadette reared up. Her face was gray and swollen, her eyes wild.

"What happened?" Tiny bits of spit collected at the corners of Bernadette's mouth. "How dare you! How dare you ask me what happened!"

When she scrambled to her feet, Jazz did, too, and when Jazz stepped closer, Bernadette threw out a hand. She held a prayer card in that hand, one of the ones she gave out to the girls who did especially well on tests, and she gripped it tightly in desperate fingers. "You stay away from me! You all stay away from me! You just want to laugh at me. It's all you've ever wanted to do. Well, now you can do it, can't you? Now you know how stupid I am, how gullible."

The cross on Bernadette's chest did a wild rumba to the tempo of her rough breaths, and watching the fake jewels in it catch the light and flash, Jazz couldn't help but think of everything she'd learned about dealing with frightened animals. She kept her voice down. She moved slowly. She stayed calm.

"I'm not sure what you're talking about," Jazz told her. "But if you want to sit down . . ." She motioned toward the nearest pew. "You can tell me what's bothering you."

Bernadette was not a tall woman, but when she stiffened her spine, threw back her shoulders, and lifted her chin, she looked formidable. Savage. "I'll tell you right here and now what's bothering me. You should know. The whole world should know. What we hear . . . what we . . ." Her voice choked over a sob. "What we believe . . ." She glanced over her shoulder toward the choir loft, then spun to aim a laser look at Jazz. "Sometimes we want to believe so much, so hard, that we deceive ourselves. Then the truth dawns." She clutched at the prayer card and it crumpled in her fingers. "It's not always the voice of God we hear. Sometimes the angels aren't angels at all; sometimes they're devils."

By the time she was done telling the story, Jazz's coffee was cold. Nick got up to refresh both his and hers, and when he came back in the dining room he had a bowl of grapes with him, too.

"Donuts," he said, and set the bowl in front of Jazz. "At this time of night, we should be eating donuts, not healthy food. All you have around here is fruit and yogurt and stuff no person in his right mind should eat at three in the morning. Where's the cold pizza? Where are the donuts? Everyone should have a supply of donuts for emergencies."

She gave him a one-sided grimace at the same time she plucked a grape from the bowl. "Spoken like the cop you are."

Oblivious to the sarcasm, his gaze drifted over the bits and pieces of the angels and saints laid out on the table, and Nick sat back down. "So what happened after that day in the chapel? To Bernadette?"

The thought still made Jazz uneasy, especially when she considered that the end of the story was not a happy one. "She was different after that night. Quiet. Withdrawn. There were complaints from the girls in her classroom. Bernadette had always made her classes interesting and challenging. After that night, we heard she was just going through the motions. She was never good talking to parents, but she at least made an effort. After that night, parents complained that she wasn't even returning phone calls. Other teachers said . . . well, she'd never been overly friendly, but the other teachers saw a different side of Bernadette. They said she was short-tempered, crabby. One of the girls told us Bernadette even forgot to lead them in prayer before class. And she always started every class with a prayer."

"Despair." The single word carried so much weight, Nick sat back in his chair. "She'd lost her enthusiasm."

Jazz looked at the ripped images of the saints and angels. "I think it goes deeper than that, Nick. I saw her in the chapel. She was frantic. Desperate. It was like her whole world had turned upside down, like the most important thing in her life —" Jazz sucked in a breath. "You know, she never would have destroyed or disrespected a prayer card. It just wasn't in her makeup. But the one she was holding that night, she crumpled it like it was a piece of garbage. It was like whatever happened there in the chapel, it had caused her to lose her faith. She was suddenly in a free fall and she didn't know how to stop it. How sad, especially when you think she was dead just a couple weeks later."

Their sighs overlapped.

Nick grabbed a handful of grapes. "What do you think happened?"

A shrug was hardly an answer. "It was around the time Bernadette found out that Taryn Campbell plagiarized her scholarship essay. Even after the Titus incident, Bernadette never lost faith in Taryn or Juliette or Cammi." A thought hit and Jazz sat up like a shot. "The Titus incident! I should have thought of that before. Taryn, Juliette, and Cammi had tricked Bernadette once with the cat. What if they kept on playing tricks on her? It explains why they were never at Drama Club practice, Nick. They'd hang around school, but they weren't where they were supposed to be. What if they waited for Bernadette to go up to the chapel after school? Everyone knew she did it; that was no secret. That's what Taryn was talking about when she said I should ask Juliette and Cammi about the angels. Could anyone be that mean? What if . . ." It was nearly impossible to comprehend, but Jazz put her theory into words. "What if the three of them, they were the angels?"

Nick groaned. "You mean the walls in the chapel —"

"Yeah, the whispering walls. The girls . . ." There was no reason Nick would know the details, so Jazz explained. "They got in

266

plenty of trouble for Titus. Seems to me this would be the perfect revenge. They whispered to her while she was praying and made her believe she was being talked to by angels."

"And that night you found her crying —"

"I heard the girls run out of the chapel. Maybe Bernadette did, too. Maybe that's when she finally figured out there was a very real human explanation for what she thought were angel voices." She glanced at the prayer cards. "Bernadette didn't just want to believe that the angels were talking to her; she did believe it. Then maybe she caught a glimpse of the girls. Or maybe one of them gave away the hoax by laughing or something. That's when Bernadette realized what was really going on. She found out she'd been tricked and it broke her heart. It destroyed her faith. How sad."

"What are you going to do about it?" Nick wanted to know.

"I'll have to tell Eileen." The prospect made Jazz feel awful. "I'll leave it up to her and the board. Maybe if the girls confess to what they did . . ."

"They won't get expelled?"

Jazz put her face in her hands. "I thought the Titus hoax was cruel. This was even worse."

"You'll deal with it." Nick put a reassuring hand on her shoulder. "For now . . ."

He stood and peered into the box. "There's a ton of other stuff in here," he said. "It's going to take us days to go through it." He pushed that box to the side and retrieved the box from the long-closed department store. "This one's smaller. How much junk could be in here?"

He was right. There wasn't any junk in that box. Just a white blanket, carefully folded and tucked between pieces of tissue.

Knitted or crocheted?

Jazz never could tell the difference. "Pretty," she said.

"And we can at least eliminate this box as telling us anything." Nick popped the lid back on the box. "One more?" he wondered, but he didn't wait for Jazz's response. He grabbed the last of the archive boxes.

"Looks like stuff from a desk," he said, and taking out the contents, he piled it on the table. "A calendar. That might be helpful except it's from a few years before Bernadette was killed. Pens. A tape dispenser. A stapler. And . . ." He was nearly through the contents of the box, and his hands stilled over his work.

"That thing with Maddie . . ." He looked at Jazz at the same time he scooped some papers from the box. "Bernadette said there was nothing to it, right?"

"You mean the Parkers thinking Bernadette was stalking Maddie? No proof. Not a shred."

"Then what about these?"

What he'd found were photos, probably taken by a phone, definitely printed at home on eight-by-ten pieces of computer paper.

Maddie buying popcorn at the movies.

Maddie in the park on her bike.

Maddie at the mall, walking beside her friend Della.

Jazz's blood went cold. Her stomach bunched. She'd been about to pop down another grape, and she knew it would never get past the lump that suddenly blocked her throat. She tossed the grape back in the bowl. "The Parkers were right. Bernadette *was* stalking Maddie."

"It sure looks that way."

Jazz's insides twitched. "What does it mean, Nick?"

"I'll have to show these to Lindsey. It could have something to do with motive."

"You mean Maddie's parents found out and . . . ?"

"Or Maddie didn't like what was going on."

"No." Jazz refused to sit there and listen

to that kind of nonsense. She refused to even consider that Maddie — sweet, sincere Maddie — could have possibly had anything to do with the skeleton on the fourth floor. "You can't possibly think —"

"I don't know what to think. And neither do you. I only know these pictures might be important."

"But Maddie said she didn't have a problem with Bernadette."

"Maybe Maddie didn't know she was being followed."

Jazz wrapped herself in a hug. "That makes it creepier than ever."

"Here's more creepy."

Carefully, he drew one last thing out of the box. It was a wreath of what had once been white and red roses. Now the flowers were brittle, brown. The tiny pieces of baby's breath that were tucked between the roses crumbled when Nick lifted the halo out of the box and they sprinkled the table like snowflakes.

"Maybe not so creepy." If only Jazz felt as assured as she tried to sound. She looked at the dead flowers, thought of the dead woman. "Flowers don't mean anything. Maybe Bernadette was a bridesmaid or something."

When Nick set the halo of flowers on the

table, Jazz touched a finger to the nearest rose. A petal dropped off. The petals beneath it were crusted with gray mold.

Nick pulled one last thing from the box, an envelope. He opened it and unfolded the letter inside. He read it over quickly and whistled low under his breath. "You were right. Bridesmaid or something. Listen to this."

The letter was short and to the point.

" 'Every soul has its mission and there are as many different missions of redemption as there are souls on this earth. It is with the deepest sadness and regret that we inform you that after a great deal of discussion and even more prayer, we have decided that your mission is not in alignment with ours. As of this day . . .' "

Nick checked the heading on the letter. "It's dated about sixteen years ago."

"From who? To who?" Jazz wanted to know.

He held up a hand to tell her to be patient. " 'As of this day, you are released from all obligations, responsibilities, and association with the Little Sisters of Good Counsel. From this day forward, you will no longer be Sister Mary Philomena but will be known once again as Bernadette Quinn.' "

CHAPTER 16

The Little Sisters of Good Counsel was a teaching order of nuns whose mother house was located near Niagara Falls, Canada. It was a three-and-a-half-hour drive, but after she and Nick found the letter from the convent Jazz gave in to the exhaustion that overwhelmed her once the adrenaline drained. She was able to get a couple hours of sleep before an officer from the local precinct called to say he was on his way to take her statement about what had happened the night before, and ready to go by the time the officer left.

She was just going into the kitchen when she banged into Nick just coming out of it.

"What are you still doing here?"

He put a hand to her forehead, though how that was supposed to help she wasn't sure. "Maybe you have a concussion. You don't remember I slept on your couch last night?"

"Of course I remember." Since Wally's leash wasn't on the hook where she always kept it, she knew Nick had already walked him and he'd fed the dog, too, by the looks of the smears of yogurt in his bowl, so she poured herself a cup of coffee and took a long drink. There was nothing like waking up to really good coffee. Nothing like waking up to a man who was considerate enough to walk the dog, feed the dog, and get a pot brewing while she was still in the shower.

Jazz twitched the thought away. "It's a Saturday in June," she said. "It's noon and . . ." She didn't need to confirm it, but she peered out of the window anyway and tried to sort the facts in her head. One of the things Nick loved most was coaching kids baseball and he did a good job of it. Every Saturday, come rain or shine, as long as his work allowed it. He was dedicated, devoted. There were times back in the day when she clearly remembered telling him he was obsessed. It wasn't like she could blame him. She was convinced he was making up for all the attention he'd never gotten when he was a kid. Jazz got it. She really did. She knew it was why he never made an exception. He'd never let the kids down. "The sun is shining. Shouldn't you be at the baseball field?"

"Just got off the phone with Patrick." He was Nick's assistant coach, a young guy who taught phys ed in the Cleveland public school system. "He's taking over for me today."

"You're missing baseball?" It was Jazz's turn to put a hand to his forehead. "Because . . . ?"

"Because I'm going to Canada with you, of course. I'll drive. My car is more comfortable than yours." It was as easy as that. At least to Nick.

To Jazz it was the equivalent of a hug, or a declaration of undying love, and for a moment all she could do was drink in the wonder of it all and the way warmth tangled around her heart.

Nick went right on. "We'll have to stop by my house and pick up my passport." At that moment, the toaster popped, and he took two pieces of toasts out of it, slathered them with butter and apricot jam, and gave them to her, then gave the dog a look. "What about Short Stuff? He'll be okay here until we get back tonight?"

Jazz had just taken a bite of toast and she washed it down with a sip of coffee. "I called Greg Johnson as soon as I got up. He's going to take Wally to his house for the day."

"So we're set." Nick rubbed his hands together. "If traffic's not too bad, we might even have time to stop and look at the falls."

They didn't, but then, it took longer than they anticipated to find the convent. It was outside the city of Niagara Falls in an area lush with vineyards and wineries that on an afternoon so beautiful were packed with tourists. Traffic was snarled and they made wrong turns once, twice, three times before they finally found what they were looking for.

The Sisters of Good Counsel were head-quartered in a massive building that looked like it came right out of a fairy tale. Or a medieval history book.

Stone turrets. Steeples. Stained glass. The windows along the front of the convent were arched, the gardens between the parking lot and the front door were filled with statues of angels and saints, and the deep, bonging sound of a low-pitched wind chime, like a cathedral bell, carried on the breeze. The wide front steps they climbed were bordered by rhododendrons, their purple flowers just popping.

Inside the front door in an entryway with a polished stone floor, a fresh-faced young woman in a gray skirt and trim white blouse welcomed them, and when they told her they wanted to talk to Sister Mary Henry, who according to the convent's website was the Mother Superior of the order, she escorted them down the hallway and deposited them in an office that reminded Jazz of her own office back at St. Catherine's with its high ceilings, its glass-fronted bookshelves. There was a portrait of a veiled woman above the fireplace to Jazz's left, and a statue of the Virgin Mary on her right. The walls, paneled with dark wood, were filled with photographs.

"Nick, look. All the nuns in these pictures, they're wearing flowered crowns. Like the one we found in Bernadette's things. Look at what's printed on this one. It says this is the day the nuns took their final vows." Jazz didn't need to point it out. Nick had picked right up on the flowers, and while Jazz was still thinking about what it meant and what it could tell them, he was already going from one photo to another, reading the dates on the brass plaques on each oak frame and the names of the nuns printed below where each sister stood.

"She was how old?" Nick wanted to know.

"Bernadette?" Jazz really didn't need to ask. "I'd say thirty-five or so at the time of her death."

"So we don't have to bother with these." Nick ignored the pictures that were obviously old. Sepia-toned prints, black-and-white group shots. The older the photos were, the more young women they featured. The more modern photos . . .

Jazz went to stand at Nick's side and look at the picture he was examining.

"This one's dated 1979. Dozens of girls back then . . ." She looked over her shoulder toward the older pictures. "And after that . . ."

"Not an easy life, I don't imagine." Scanning the dates, Nick skipped past an entire wall filled with pictures. "I'm thinking we at least need this century. Bernadette wouldn't have been here any earlier."

They found the newest pictures — and the smallest groups of new nuns — and discovered what they were looking for.

A line of seven newly minted nuns in their gray habits and wearing crowns of red and white roses.

"Sister Mary Philomena." Jazz poked a finger against Bernadette's nose. "There she is right in the center. She looks so happy." She stepped back to take in the whole picture. Like all the nuns in it — the tall, skinny girl, Sister Mary Margaret, to Bernadette's left and the short, round African-American girl, Sister Mary Veronica, on her right — Bernadette's shoulders were back, her head was high, her smile was a mile wide.

Jazz felt a pang of sadness. "It was all she ever wanted. That's what Eileen and I always said about Bernadette. All she ever wanted was to be a nun. We thought we were only kidding. We didn't know how spot-on we were. But why —"

Her question had to wait. The door opened and a woman with a round face and busy hands strode into the room and introduced herself as Sister Henry. Like all those nuns in all those pictures, she wore a long gray habit, but unlike the nuns in the early pictures, her head wasn't completely swaddled in a wimple and a veil. She wore a simple white veil bobby-pinned toward the back of her head and her hair, a glorious silver, peeked from beneath it. Her skin was pale and smooth, but there were wrinkles around her eyes and mouth. Maybe because she smiled so much. Maybe because she always had her eyes closed when her lips were busy with prayer.

Sister Henry directed them to the guest chairs in front of her desk and sat down, her hands clutched together on the desktop.

"What can I help you with?" the nun wanted to know.

This was Nick's bailiwick. Questions. Answers. Cooperative informers. Uncooperative witnesses. But he looked Jazz's way and let her take the lead.

She explained that she had worked with Bernadette Quinn, the woman who was once Sister Mary Philomena.

"Oh." Sister Henry's expression gave nothing away, but her hands fluttered over the blotter on her desk. "That's a name I haven't heard in a very long time."

"According to the picture over there . . ." — Nick looked that way — "she took her vows here seventeen years ago."

"Seventeen? Is it?" Sister Henry's smile came and went like the wrens that fluttered around the feeder outside her window. "The years blend together so easily. Yes, as you saw from the picture, Sister Philomena did take her vows here. But if you've come to see her, I'm sorry to tell you, she's no longer with us. She hasn't been for a good many years."

Jazz had wondered how she would break the news, but really, there was no other way than to get it over quickly. "Bernadette is dead."

Sister Henry bowed her head and made

the sign of the cross on her chest, taking the moment to collect herself. When she was done, she looked from Nick to Jazz. "I'm sorry to hear it, but I don't understand how we can help."

"She was murdered." They were everyday words to Nick. Part of his job. Still, he gave them their due, and gave Sister Henry a moment to suck in a breath, stifle a sob.

"I'm so very sorry to hear that." Her voice was low, pensive. Her bottom lip trembled. "What happened?"

"That's what we're trying to find out," Jazz told her. "She was teaching at St. Catherine's school in Cleveland at the time of her death. But none of us knew . . ." Thinking about it now, it seemed incomprehensible. "When she filled out her employment application, when she sent in her résumé, when she went through a series of interviews, Bernadette never mentioned that she'd been a nun."

"I imagine that's because she didn't stay with us," Sister Henry said. "But what a blessing it is to hear she had the opportunity to teach. It's what she always wanted, and she'd already begun taking college courses when she was here. She was meant to be a teacher."

"And she was a good one," Jazz told her.

She ignored the memory of the torn holy cards, of the picture of the angel mangled in an angry fist. "She was dedicated and devoted to her beliefs. That's why we're wondering why you told her to leave."

Sister Henry sat quietly for a moment, her hands flat and suddenly still against the desktop. "It was a very long time ago," she finally said. "Let me . . ." She got up and crossed the room to a row of file cabinets, opened a drawer, looked through it. She shut the drawer and turned around.

"Those records must have gone to our IT facility. There's no reason we would keep them, not when they're so old."

"But you were here then, right?" Jazz knew she was. According to the website she'd consulted before they left Cleveland, Sister Henry had been involved in the administration of the convent for nearly thirty years. "You must remember. A promising teacher. Very devoted. Very religious. She didn't just up and decide to quit. The letter you sent her —"

The color drained from Sister Henry's cheeks. "She showed you the letter?"

" 'Your mission is not in alignment with ours.' That's what you told her. You signed the letter, Sister."

"I really can't help you." Sister Henry hurried back to her desk, but she didn't sit down, a clear signal that she expected Jazz and Nick to stand, too, to leave. "I wish I could. I have a feeling you're looking for something that might connect Sister Philomena's experiences here to the awful thing that happened to her, but obviously if there was anything like that, I'd remember it. And I don't. I can only tell you she wasn't suited to this life. We had no choice but to ask her to leave."

"It wasn't because of angels, was it?" Jazz wanted to know, wondering if somewhere along the line, sometime before she'd been fooled by three mush-headed teenagers, Bernadette had been lured by the promise of angel voices. But even before Sister Henry answered, she knew what the nun would say. Her expression was blank, confused. If Bernadette had told her she talked to angels, if the convent had cut her loose because they didn't want to be associated with a woman who was delusional, Sister Henry would have at least flinched. It wasn't the kind of thing anyone — especially a nun — could pretend had never happened.

"I have no idea what you're talking about," Sister Henry assured Jazz. "We have angel statues here, of course. Angel meditations.

We pray for the guidance of our guardian angels. But Sister Philomena . . ." She gave her shoulders a shake. "She was no more or no less devoted to angels than any of our other sisters. Not that I remember."

Sister Henry moved toward the door and Jazz knew she wouldn't have another chance.

"It's unusual, though, isn't it?" she wanted to know. "Once a nun takes her final vows —"

"We're not the Mafia, dear." Sister Henry's smile was as wide and as innocent as all those smiles on all those nuns in all those pictures. "If things aren't working out, we're not going to make you stay. Or put cement shoes on you."

"So you don't remember much about why Bernadette was asked to leave, but you do remember things weren't working out?" Nick asked.

At his question, Sister Henry turned a laser look on Nick. And a blind eye to the question. "While you're here, I'd suggest you stop into the chapel. It's quite lovely. It's on the Canadian Register of Historic Places, you know. I can send someone with you if you'd like a tour."

"That won't be necessary," Jazz told her. "We've got a long drive back home. Thank you, Sister."

"Thank you for letting us know what happened." She strode to the door and opened it so they could leave. "You can be sure we'll pray for Ms. Quinn's soul."

"Well . . ." Outside in the hallway, with Sister Henry's door closed behind them, Jazz turned to Nick. "That was odd, don't you think?"

"People are odd when they don't want to talk."

"What is it you suppose she doesn't want to talk about?"

His shrug wasn't encouraging. "Maybe Bernadette was a drinker. Maybe she beat little children. Maybe she stole relics from the chapel and sold them on the black market."

"Maybe," Jazz had to admit. "But if that was the case —"

"If that was the case" — Nick wound his arm through hers and they headed for the door — "Sister Henry is going to keep her mouth shut because she doesn't want to admit the convent knew what Bernadette was up to."

"Which means what we pretty much found out was nothing." Outside, Jazz drew in a breath of late-spring air, hoping it would make her feel better. It didn't. Neither did the birdsong that filled the air or the scent of the roses in glorious bloom nearby. She was faced with the prospect of three-plus hours in the car, with ribs and a back that still ached and knees that stung like the devil. That, and the sad reality that they'd come a long way and were no further along in figuring out what happened to Bernadette now than they were when they left home.

Nick tried his best to cheer her up. "You want to stop at a winery on the way home?"

"You want to drink and drive?"

He rolled his eyes. "Of course not. But we could buy a bottle and sit out on your front porch with it tonight. What do you say?"

"You're not working?"

"Not until Monday."

"And you don't have other plans?"

"Are you dog training tomorrow?"

It was a fair question and a few weeks ago — heck, a day ago — she might have had to think about her answer.

She wrinkled her nose. "My knees hurt too much to go to training."

"I'm thinking that means a bottle of wine tonight and a couple sandwiches from La Bodega sounds like a plan?"

It wouldn't help with the investigation, but it was the best idea Jazz had heard in a long time and she grabbed Nick's hand. At the bottom of the wide stone steps, a movement over on their left caught her eye and she turned that way.

"Chapel," Nick said, looking where she was looking, at the stone building with its steep roof and the single nun who was heading toward its door. "I hear it's historic."

"Not at all what I'm thinking," she told him, and she took off in that direction.

She got there just as the chapel door closed and pushed it open so she could hurry inside where a nun — a short, squat African-American woman — was just getting ready to genuflect toward the altar. Jazz waited until the nun had paid her respects and stood.

"You're Sister Veronica."

The nun stuck out a hand to shake Jazz's. "I am. But I don't think we've met. How do you —"

"We've just been looking at the photos in Sister Henry's office," Jazz explained. "There aren't many other African-American nuns in them. You took your vows at the same time Sister Philomena did."

Sister Veronica laughed. "That was a very long time ago. We were kids."

"And now?" Nick asked her.

She patted her tummy, round beneath her

gray habit. "A few more years, a few more pounds. I'm not the sacristan, but I can show you around the chapel if you like. We have some lovely late-Victorian stained-glass windows, a few relics that are interesting."

"Actually" — Jazz thanked her for the offer with a smile — "we came to find out why Sister Philomena left the convent."

"Oh." Sister Veronica tucked her hands into the sleeves of her habit. "I remember the day it happened. Sister Philomena . . . well, we were told not to call her that once she left so I'll just call her Bernadette. Bernadette and I, we were good buddies. We loved watching Cary Grant movies and sipping hot chocolate together in the evenings!" Her smile faded. "I missed her for a very long time. I guess I still do. I hope she's teaching. My goodness, that's all that girl ever wanted to do. Bernadette was still learning the ropes, but we could all tell that someday, she'd have a sort of magic around her when she stood at the front of a classroom. These days . . ." Sister Veronica sighed, and the cross she wore around her neck rose and fell along with her chest. "Every time I walk into a classroom, I think of Bernadette. That's a good legacy, don't you think?"

With a cough, Jazz cleared the sudden

lump in her throat. Still, it wasn't easy to find her voice, or the words, and Nick must have known it.

"We're sorry to tell you," he said, "that Bernadette Quinn is dead."

Sister Veronica's eyes welled and she sniffled. "Poor dear." She shook her head. "Poor, dear Bernadette. I'll never —" Her voice broke, and from somewhere deep in the folds of her habit she pulled out a handkerchief and wiped her cheeks. "I'll never be able to watch another Cary Grant movie without crying."

They gave her a minute to compose herself, but delivering the news about Bernadette wasn't the reason for their visit and Jazz knew they couldn't leave Sister Veronica alone with her grief, not until they'd done what they'd come to do.

"Do you know why she left here?" Jazz asked the nun.

Sister Veronica bowed her head. "It wasn't her choice."

"We saw the letter," Nick told her. "Sister Henry says she doesn't remember the details. You were friends. Maybe you —"

Sister Veronica shook her head. "It was a hard time. I remember how she cried and cried, even before Sister Henry and the others delivered the news that she could no longer stay. It broke her heart."

"What did she do?" Jazz wanted to know.

"Do?" With a shake of her shoulders, Sister Veronica pulled herself away from her memories. "She didn't do anything. Not that I know of. I always just assumed . . ." Her mouth twisted. "I wonder why Sister Henry didn't mention it. Before Bernadette left here, she was not well. She wasn't eating. She wasn't sleeping. She had always been so enthusiastic about wanting to teach, about life. And yet in those weeks, she was a different person. Quiet. Withdrawn. I tried to talk to her. Of course I did. She told me she was fine. Then she was told to leave and after that . . . well, Bernadette never spoke another word. Not to me. Not to anyone here. I tried to contact her once she was gone, but I never heard back. I'm sorry I can't help you more than that. I always assumed she left because she was just too ill to stay on. I hope . . ." A bittersweet smile lit Sister Veronica's face. "I pray she had some years of happiness."

CHAPTER 17

Was Bernadette happy?

The thought haunted Jazz even while she and Nick shared that bottle of wine. Even when he asked if he could stop by the next day, just to check on her.

She thought about it while they went out for coffee on Sunday afternoon, while she took her days off — Monday, Tuesday, Wednesday — and worked with Wally on long stays and handled the admin work that went along with keeping things in the search and rescue and cadaver dog group running smoothly.

She was still thinking about it Thursday morning when she arrived at St. Catherine's to do the million last-minute things to prepare for the first session of summer school.

It was early, and the school was dark, empty. Jazz's sneakers slapped against the floor, the sound echoing back from the high ceilings.

She hit the security code on the pad outside her office door and got herself settled.

If only it was so easy to quiet the questions that whirled through her brain.

What had happened that day on the fourth floor?

And why?

Who could have hated Bernadette enough to take her life?

Or wasn't it hate at all?

Eileen was due to come in at ten, and while she still had time and plenty of quiet to let her mind work over the problem Jazz made herself a pot of coffee and watched, lost in thought, as it brewed. She poured a cup and stopped cold. It wasn't her imagination. She'd heard the soft sounds of footsteps behind her.

She wasn't alone.

The memory of what had happened on Friday night washed over her like an icy wave. She held on tight to the coffee cup, all set to hurl its contents at the person behind her. Muscles tensed, she drew in a breath, turned.

And let out a squeal. "Why didn't you say something when you walked in?"

Sarah laughed and sidestepped Jazz to get

291

a cup of coffee. "I did say something. I said I was here to get the art studio ready for the first group of girls next week. You were so out of it, you didn't hear me."

"Sorry." Jazz went over to her desk, but she didn't sit down. She was too tense. Too dissatisfied with spending her days thinking and worrying and wondering — and getting nowhere fast.

She took a drink of coffee. "Thinking," she told Sarah.

"About your weekend?"

It wasn't the question; it was the sly smile that lit Sarah's expression, the sudden color in her cheeks that perfectly matched her pink skirt and top.

Jazz cocked her head. "What do you know about my weekend?"

"I know a certain cop stopped by to see you."

Jazz grumbled, "Nick talked to my brothers."

"Hal specifically. And Hal talked to Matt of course." Way too proud of herself for having the inside scoop, Sarah sashayed to the nearest chair and sat down. "Matt called me from the station to tell me the news."

"There is no news," Jazz told her, but even before she said it, she knew Sarah would never be satisfied. Not with an explanation that flimsy. "I got jumped on Friday." To prove it, she pointed to the bandages on her knees and elbows.

Sarah's mouth dropped open and she sat up. "Why didn't you call —"

"I knew you were out with Matt. I didn't want to bother you."

"Honey, life-and-death things are not a bother." Sarah got up, the better to take a close look at the scrape on Jazz's forehead, the tiny cut on her throat. She narrowed her eyes. "I hope Nick took the son of a bitch down."

"I didn't see him."

"How much did he get?"

"I wasn't robbed."

"Then why —"

"Why do you think?"

Sarah dropped back into her chair. "Someone wants you to stop asking questions."

"And that only makes me want to ask more questions."

"Are you getting any answers?" Sarah wanted to know.

Jazz had called Eileen on Monday and told her what she and Nick had found out about Bernadette over the weekend, so she didn't feel guilty sharing the news with Sarah, and when she was done telling the story of the Little Sisters of Good Counsel, of the convent, and the fact that Bernadette had been unceremoniously kicked to the proverbial curb, Sarah nodded.

"It explains a lot about her," she said.

"But it doesn't tell us anything about how she died." All weekend, Jazz had been thinking about what she'd do at school that morning when she thought she'd have a few hours to herself. She still had the time, and she wasn't going to let the fact that Sarah was there stop her.

She went into Eileen's office and came out carrying the ring of little-used keys. She jangled them at Sarah.

"You coming?"

Sarah gulped. "To the fourth floor? I always thought it was creepy to have a part of the school that's all locked up and never used. Now that I know there was a dead person up there . . ." She bounded out of her chair. "You bet I'm coming. I wouldn't miss this for the world!"

At the locked door that led to the fourth-floor staircase, Jazz stopped and counted off the keys.

"Number six." As if would prove something, she showed the key to Sarah. "Eileen always keeps the keys in the same order and number six is the key to this door. It's back where it belongs now, but on Assembly Day when we came up here to get the room ready for the dog demonstration, the key was out of place."

Sarah wrinkled her nose. "Eileen used it and put it back in the wrong place?"

They both knew Eileen didn't make those kinds of mistakes.

It seemed like a no-brainer to Jazz. "Or someone else used it and put it back in the wrong place."

"Like the killer." Sarah made a face. "Or maybe Bernadette. Maybe she took someone up to the fourth floor. Or invited that person to meet her there. Maybe she didn't realize how carefully Eileen kept the keys on the ring, how she kept them in a certain order."

"Except if it was Bernadette . . ." Jazz stuck the key in the lock and turned it. "How did the key get back on Eileen's key ring?" She swung open the door. "Ready?"

Sarah's gaze darted up the steps. "I'm not so sure. What do you think you're going to find up there?"

"There's only one way to find out." Jazz swung out an arm, inviting Sarah to go first, and once she did Jazz stepped into the small landing at the bottom of the stairs and closed the door behind them.

"You're not . . ." She was already on the

295

stairs, and Sarah's face was a pale oval in the half darkness. "Are you locking us in up here?"

Jazz had been examining the door and yes, that's exactly what she was planning on doing. "Just trying to figure it out," she said. "If you were meeting someone up here . . . or you were coming up here with the intention of killing someone, how would you know you wouldn't be interrupted? But see." She turned on the flashlight app on her phone, the better to show Sarah what she saw. "You don't need a key to lock the door from this side. There's this turn thingie." Jazz turned it and the old lock clunked into place. "You could be up here, locked in. And no one would know it."

"That's not very comforting," Sarah grumbled, and when Jazz gave her a poke she scurried up the steps.

Up in the dormitory, Jazz looked around. Except for the scuff marks from the shoes of so many police officers, so many technicians picking and poking at Bernadette's bones, nothing had changed from the day Jazz brought the dogs to the attic.

"Bernadette's cousin told me that when he delivered a pizza that last day before Christmas break, there was a woman in Bernadette's classroom with her," she told

Sarah. "You think the woman could have come up here with her?"

"And killed her?" It was warm outside, hot and stuffy in the attic, but still, Sarah chafed her hands over her arms. "Another teacher?"

"I wish I knew." Jazz walked the perimeter of the attic, checking out the room from every angle, looking at the stairs, the windows. "According to Nick . . ." She ignored the look Sarah slanted her at the mention of his name. "Bernadette was strangled. So I'm thinking the killer came at her . . ." She rushed up behind Sarah and wrapped her fingers around Sarah's neck, and after an initial second of surprise Sarah played along. "There probably would have been a struggle. This is probably just about right where Bernadette fell."

"Well, I'm not getting down on the floor." Sarah wiggled out of Jazz's grasp. "I just took this skirt out of the wash."

"You don't have to lay on the floor." Jazz stepped back and looked at where they were in relation to the door of the utility area where the bones were found. "It's not far, but there's a reason it's called deadweight. Bodies are heavy. My guess is especially if the killer was a woman, she wouldn't have been strong enough to carry Bernadette.

She would have had to drag the body over to the utility room."

"And she would have had to know the door was there, right?"

Jazz knew what Sarah was getting at. "You mean, she would have had to know that little room was a convenient place to stash the body? You're right, but you know what, that brings up something even more interesting."

The door was tucked into the space where the sloped ceiling and wall met, and Jazz hurried over to it and opened the door. Unlike the last time she'd fought with the door, it swung open easily. Like last time, it was dark inside the tiny room. "The killer would have had to be prepared," Jazz said. "Nothing's stored up here." Just to be sure, she looked all around the attic. "That plastic the killer used to wrap the body must have been brought up here ahead of time. It was all planned. Down to the last details. The killer knew what was going to happen before he . . . or she . . . came up here with Bernadette."

"But why here?" Sarah wanted to know. "Why would anybody willingly come up here? How did he . . . or she . . ." She echoed Jazz's words. "What do you say to someone, 'Come on up to the never-used attic because I'm planning to kill you and nobody's going to find the body up there'? It doesn't make a whole lot of sense."

"It really doesn't," Jazz agreed. "Unless there was something they had to get. Could something have been hidden up here? Stored up here? The girls, they're always talking about how the fourth floor is haunted, how they sometimes hear foot-steps. Maybe somebody —"

The theory would have to wait.

From the bottom of the stairs they heard a key slide into the lock.

"Come on!" Jazz whispered, and when all Sarah did was stand there, her gaze fixed on the stairway, her eyes wide and her cheeks as pale as the bits of dust that floated in the humid air, Jazz darted forward and grabbed her hand. "Sarah, come on! Over here."

They stooped to fit through the doorway, slipped into the little room where only weeks before Bernadette had lain forgotten, and closed the door behind them.

It was stifling, cramped, and, except for the sliver of light that flowed from the attic beneath the door, pitch-dark in the tiny place, and Jazz didn't dare use her flashlight app. She stood motionless, and when she saw Sarah twitch she put a finger to her lips, grabbed Sarah's hand, and held on tight.

Was she trying to calm Sarah? Or herself?

They listened to the clunk of footsteps coming up the stairs. They heard the shuffle of shoes on the wooden floor of the old dormitory.

Walking to her right.

Jazz made a mental note of it.

That meant the person was headed to the left of the stairway.

Now closer to that never-used roof access door.

The creek of rusted hinges made both Sarah and Jazz flinch.

Roof door. Jazz mouthed the words and pointed, but she doubted Sarah even noticed. Her body trembling, it took every ounce of courage she had for Sarah to keep still. To keep quiet.

Jazz couldn't blame her. It was hard enough to keep calm when the person who might be the murderer was walking just a few feet way.

It was even harder if Sarah, whose imagination was way more lively than Jazz's, was thinking what Jazz was thinking — they were in the dark. In the place where Bernadette had been entombed.

As quickly as the thought occurred, it raced out of Jazz's head when the footsteps came back the other way and a shadow blocked the light. The handle on the utility room door jiggled.

And a phone buzzed a text message alert.

Thank goodness it wasn't from Jazz's or Sarah's phone. Jazz slapped a hand over her own mouth to keep from gasping just as the person outside the door turned and went back down the steps.

If it was up to Sarah, they would have escaped the tiny room in a heartbeat. But Jazz stopped her, a hand on her arm. They waited a minute before Jazz let go the breath she was holding and signaled Sarah that they could leave.

"Oh, God! Oh, God! Oh, God!" Outside in the dormitory, Sarah shook off the fright and the dust that coated her newly washed skirt. "Jazz, that could have been —"

"Yeah, I know," Jazz conceded. She didn't wait. She went over to the roof access door.

"Word is this door has been nailed shut since forever," she told Sarah, and at the same time she grabbed the handle and pulled the door open.

As it turned out, the door didn't lead directly to the roof but to a small boxlike structure that had been built to provide extra insulation between the actual roof door and the inside attic door, extra protection against cold Cleveland winters.

Jazz stepped back so Sarah could see into the little room. "Something was in here. Look, you can see the way the dust is disturbed on the floor. Whoever that was, he just came and got something and took it downstairs. And if we're quick enough —"

Jazz rushed down the stairs and into the third-floor hallway, but whoever had been up in the attic with them was not around now.

"But Jazz . . ." Behind her, Sarah whimpered. "What if —"

"Shhh!" Jazz heard a door bang closed and tried to gauge where the noise came from, but in the stillness, with the sound bouncing and echoing against the walls, it was impossible. "We're good," she assured Sarah. "We're fine." She looked at the cobwebs trailing from Sarah's hair and laughed. "But whoever it was, we can't let them see us like this." She locked the door, and together they ducked into the nearest ladies' room. "Let's get cleaned up before we go back downstairs."

It didn't take Jazz long to brush her fingers through her hair, splash some water on her face, and dust off her shorts and T-shirt. Sarah's pink skirt needed a little more tending to, as did Sarah herself. After the initial cleanup, Jazz left her in the art studio, still shaking, but with a box of vegan-approved chocolates open in front of her and the electric teapot she kept near her desk nearly at the boil.

They made a lunch date, and Jazz went downstairs. She stopped short at the door to her office.

But then, she didn't expect to see Sam Tillner.

"How did you get in?" It was the wrong way to greet a guest to the school, but after the experience in the attic, Jazz couldn't help herself. Suspicion hung in the air like the dust motes that floated around the attic.

"Sorry." Tillner had been waiting in her guest chair and he stood. "I didn't mean to startle you."

"You didn't startle me; you confused me. We have a security system. How did you get in the school?"

"Oh, that!" Unlike at the funeral where he should have been in his Sunday best, he was dressed formally, in dark pants, a crisp white shirt, and a blue silk tie that was understated and all the more impressive because of it. He grabbed a plastic grocery bag that had been on the floor next to the chair.

"I tried to come in the front door, but it's locked tight, and I knocked and a guy named Eddie came by and let me in."

"Eddie should know better."

"I told him . . ." Tillner closed in on Jazz. "I told him I just wanted to stop by and give you this." He handed her the bag and Jazz peeked inside.

From what she could see, it was filled with bits and pieces of paper — a rubber-banded-together stack of cream-colored note cards with a border of blue flowers, a legal pad, a book of daily devotionals.

"It's Bernadette's," he told her. "I found it all in a drawer, a piece of furniture I'm having refinished. It doesn't look like much, but since you have the rest of her things, I thought you might want it."

"Thank you," she told him at the same time she looked him up and down. If he'd been up in the attic, his dark pants showed no traces of dust. But then, she and Sarah had taken the time to clean up. "How long have you been waiting?"

"Not long." He checked his watch. "Which is a good thing, because I've got to get to work. There's an auction today and a lot of work that needs to be done before it starts." He stepped around Jazz and out into the hallway, and a minute later she heard the front door of the school close behind him just as Eileen stepped into the office.

"Bernadette's cousin?" The principal glanced in the direction where Tillner had gone. "What did he want?"

Her mind spinning, Jazz went to her desk and deposited the grocery bag on it. "That's a very good question."

CHAPTER 18

"You know what this means, don't you?"

Jazz and Sarah had picked up lunch and they sat on a bench side by side beneath the shade of a tree in Lincoln Park.

"It means I never want to do anything like that again." At the same time Sarah shivered, she popped open the to-go top on her curried broccoli and chickpea salad and made a decidedly disapproving face at Jazz's corned beef on rye.

"I'm still shaking," she insisted, though she was not shaking so much that she couldn't scoop up a forkful of salad and chomp it down. "How can you do this investigating thing, Jazz?"

Jazz bit into her pickle and the vinegar hit her at the back of the throat. At the same time she shook off the sharp tang, she told herself that the only place she'd get by dwelling on what had happened earlier up in the school attic was into a state of panic.

"Not what I'm talking about. Sure, it was scary at the time, but we're fine. It's over," she said, and she sounded confident enough to convince Sarah and, very nearly, herself. "I'm talking about the fact that someone was up there in the attic."

"Yeah." Sarah shivered. "Someone who wasn't us. That's exactly why I have the willies."

"So how did that someone get up there?" Jazz wanted to know.

Sarah looked at her like she was crazy. "Up the stairs, of course."

"Uh-huh." Jazz stared at her, waiting for the lightbulb to click on. "And . . ."

Sarah set down her fork long enough to think, her eyes squinched, her nose wrinkled, and when all thinking did was make her muscles cramp she groaned. "And what?"

"And we had the key."

The light dawned, and Sarah's mouth fell open. "You mean —"

"Eileen's key isn't the only key."

"And the other one might belong to —"

"I'm going to guess it's the murderer."

Sarah gulped. "That means we were up there with a soulless killer."

Jazz didn't put a lot of stock in melodrama. She re-wrapped her sandwich and handed it to Sarah. "Take that back to school for me and tell Eileen I'm going to be a little late coming back from lunch." She slid off the bench.

"And you're going where?" Sarah wanted to know.

"Wherever a killer would go to have a key copied."

It took three tries, and Jazz wasn't really surprised. Any killer worth his (or her) weight in salt would know better than to have a stolen key copied in the one and only hardware store close to the school. She tried a different lock and key shop downtown, and when no one there remembered copying an antique key she made one last stop. It was already mid-afternoon, and she needed to get back to St. Catherine's.

The store, just on the outskirts of downtown, had been an anchor in the area of small businesses, dive bars, and strip clubs since forever. It was dark, musty, and cramped with coils of rope and bins of nails, and tools hanging from pegboards on the walls the likes of which Jazz couldn't identify. The man behind the counter looked like he'd been there since the place opened. He was thin, bald, and as wrinkled as an old blanket, and he had the wheeze and the smell of a habitual smoker.

"This key." Jazz had hung on to the one from St. Catherine's, and like she had at the other shops she'd visited, she showed it to the man. "Have you copied one like it?"

He had Coke-bottle glasses and he took the key out of her hand and held it an inch from his nose. "Not lately."

Something she didn't dare admit felt like hope fizzed inside Jazz. "What do you mean, not lately?"

The man handed the key back to her. "Been a while."

It lined up with Jazz's theory. The killer could have taken the key off Eileen's key ring, had a copy made. That would explain why the key wasn't on the ring where it was supposed to be when Eileen went to look for it on Assembly Day. It also explained why someone else was able to get upstairs earlier that day when the attic door was locked from the inside.

And a few years? Yes, the key would have been copied more than three years earlier if it was copied by the murderer, before Bernadette was killed.

"Do you keep records?" Jazz wanted to know.

"For key duplicates? Supposed to, but if you ask me, it's more trouble than it's worth." He waved a dismissive hand and the smell of stale cigarettes oozed from him and washed over Jazz, a noxious cloud. "Not worth it for a sale so small."

"Then do you remember —"

"Who asked me to duplicate a key three or four years ago?" He laughed, then coughed and kept on coughing, and he hung on to the front counter with one hand and rocked back and forth.

It was only polite to wait until he was done hacking to thank him and back away, and Jazz did just that.

"No sir, I wouldn't remember nothing at all. If not for that woman."

Almost to the door, she stopped in her tracks and turned around. "What woman?"

"The one who was murdered. You know, it was all over the news. That skeleton they found at that hotsy-totsy school over on the west side. They showed her picture on the TV. Not the skeleton, mind you. A real picture. From when the woman was alive."

She zipped back to the front counter. "What does the key have to do with the woman who was killed?"

"That's what made me remember the whole thing," he explained. "Because keys like that . . ." Jazz had already tucked the key back in her pocket and he looked that way. "Not a dime a dozen, if you know what I mean. And thinking about that key, that made me think about that there woman. And about the other key."

By this time, Jazz's head was spinning, and she shook it in the hopes of clearing it. "There were two keys? Or two people?"

"One key, I guess. That key. The one you have. I can tell just by looking at it 'cause I know a thing or two about keys. What you have there, that's the original. And that young man, he came in here with that same original key and he asked me to make a copy."

Jazz didn't want to look too eager, so she thought this over, took her time. "Can you describe him?"

He scratched one bony hand across the back of his neck. "Tall kid. Dark hair, the way I remember it. Wearing gray clothes. Like he was a janitor or something. Oh, and bad skin. Yeah, I remember that. Bad skin."

Eddie Simpson.

Still, it didn't explain . . .

"What does that dark-haired kid who came in here have to do with the woman who died?" she asked.

"That's easy." The phone rang and the man stepped toward it, one hand out to answer. "When I made a copy of that key for the kid, that's what made me remember that a few years ago . . . like I said, maybe three or four, a woman came in. That woman who was murdered. And she gave me the same key and asked me to make a duplicate for her."

Jazz was tempted to call Nick, but she knew better than to rock the procedural boat. She didn't give a damn what Detective Gary Lindsey thought of her, but there was no use making things at the office hard for Nick. She waited until she got back to St. Catherine's and phoned Detective Lindsey to tell him what she'd learned.

He arrived at the school about a half hour later, and from the looks of the shirt half-tucked into his pants and the fact that he was wearing white sports socks with his black loafers, she guessed it was his day off. He'd been busy with something else, and he dropped what he was doing and changed in a hurry.

Like it or not, she had to give him kudos for that.

He was followed into the school by two uniformed officers, and they asked where they could find Eddie and went out back where he was supposed to be weeding the flower beds that surrounded the garden shed where, once upon what felt like a very long time ago, Jazz had uncovered the cat switcheroo and the dead body of poor little Titus. When they brought Eddie inside so they could talk to him and get the story straight about the key, Eileen offered her office and stepped into Jazz's. Eddie wasn't handcuffed, but he was plenty pissed. His cheeks were red and spittle pooled at the corners of his mouth.

"I don't care what she says." He spit out the words at the same time he sent a glare at Jazz. "I never touched the bitch. She's making it up about how I jumped her over near the park."

Jazz sucked in a breath. She wasn't sure if she was supposed to be outraged by Eddie's confession or just plain stunned. Eddie was the man who'd jumped her and nearly caused her to lose Wally?

Outrage won out over stunned and Jazz had already taken a step toward Eddie, her fists clenched and her Irish temper stoked

Sure, a bigger person would just have ignored Eddie's sputters and moans when he realized he'd just made a huge mistake. But then, that person probably wouldn't love Wally the way Jazz loved him. Watching Eddie step in it was at least a little revenge. Jazz gave Eddie a great big smile. "Since I haven't talked to Eddie since last week," she told Detective Lindsey, "it's strange, don't you think, that he knows I got jumped on Friday night?"

"Strange, indeed." Lindsey's pursed lips told her he'd heard suspects say dumber things, but not lately.

"He told me to mind my own business," Jazz said.

Eddie sputtered. "It wasn't me. It was —"

"Shut up!" With a tip of his head, Lindsey instructed the cops to take Eddie into Eileen's office and he stepped closer to Jazz. "You want to tell me what's going on?"

"There's no way he could know what happened to me Friday. Except if he was the one who did it. I filed a police report on Saturday morning. All the details are in it."

Lindsey nodded and she went right on.

"And this morning, someone came up to the fourth floor when I was already up there and had the door locked behind me."

"Someone with a key."

She gave him credit for being quick on the uptake, nodded, and wrote down the name of the hardware store where she'd talked to the coughing man. "He had a copy of the key made there. And he's not the only one." She hadn't had a chance to fill Eileen in on the details, so Jazz looked her way.

"Bernadette got her hands on the key, too. She had a copy of the key made in the same place."

"Why?" Eileen wanted to know.

All Jazz could do was shrug. "We'll let Detective Lindsey figure that out."

He mumbled what might have been an agreement, but he had a suspect in the other room, and more information to find out before he talked to Eddie.

"So up in the attic today . . . ?"

"There was something inside that door out to the roof," Jazz told him. "And someone, maybe Eddie, who came up there this morning and took it away. I'd say it was about . . ." She held her hands about a foot apart. "Probably about that big from the shape of the dust marks on the floor. Whatever it was, maybe it has something to do with Bernadette's death."

"Maybe," Lindsey conceded, but it was all he would say. He called the station and asked for backup and a tech who could look over the attic again, and when he was done he went into Eileen's office and closed the door behind him.

"Eddie?" Eileen's voice shook, and she dropped into the chair behind Jazz's desk. "I know Loretta always said he was a screw-up, but a murderer? It's hard to believe."

"It is. Still, you'd be the first to tell me none of us can ever know the secrets of another person's heart," Jazz reminded her. "Sometimes there's great good hidden."

"And sometimes, great evil." Eileen shook her head. "And he attacked you?"

"It sure looks that way. Whatever he was hiding up there in the attic, he didn't want to take the chance of me poking around and finding it. I was asking questions, and I guess he thought he could scare me off."

"You should have called me Friday night when it happened."

"I called Nick."

A smile lightened Eileen's expression. "See, sometimes good things can come out of bad." A car door slammed outside and she glanced toward the door. "Go and let the other cops in, will you, Jazz?"

She did, and when she let Lindsey know the cops were there he instructed them and the tech who arrived soon after to go up to the fourth floor. Jazz led the way, unlocked the door for them, but knew better than to butt in where she didn't belong.

She got back downstairs just in time to see the two cops haul Eddie out of Eileen's office. This time, there were handcuffs around his wrists.

"It was just a little weed, man!" Eddie's

voice was tight, desperate. "And yeah, sure, so I did jump Jazz. I didn't really hurt her, and I didn't kill nobody. I swear, I never laid a hand on that crazy teacher."

He was still saying it when they hauled him out of the school, and as she watched them go a thought hit Jazz out of the blue. "Eddie's the one the girls have been hearing walking around upstairs."

Eileen sucked in a breath. "The haunted attic! We should have known. You don't suppose . . ." She made a face. "He wasn't the angel Bernadette heard?"

"I think Taryn spilled the beans about that. She told me to ask Cammi and Juliette about the angels. It was them. That explains why they weren't doing what they were supposed to be doing at Drama Club. They'd wait for Bernadette to go up to the chapel after school, cut out of play practice, and —"

"Whisper so that the walls caught their voices and Bernadette thought it was angels." Eileen sighed. "It was cruel."

"And I have no proof," Jazz admitted. "But I'll bring them in anyway. Along with their parents."

"Bernadette knew it!" Jazz thought about the prayer cards that had been destroyed, about the day she found Bernadette dis-

317

traught outside the chapel. "It's why she lost her faith."

"Poor thing." Eileen shook her head. "She thought she was communicating with heaven and she found out it was just a prank. If they admit what they've done —"

"You'll forgive them?"

Eileen's jaw tightened. "I'll expel them. There's no excuse for being that mean. We should have looked into it more. We should have checked the attic when the girls talked about ghosts."

"Don't beat yourself up about it. There was never any reason. But if Eddie was stashing drugs up there . . ." Jazz let the thought float around in her brain for a bit. "I don't suppose it's odd he never found Bernadette's body. It was in that little room and that's not where he was hiding the drugs." Thinking it through made her brain hurt, and Jazz scraped her hands through her hair. "Why would Bernadette want a key to the attic? And if she had one . . ."

She thought back to coming down from the attic earlier that day, to finding Sam Tillner waiting in her office.

"He could have gotten hold of it," she said. "Sam Tillner. If Bernadette had the key, and if Sam found it . . ."

"He claims he never saw her. That they

never spoke, except for the day he delivered the pizza."

"There is that." Jazz's shoulders drooped along with her spirits. She looked over at the grocery bag Tillner had brought with him that morning. "He delivered more of Bernadette's things."

"Worth looking through?" Eileen wanted to know.

"Probably not," Jazz admitted, but she got the bag anyway and dumped it on her desk.

The blue and cream note cards fell out first. They were unused, and she set them aside. Eileen paged through the book of daily devotions, but except for a prayer card from Bernadette's mother's funeral, there was nothing in between its pages.

"A stub from a movie ticket. The twentieth-anniversary showing of *Agnes of God*. Why am I not surprised?" Jazz set it aside. "A printout from the library. She took out a book . . ." The print on the receipt from the library was faded, and Jazz squinted to read it. "A book about forensic investigation. That's weird, considering." She set that aside, too.

"Here's a note from Odessa Harper." Eileen held it up for Jazz to see. They both knew the name, the attorney Bernadette was consulting about suing the school. Eileen read over the note quietly, then passed it to Jazz.

" 'I had no idea. I need to explain,' " Jazz read the note aloud. " 'Can we talk?' " It was dated three years earlier, two days before Christmas break.

She looked at Eileen. "You think there's any chance Odessa Harper was the woman Sam Tillner saw in Bernadette's office when he delivered the pizza?"

There was a clock on the wall opposite Jazz's desk and Eileen checked it. "It's not five yet. I bet she's still at the office. I hear attorneys keep long, lousy hours. Kind of like school principals."

CHAPTER 19

For the second time that day, Jazz made a trip to downtown Cleveland. The offices of Forestall, Clemons, and Stout were located just at the spot where downtown dipped into what was known as The Flats, the area on both the east and west banks of the Cuyahoga River that was once the city's industrial heartland and these days was all about clubs, restaurants, and upscale real estate.

The building had stood looking over the river for more than one hundred years. It was solid and strong. No doubt that's why the law firm had decided to anchor itself there. Solid and strong was good for business.

The law offices were on the third floor and the reception area featured a window that looked out over the slow-moving boat traffic on the river, a way to entertain waiting clients, no doubt, especially when an ore carrier went by, guided down the impossibly twisting river by a hardy tug. The maneuver always fascinated Jazz — a little technical prowess, a little magic — and she wouldn't have minded waiting and hoping for a freighter to come through, but she never had a chance.

"Odessa Harper?" she asked at the receptionist's desk. The nameplate said she was Miranda.

The girl was young and eager looking when Jazz walked in, but at the mention of the name her brows dropped and her mouth pursed. "Who?"

It had been a long and eventful day, so Jazz congratulated herself when she managed to keep her smile in place. "She's an attorney. Her office is here."

"I don't think so." A woman in a trim dark suit walked into the reception area and Miranda called her over. "Ms. Hyland, this woman is looking for someone named . . ." She glanced at Jazz.

"Odessa Harper," Jazz told Ms. Hyland.

The woman was whip thin and stood as upright as if there was a steel bar in her spine. She had iron-gray hair and a pinched mouth that at the mention of the name puckered even more. "Ms. Harper? Hasn't worked here in years," she said. "Is there something I can help you with?"

Jazz bit back her disappointment. "I hoped to talk to her about one of her former clients, Bernadette Quinn. You might have heard about her on the news; Ms. Quinn, she was —"

"The skeleton!" Miranda was a news watcher. Or a news reader. She flushed the color of strawberries. "Wow! Are you a cop or something?"

Her question dissolved into a burble at an uncompromising glare from Ms. Hyland.

The look might have been enough to intimidate poor Miranda, but it wasn't about to stop Jazz. "Ms. Harper sent a note to Bernadette Quinn, asking for a meeting. I just wondered if you had any idea if that meeting actually took place, and what they talked about."

Ms. Hyland's eyebrows rose a fraction of an inch. "Attorney-client privilege" was all she said before she turned away.

"Except her client is dead. Murdered." Jazz took a step toward Ms. Hyland and stopped when she did. "If you could just tell me where Ms. Harper is working now, I can contact her there."

Ms. Hyland turned and gave Jazz the same look Miranda got when she dared to show some interest in the purpose of Jazz's visit.

"I have no idea where she's working. And there's no use asking anyone else. I'm the office manager. If anyone knew, it would be me. You did the right thing asking me about this matter, Miranda." She turned to the receptionist. "And the wrong thing injecting lurid sensationalism into the discussion. See me in my office. Now."

Ms. Hyland sailed on and Miranda, still red-faced but no longer from excitement, scampered after her and disappeared into the first door down a long, paneled hallway.

"So much for that," Jazz mumbled to herself. She'd already turned to leave when the door of the reception area popped open and Mark Mercer walked in.

"You!" His expression said he knew Jazz; he just couldn't say from where. At least not at first. "I met you at the cemetery."

"That's right." She closed in on him. "I just stopped by to talk to Odessa Harper, only I found out she's no longer with the firm. Ms. Hyland couldn't tell me where she's working now, but you worked side by side with her, right? You must know."

Mercer glanced down that long hallway to the door of the office, now shut.

"It's a beautiful afternoon," he said.

It took a second for Jazz to catch on. "Nice enough for a walk." She slipped out the door and rode the elevator to the first floor. She stood out on the sidewalk for a minute or two, and just when she was finally convinced Mercer had given her the slip he stepped out of the building, put a hand through her arm, and walked her around the corner and into the alley between the building they'd been in and the Spanish restaurant next door. He was right, it was a beautiful afternoon, but in the shade of the stone building it was chilly. Jazz untangled herself from him and stepped back.

"What's going on?" she asked.

"Nothing. Honestly. But if Hyland the Harpy found out I'd talked to you at the cemetery . . ." He whistled low under his breath. "There are some things she's better off not knowing."

"And some things she's better off not knowing you know?"

He nodded.

"Like the fact that even though she was a client, you and Bernadette had a relationship?"

Mercer's shoulders shot back and his mouth twisted. "I wouldn't call it that."

"Except you went to the cemetery to pay your respects."

"Yeah. Well." A moment of bluster was all he could maintain. He shuffled his feet and looked at the pavement. "I . . ." When he looked back up at Jazz again, there were tears in his eyes. "We didn't know each other very long, me and Bernadette. But there was a real connection, one I've never felt before with anyone. I loved her."

Somehow, she'd never thought of Bernadette as a woman who could be loved, and Jazz took a few moments to align this new reality with what she knew about Bernadette. She hoped for a cheery comeback. Something like *How wonderful!* or *I'm so happy for you.* But all she could manage was "She could be difficult."

"Yeah." Mercer chuckled. "It was one of the things about her that was so adorable."

Adorable was another word that did not come to mind when she thought about Bernadette. Jazz tried it out for size. "Adorable. Right. That's why you came to the school to see her."

He nodded.

"Then why did you argue?"

"Because she was adorable. And difficult." Two men in suits walked by out on the sidewalk and Mercer stepped farther into the alley and stood as still as a statue until they passed, and when they did he let go a breath. "Forestall and Clemons," he said. "They'd wonder what I'm doing out here by the Dumpster talking to you."

"You could tell them you were explaining. About the woman you loved and why you fought with her."

"Because she . . ." He threw his hands in the air, turned, and walked as far as the door that led into the kitchen of the restaurant next door, then came back again in Jazz's direction. "I wanted to marry her."

"And she . . . ?"

"She said it was sudden. She said it was too soon. But then, she said yes. I can't tell you how happy it made me! Bernadette was everything I've ever wanted in a woman. She was dedicated to her work and she was so loving. She really cared about her students."

Jazz remembered what happened at the cemetery, how Mercer had turned tail and run at the mention of Maddie's name, so she moved to the very center of the alley, blocking his means of escape. "She cared about one of them a little too much."

He glanced out to the sidewalk, but Mercer knew he didn't have a chance to get by her, not without bowling her over. He wasn't the type, Jazz knew. No man who could actually be in love with Bernadette Quinn would ever be that nasty.

"Maddie Parker, yes." Mercer nodded.

"She loved Maddie."

"Why her?"

"Because she knew . . ." Mercer's mouth twisted. "The secrets, they belong to Bernadette."

"But maybe if you share them, we can find out what happened to her."

"Really?" There was a flash of hope in his eyes, but it lasted only a moment before it faded, then flared into fear. "You don't think I killed her, do you?"

"You fought with her."

"It was about Maddie," he admitted. "Bernadette had been warned by the school. She wasn't allowed to tutor Maddie any longer. She came here to see Ms. Harper. That's how I met her. We discussed her case. She explained how the people over at the school wanted her to keep away from Maddie and how she couldn't. She said Maddie really needed a friend."

"Because . . . ?"

"Well, because of her family situation for one thing."

"The mother and father who are doctors? The big home in the suburbs? The chance to have an experience living in a foreign country this coming year? To attend the college of her choice?"

"Bernadette knew Maddie's parents were

successful. She thought that was good. Of course she thought that was good. But she also knew there was a thread of sadness in Maddie, a feeling of not being connected. You know, because she's adopted."

Jazz didn't know, but she made a mental note to ask Eileen about it. "You fought about Maddie being adopted?"

"We fought because I suggested to Bernadette that maybe she should back off a little. Give Maddie some space. Let things cool down at school. Not rock the boat. I knew how much she loved teaching, and I didn't want her to lose her job. And she told me —" His voice broke. "And she told me she could never abandon Maddie. She told me that if I didn't understand that, then I was not the man she thought I was. That was right before she told me she never wanted to see me again."

"She broke up with you? Over Maddie?"

Jazz could barely believe it, but then Mercer couldn't, either. Now, like it must have done when Bernadette broke the news, heartbreak etched his expression. "I told her that if she toed the line and kept her job at St. Catherine's, well, maybe she wouldn't be tutoring Maddie every day, but they could still see each other. Bernadette could still offer the girl encouragement. I pointed out that we'd have children of our own, but that didn't matter to her. And now, with Bernadette gone, none of it matters."

Jazz was afraid he was right. All that mattered now was the bones that had once been a woman, the killer who needed to be held accountable. All that mattered was finding out the truth.

"Where can I find Odessa Harper?" she asked him. "I think she might have met with Bernadette shortly before the murder."

Drawing himself from the past, Mercer twitched his shoulders. "No one knows. . . ." A breeze zipped down the alleyway and Jazz shivered. "She left," he said, as simple as that. "One day she was here, and the next day she was gone."

A curl of uneasiness coiled in Jazz. "Wait a minute, you're telling me that first her client disappears, then Ms. Harper does. And no one thought anything of it?"

"No, no. It was nothing like that. Nothing mysterious or anything. Ms. Harper, she sent a resignation letter."

"Just like Bernadette did," Jazz murmured.

"Well, I guess that's not all that unusual, is it?" Mercer asked. "If you're unhappy with your job —"

"Was she? Unhappy? We knew Bernadette was; that's why we never questioned her leaving. But Ms. Harper, was she unhappy here?"

Mercer made a face. "Do you know attorneys? Sometimes it's hard to tell if they have hearts and souls. Knowing if they're happy or unhappy is way out of my league."

"She never said anything to you? About leaving?"

"Well, she wouldn't. Not to me. I'm only a lowly paralegal."

"And she left when?"

He thought about it, but only for a moment before his mouth fell open. "Right around the time Bernadette disappeared!"

It was too strange. Too coincidental. Jazz closed in on Mercer. "Can you get me a copy of Ms. Harper's resignation letter?"

He reared back, not just away from Jazz, but away from the very idea. "Are you nuts? I can't just go rooting through old files and —"

"Why not?"

"Because I need my job, that's why not. And because I'm not crazy. You met Hyland the Harpy. Can you imagine what she'd do to me if she found me looking through files I'm not supposed to access? She'd skin me alive!"

"You could say you were doing research."

"And you can send flowers to my funeral."

This time he didn't care if Jazz was between him and the freedom of the sidewalk. Mercer pushed her aside. His uneven gait making it look like he rolled from side to side, he fled out of the alley.

"It might help!" Jazz called after him. "What if it did? What if it helped us find out who killed Bernadette?"

CHAPTER 20

By Monday morning Eddie had been charged with possession with the intent to sell for the weed and assault for his attack on Jazz. He was promised a deal on the charges if he'd talk about Bernadette's murder, but — at least according to Nick, who heard it from Gary Lindsey — he still insisted he had nothing to do with that. Who did? Jazz only wished she knew. Sam Tillner was plenty suspicious. He'd been at school on the day Bernadette disappeared and he'd moved into her home. Taryn Campbell's dad, Leon, was never far from Jazz's mind, either. He openly admitted his dislike of Bernadette.

And then there was the curious fact of Odessa Harper's resignation.

It had niggled at Jazz all weekend, and when Nick called to tell her what was going on with Eddie she asked him to see what he could find out. The results weren't encouraging. Odessa wasn't married and had no children. She lived alone. Interestingly enough, right in the neighborhood. No one filed a missing person's report and no one was likely to except the people at work, and as far as they were concerned, she'd resigned. On to greener pastures. New adventures.

Odessa Harper was never officially missing.

Of course, that's what they all thought about Bernadette, too.

Maybe that's the reason thinking about Odessa didn't sit well with Jazz. The reason it tapped at her brain, interrupted her sleep, stayed with her like the remnants of a bad dream, haunting and disturbing.

Maybe that was the reason she was still thinking about it on Monday morning when the bell rang to let summer school students know they had fifteen minutes to finish up at their lockers and get to their classrooms. Jazz had been so deep in thought, she nearly jumped out of her skin.

She slapped a hand to her heart, sucked in a breath, and told herself to get a grip.

There was no better way of doing that than getting out into the hallway to help usher their summer school students — many of whom had never been to St. Catherine's before — in the right direction.

She waded into a sea of young girls, some with buddies at their sides, others alone and looking as lost as if they'd been dropped on the moon. She helped a student named Tanya who was having trouble with her locker combination. She showed a girl named Jess the way to the art studio. And then there was Becka, a tiny thing with big eyes and a head of the most amazing curly hair. She was on the verge of tears trying to find the library for a session on Jane Austen and Jazz took pity on her, walked her all the way there, and left as fast as she could. If anyone asked her anything about Jane Austen, she was in big trouble.

She was going back down to the first floor when she met Maddie coming up to the second.

"Good morning!" Out of her uniform, in yellow shorts and a shirt tie-dyed in blue and red and purple, Maddie looked younger than a senior. There was a spring in her step and a smile on her face that was as bright as the sunshine outside. "How are you today, Ms. Ramsey?"

It took a moment for Jazz to line up this new, sunshiny Maddie with the morose girl she'd seen only a week earlier. It took another moment before she was able to spit out, "I'm fine, Maddie. How are you?"

"Fabuloso! That's Spanish for fabulous," she added, in case Jazz didn't get it. "All set to spend a couple of weeks learning all I can before we head out."

"Then you're excited about going to Honduras with your parents?"

"Ms. Ramsey, I'm excited about life!" With a laugh, Maddie took the steps two at a time, did a pirouette at the landing, then sailed into her classroom.

Jazz was still standing there with her mouth open when Eileen came up beside her and looked toward Maddie's classroom. Eileen knew where every class was scheduled, of course, and she knew which girls were in each class.

"Maddie?" she asked, her tone clearly saying she wasn't sure she wanted to hear the answer.

"She's . . ." Jazz searched for the right word. "She's great. She's . . . happy and excited."

"I guess she had a good weekend." Eileen turned to go down the steps and Jazz shook herself back to reality and walked along with her. "The young are resilient."

"That resilient?" Jazz wanted to know, but since she knew even Eileen couldn't answer that, she asked a different question. "Did

336

you know she's adopted?"

Eileen slanted her a look. "I've known since she applied here. How did you find out?"

"She told Bernadette. And Bernadette told Mark Mercer, that paralegal who was helping with her lawsuit against us."

"And he told you."

"Does Maddie know?" Jazz asked.

"Of course." They were back in the office now, and they found two students lost and looking for computer programming. Eileen took them out in the hallway and pointed them in the right direction, then came back into the office. "It's not the nineteenth century. Most families don't have secrets when it comes to things like adoption. It's something they treasure. Something they celebrate."

"Bernadette thought Maddie was sad because she was adopted. That she didn't feel . . ." She thought back to everything Mercer had told her. "That she somehow didn't feel complete."

"That doesn't mean she's not happy. Her parents adore her."

"And she's thrilled about going to Honduras." Jazz thought about the smile that wreathed Maddie's face. "Do you think that's enough to make her forget how miser-

able she's been since she found out Bernadette was dead?"

"All we can do is hope," Eileen told her,
and went into her office. "All we can do is
hope."

Jazz wanted nothing more than to believe
it was true. Bernadette and Maddie had
been close. Too close if those pictures of
Maddie she'd found among Bernadette's
things meant anything. Still, that wasn't
Maddie's fault. She missed a favorite
teacher. She felt bad about holding a grudge
thinking Bernadette had just up and left
without saying good-bye. She was miserable
when she learned of Bernadette's death.

"If she can have one day of happiness,"
Jazz said to herself, "I guess that's all we
can ask."

One day of giddiness grew into two and
two turned into three. On Wednesday,
loaded down with Spanish homework and
with torrential rain falling outside, Maddie
practically skipped out of school.

It was good.

It was better than good.

And Jazz couldn't help but be worried
about it.

"You're looking thoughtful." Working a
kink from her neck, Sarah came into the office and went to the windows, checking out

the driving rain. "Matt and I were supposed to go to an Indians game with the boys tonight. They'll be disappointed."

"They like Matt?"

"They do." Sarah spun around and leaned back against the sill of the leaded-glass windows. "It took them a couple times meeting him before they warmed up, but you know how kids can be. Then again, Matt forgot the rules of our house. The first thing he asked them to do with him was go out for burgers."

Jazz could only imagine the scene! Thanks to their mother, Sarah's boys were all about veganism.

Sarah tapped a foot against the hardwood floor. "You know, for a moment there, I thought Dhani was going to take him up on the offer."

Dhani was Sarah's oldest and would be in high school the next year. It couldn't do much for his popularity quotient for him to eat chickpea salad while his schoolmates chomped down burgers and fries.

"I bet Loser lets them eat meat," Sarah grumbled. "When they stay with him, I bet he lets them eat anything they want."

"Maybe that's a good thing," Jazz dared to suggest. "They can try both lifestyles and make up their own minds."

Sarah harrumphed. "Matt swore he'd never forget the rules again. He says he'll always make sure the boys keep on the straight and narrow, food-wise." She smiled. "Matt's great."

"He is."

"And Nick?"

"Nick is busy."

"Nick is always busy."

"Yes." Jazz had paperwork to finish before she left for the day and she went to her desk and sat down. "But it's okay, Sarah."

"Really?" She pushed off from the window. "If he's putting you off —"

"He's not. But he's not pushing, either. That's good."

"Is it?"

"It is." Jazz was certain of it. "We're taking it slow, enjoying each other's company. We're talking."

"And last time, what you mostly did was —" Sarah remembered herself and glanced at Eileen's door.

"Maybe we'll get there again. When and if we're both ready. For now . . ." She tapped the stack of papers on her desk. "If I don't get this done, I don't get home on time, and if I don't get home on time, Wally's going to pee in his crate."

Sarah threw up her hands in surrender. "I

get the message! I've got to get going, too. If we can't do the ball game tonight . . ." As if the weather might actually have changed since last time she checked, she looked out the window again. "There is this new Middle Eastern restaurant I've been reading about. I bet the boys would love to try their lemon and coriander falafel."

Her menu choice selected, her mood improved, Sarah swept out of the office, and Jazz got down to work. She wasn't finished until nearly four, and by then Eileen had gone off to a meeting at the hunger center where she volunteered and Jazz had the school to herself. Now that she didn't have to worry about Eddie, getting jumped, or hearing mysterious footsteps from the fourth floor, it actually felt like a luxury.

If only she could put aside her worries about Maddie.

An idea hit, and at the same time Jazz told herself it wasn't just wrong, but underhanded, sneaky, and unethical, too, it refused to leave her alone.

"Forget it, Jazz," she told herself, her voice hollow in the empty school. "Go home. Make dinner. Take Wally for a walk in the rain. Maybe that will wash the craziness out of your head."

Good advice.

She didn't follow it.

Instead, she went to the locked file cabinet where they kept the master key to all the school's lockers. Each summer school student had been assigned a locker that would be used by an incoming seventh grader in the fall. St. Catherine's girls were allowed to keep the lockers they'd used all year.

Jazz knew what she had in mind was a betrayal of trust.

An invasion of privacy.

It didn't keep her from clutching the key in one hand and heading upstairs.

As if she was right there, Jazz heard a lecture from Eileen spin around inside her head. Sure, administration was allowed to examine a girl's locker, but only in the most serious instances. Like the time one of the older girls was reported to be stashing uppers in her locker so her boyfriend's parents wouldn't find them at home. Or the time one of the younger girls — Jazz still cringed at the memory — wanted to surprise her mom for Mother's Day with a cake. She bought it before she could squander her allowance money and stored it in her locker for two weeks.

Bugs made for a serious instance, indeed.

Was Maddie's current good mood just as critical?

Jazz wished she knew. And to her way of thinking, there was one way that might help her find the truth.

On the second floor at the row of lockers used by last year's juniors, Jazz weighed the locker key in one hand and the questions in her mind: Was this likely to help? Or was she just being nosy? She was all for kids being happy.

Kids being suddenly and inexplicably happy?

As far as Jazz was concerned, that fell into the serious instance category.

She had just inserted the master key into the lock on Maddie's locker when Jazz heard Eileen call from the bottom of the steps.

"You up there?"

She groaned, hung her head, and actually thought about not answering, but Jazz already felt guilty, and that would only make it worse. "Second floor!" she called back. "Junior lockers!"

Just as she expected, she heard Eileen's footsteps on the stairs.

"Maddie?"

There was no use lying about it. Jazz looked over her shoulder at the principal, but she didn't take her hand off the key in its lock. What was the use now?

"Yeah."

Eileen stepped nearer. "You don't think a volunteer committee for the hunger center actually meets on Wednesday afternoon at four o'clock, do you? I was hoping you'd be gone when I came back so you didn't know I was about to violate every rule I hold sacred."

"You mean you're not going to —"

"Yell and scream about privacy violations? Take you to task because you didn't ask my permission? Read you the riot act because you went over my head and did something I'm totally and completely opposed to? What do you think?"

"I think I feel like I'm committing a mortal sin," Jazz admitted.

Eileen waved a dismissive hand. "Not even close. Besides, did you see Maddie today?"

Jazz had. "She was singing in Spanish at lunchtime."

"And doodling during study hall. Flowers. Sunshine. Hearts."

"You think she met a guy?"

Eileen wrinkled her nose. "I hope that's all it is. So . . ." She looked at the locker, at the key. "Since you beat me to it, what are you waiting for?"

Jazz turned the key and pulled open the locker door.

Like so many of the St. Catherine's girls' lockers, this one had a small mirror attached to the inside of the door, a little tray under it had lip gloss and breath mints in it. There was no coat hanging on any of the hooks. The single shelf, though, was packed with papers, and Jazz reached up to haul them down. Her hand slipped, the papers tipped, and Jazz had to scramble to keep them from falling. She moved fast enough to avoid a disaster, but not fast enough to keep one paper from fluttering out and landing on the floor at her feet.

Her arms still raised to stem the avalanche of papers, Jazz looked down. Her breath caught.

The paper that had fallen to the floor was a cream-colored note card decorated with blue flowers.

Just like the ones Bernadette had once owned.

As carefully as she could, Jazz pulled all the papers out of the locker, tucked them under her arm, then bent to retrieve the note card.

"My office?" Eileen suggested, and together they went downstairs and into the principal's office. Eileen shut the door behind them.

"I think we've got the place to ourselves, but there's no use taking any chances," she said. "We don't need someone walking in on us and asking why we're rooting through a student's locker." Hands on hips, she glanced over the stack of papers. "I feel like a traitor to my girls! Remind me again, why are we rooting through this student's locker?"

"This, for one thing." Jazz picked up the note card and showed it to Eileen. "There were unused cards just like this in the bag of stuff Sam Tillner brought over the other day."

"Does that mean that note is from Bernadette?" Eileen shivered. "I don't suppose it's unusual for a teenaged girl to keep a memento like that."

Jazz looked inside the card.

"Blue ink," she said, though how that could possibly matter she didn't know. "Nice, neat handwriting. The letters are very straight, nothing fancy. It's not signed," she said. "Would you recognize Bernadette's handwriting?"

"Not a chance," the principal admitted.

"But we do have . . ." She raced out to her office for Bernadette's personnel file, flipped it open, riffled through the papers inside. "Does her signature on her employment application help?"

They examined it, then the writing inside the note card. "Looks the same," Eileen decided. "So the note is from Bernadette. And what does it say?"

" 'I always keep my promises.' Then at the very bottom of the card, she's written what sounds like a quote of some sort." This writing was smaller and Jazz squinted to read it. " 'Come from the silence so long and so deep.' Sound familiar?"

"Not to me," Eileen admitted. "You're young. You know the music the girls listen to. Something from a song?"

"Not one I recognize. And it's kind of . . ." Jazz searched for the word. "It's kind of gloomy, isn't it? 'The silence so long and so deep.' Like Bernadette was talking about her own death." Jazz's comment was punctuated by a roll of thunder that shook the windows. She waited until its echoes died down.

Eileen shivered. "It sure doesn't tell us much, does it?"

Jazz was hardly listening. She'd caught a glimpse of blue in the pile of papers from the locker and she picked through graded homework assignments, notes, and empty granola bar wrappers and found a stack of the same blue and cream note cards tied together with yellow ribbon.

"Maybe these will," she suggested at the same time she set aside the rest of the papers and pulled one of Eileen's guest chairs closer to the desk. She sat down and set the stack of notes on the desk in front of her, pointing to the ribbon. "You want to do the honors?"

"You go ahead." Eileen sat down. "I feel —"

"Devious. Yeah, I know." Jazz scraped her palms on the legs of her pants. "Like we're eavesdropping."

"Spying."

"Except it might help," Jazz told Eileen, and before her conscience could stop her she stripped the ribbon from the bundle of cards.

The notes were arranged by date, all of them at least three years old.

" 'I hear your grades in English are improving. Good for you,' this one says." Jazz showed the oldest of the notes to Eileen. "And there's another line at the bottom, written smaller, just like in the other note. 'I see you in gleams pale as star-light on a gray wall.' " Jazz glanced up at Eileen, but the principal looked as confused as Jazz felt.

"How about the next one?" Eileen asked.

348

Jazz read it aloud. " 'Bs in all your classes! Your hard work is really paying off.' And the bottom line on this one is, 'And may you happy live, And long us bless; Receiving as you give Great happiness.' I didn't realize Bernadette was a poetry lover."

"She did like to give her students puzzles to work out as class assignments," Eileen reminded Jazz. "I don't suppose . . ."

"That the last bits were meant as something for Maddie to figure out?" Her own question sounded weird, even to Jazz's own ears. "I guess it's possible."

"Look at the rest," Eileen suggested. "Maybe they'll help us make more sense of the whole thing."

Each note was nearly the same. An encouraging line or two for Maddie. A line at the bottom that sounded like song lyrics. Or poetry.

Jazz reached for the last note just as another crack of thunder split the air and a streak of lightning brightened the room.

"Here's a change. This one doesn't have a message for Maddie," Jazz told Eileen. "Just another quote. 'If I were damned of body and soul, I know whose prayers would make me whole.' "

CHAPTER 21

They made copies of the notes and put the
originals back in Maddie's locker so she
wouldn't know they'd ever been missing,
and Eileen and Jazz might have puzzled over
the mysterious quotes long into the evening
if a crash of thunder didn't shake the building and the power didn't snap off.

The emergency lights in the office and out
in the hallway flashed on and Eileen grumbled.

"I'll call Frank," she said. "Jazz, you go
home. There's nothing else we can do here
tonight."

Jazz didn't leave. Not right away anyway.
She waited with Eileen until Frank arrived.
Now that Eddie was in the slammer, Frank
was the only one on the maintenance staff,
an older-than-middle-aged guy who had
been livid when he found out what Eddie
was up to and, as if he could somehow make
amends in the name of maintenance work-

ers everywhere, was only too happy to help Eileen in any way he could.

The entire neighborhood was without power and Wally wasn't used to the routine — Jazz's arrival, treat time, walk, and back home for dinner — getting turned upside down. Jazz took him for a quick potty break in the backyard in the driving rain and came right back in to feed him by the light of the LED lantern her dad had once given her "just in case." They'd go for their longer walk in a little while, she promised Wally. She didn't bother to tell him — or admit to herself — that even though Eddie was in police custody and she didn't have to worry about being followed, being threatened, or getting jumped, she would feel more comfortable walking the neighborhood once the streetlights were back on again.

It took close to an hour for that to happen, and by that time Wally was a ball of pent-up puppy energy.

Even though they were pelted with rain while they walked, Wally insisted on sniffing every inch of the ground, every bit of litter, every discarded cigarette butt. He didn't listen when Jazz told him to sit. He strained at the leash, intent on chasing Marvin, the cat who lived at the house on the corner and had the bad luck of darting out from under a rosebush just as Wally walked past. The dog was, in general, a royal pain, and by the time they got home he was heavy with the scent of wet dog and Jazz was soaked to the bone.

She put him in his crate (he was not happy about that, either) and took a quick shower, then went downstairs and grabbed a tub of salsa out of the fridge and a bag of chips from the cupboard before she flopped onto the couch.

When Wally whined, she took pity on him and let him out of his crate. But not enough pity to share her salsa.

"You sit and be good," she told him. "If you remember how."

He was good, at least for a few minutes, and Jazz took the time to let her mind wander.

" 'If I were damned of body and soul, I know whose prayers would make me whole.' " She scooped up salsa with a chip before she glanced to where Wally was stretched out at her feet. "Odd, huh? Maybe Bernadette was thinking about how she didn't believe in the angel voices anymore?"

Wally didn't offer an opinion.

"Except . . ."

Jazz thought about all the notes. Bernadette had started writing them long before she realized she was fooled into thinking the angels were talking to her in the chapel. So that last note — dated just before Bernadette died — might have had something to do with her angelic illusions being shattered.

But the earlier notes?

Jazz might know everything there was to know about training dogs to find the dead, but she knew less than nothing about poetry.

She'd brought home the copies they'd made of the notes — "Better than someone finding them here at school," Eileen had said — and she pulled them out and got onto Google.

She started with the oldest note and discovered that the line Bernadette quoted, the one about pale starlight on a gray wall, was from a poem by someone named Lola Ridge. It was published in 1920 and titled "Mother."

"Not very helpful," Jazz grumbled, and Wally might have actually cared if he wasn't sound asleep and snoring softly.

She got to work on the second quote, reading it out loud while she keyed in the words.

" 'And may you happy live, And long us bless; Receiving as you give Great happiness.' "

Another easy search. The poet was Christina Rossetti. The poem, "To My Mother."

"Well, obviously Maddie wasn't Bernadette's mother," Jazz told Wally. "Maybe Bernadette might have been talking about her own mother. Or maybe about Doctor Parker. Or about something else completely different."

She tried the disturbing quote, the one about being damned.

"Rudyard Kipling," Jazz said. "And in case you're interested, Wally . . ." She looked down at him. He was not interested. "The poem is 'Mother o' Mine.' "

A coherent theory hadn't formed in her brain yet. Not completely. But Jazz knew it was coming. She could feel the buzz in her blood, the rush in her veins. She sat up as straight as if the lightning that flashed outside sizzled up her spine. And she keyed in the last quote.

" 'Come from the silence so long and so deep.' " The poem was by Elizabeth Akers Allen and called "Rock Me to Sleep." It was about the poet's mother.

This time, Jazz swore the lightning wasn't outside. It was right there in her living room, right there inside her, and Wally felt it, too. He sat up and barked just as Jazz grabbed her phone and called Eileen.

There was no answer.

"Sorry, buddy." She looped a hand around Wally's collar and piloted him into the kitchen to his crate, grabbed her keys, and headed out.

The first place she checked was St. Catherine's, but Eileen's car wasn't in the parking lot.

Frank's was gone, too.

She tried Eileen's phone again, and this time when she got no answer she wheeled out of the school parking lot and drove toward the boundary of the neighborhood.

When St. Catherine's first opened, one of the girls' parents was working on a development of new condos in the area. The condos he built were spacious, stylish — and pricey. He gave one to the school, but only on the condition that Eileen would live in it. It was no surprise that she turned him down, but he persisted and they worked out a deal. Eileen would live there rent-free until he found a buyer. Once the condo was sold, the money would go to the school.

Funny that in fifteen years, no buyer had ever come forward.

The complex had been built to make the new construction look just right in the historic district. Rows of condos in muted colors, pole lamps along the sidewalks, their light fizzy and muted by the rain. The back of the condos on this particular street looked out over Cleveland's steel mills, but from the front every time Jazz visited she thought she just as well could have been in Mayberry.

She parked as close to Eileen's place as she could and raced through the rain to the front door, where she rang the bell. When Eileen didn't answer, she pounded on the door.

Finally, a light flicked on in the front hallway and Eileen pressed her nose to the window to the right of the door.

"What . . . ?" She opened the door and stepped back to let Jazz in. She was wearing a white terry cloth robe and she had a towel in one hand. She scrubbed it over her wet hair. "What's wrong?" she asked.

"I'm not sure." Jazz rushed into the living room. Though the condos were prime Tremont real estate and most were inhabited by young professionals who cared about things like interior design, Eileen lived simply. The living room was furnished with a gray couch with a coffee table in front of it and a chair across from it. On the table next to the chair was a book and a light for reading.

Jazz had thrown on a rain slicker, and

before she could soak the furniture or the carpeting with the raindrops that cascaded off it she stripped it off and carried it into the kitchen. She came back and waved the file folder that she'd kept dry by tucking it inside the slicker. Inside were the copies of the notes.

"I've been Googling," she told Eileen.

"The notes from Bernadette? Those lyrics?"

Jazz shook her head. "Not lyrics. They're all lines from poems. Poems about motherhood."

Her head cocked, Eileen considered this, and Jazz knew exactly when the same idea that had rocked her to the core hit the principal. As if she'd been flash frozen, Eileen stood as still as a statue, then slowly, slowly, sank onto the couch.

"You think Bernadette is —"

"It makes so darned much sense, I don't know why I didn't think of it sooner!" Jazz was too hyped to sit. She paced the living room. "It explains why Bernadette was so obsessed with Maddie. And it explains . . ." She would have slapped a palm to her forehead if she thought it would do any good. "Mark Mercer told me Bernadette broke up with him over the whole Maddie thing. And that seems weird, doesn't it? Why would you feel more strongly about a student at school than you do about the man who wants to marry you? And at the convent in Canada, Sister Veronica told us that before Bernadette left there she was sick. She wasn't sleeping. She wasn't eating. She cried a lot."

"It happens, of course." Eileen's voice was as quiet as the patter of the rain on the windows. "Never to any of the nuns I've known, but I've heard stories. Bernadette took her vows, then she met someone, and . . ." Eileen's shoulders rose and fell along with the deep breath she drew in and let out in a whoosh.

"She loved to give her students puzzles and games. She left Maddie the clues." As if there was any chance Eileen might have forgotten about them, Jazz opened up the file folder, and the copies of the cream and blue note cards spilled out on the coffee table.

"What if Bernadette was Maddie's biological mother?"

Jazz knew Nick was at a meeting of the Cleveland Police Patrolman's Association that night. She was grateful he picked up the phone.

"Say it again." There was chatter in the

358

background and she imagined Nick folded into one corner of the room, his phone pressed to one ear, his finger in the other, just so he could hear her better. "You think Bernadette was —"

"Maddie's mother. Yes. I think we found proof."

"Okay." He didn't sound convinced, and Jazz couldn't blame him. She would lay out her theory in detail when he had more time to listen and a better chance to hear. For now, she had a request. "Can you ask the coroner, Nick? Can you find out if they can tell if a woman has had a child? I mean from the skeleton. Would they know from her remains if Bernadette had given birth?"

He said they'd had a guest speaker at the meeting and then she heard his voice raised, the phone away from his mouth. "Fred!"

Whoever Fred was, he must have come over when Nick yelled for him, because the next thing Jazz knew Fred was on the phone.

"Fred Crile. Nick says you want to know —"

"If there's a way to tell if a woman's given birth. From her remains."

Fred must have been a scientist. Or a cop. She knew this because he took his time answering. He was thoughtful. Careful. He wanted to be sure what he told her was accurate.

He cleared his throat. "There are different theories, of course," he began. "And some pathologists do dispute it. But if we were to study the presence of any dorsal pitting and the shape of the preauricular groove in conjunction with the marking of the interosseous ligament of the joint —"

Scientist.

Jazz groaned. "In English, please!"

At least Fred had a sense of humor. He laughed. "In short, I do think it's possible to tell if a woman has given birth from her skeletal remains."

"Yes!" Jazz punched a fist in the air. "Thank you. Put Nick back on the phone."

Fred did.

"Can you have the folks down at the morgue check?" she asked once she'd told him what Fred told her. Or at least once she'd told him what she thought Fred told her.

"I can talk to Gary Lindsey," he replied. "He'd have to put in the request."

"Can you do that?"

"Do you think it's important?"

"Don't you?"

"Well, it's certainly strange to think she just happened to be teaching at the school her biological daughter attended."

Jazz held in the screech that would have betrayed her frustration. She couldn't blame Nick. He was doing his job, getting his facts lined up. There was no way he could understand how finding out something so big made her feel as if they were finally inching their way toward the truth.

"I'd bet anything it's exactly why Bernadette applied for the job," she told Nick. "You saw the photos, Nick. You know Bernadette was stalking Maddie. But what if she was watching her even before she started teaching here? What if she found out Maddie was going to attend St. Catherine's and that's why she decided to work here? We might never find that out for sure, but it makes sense, doesn't it? Just like we might never find out how she located Maddie and her family in the first place. But she did. I'd bet anything that's why she came to St. Catherine's, to be close to Maddie."

"And you think this might have something to do with what happened to Bernadette?"

If only she had the answer!

Before she was obliged to come up with one, Jazz told Nick she'd talk to him soon and ended the call.

"Well?" Eileen wanted to know.

"He's going to talk to Detective Lindsey.

Then we'll see."

"And you think —"

It was only natural for Eileen to ask exactly what Nick thought.

"I don't know what to think," Jazz admitted. "But I'd bet anything there's something going on, something about Maddie and her parents, something about Bernadette giving a baby up for adoption, that led to her murder."

CHAPTER 22

By the time Nick called the next day, it was after noon. Sitting at school and waiting for the phone to ring, Jazz felt as if she would jump out of her skin. She answered on the first ring and started talking before he even had a chance to say hello.

"Did you know dyslexia can be inherited? I found that out this morning, Nick. Maddie's dyslexic and Bernadette told us she was, too. No wonder she was so anxious to help Maddie with her learning disability. She probably felt responsible. There's another fact that proves my theory. What do you think, huh?"

Silence on the other end of the phone.

"Nick?"

He cleared his throat. "I . . . uh . . . I talked to Gary Lindsey. He talked to the people down at the morgue."

She was too antsy to keep still and she walked over to her office windows and smiled out at the world. Sometime during the night the rain had ended, and sunlight glinted against the puddles on the sidewalks in the park. "And I bet they're amazed we've come this far and found out so much. What did Lindsey say, huh? Is he jealous?"

"He . . . uh . . . ."

Nick was not the type to hem and haw. He was plainspoken, direct, truthful. Except for the time he was playing ball with Manny in Jazz's living room and knocked the framed autographed jersey of Omar Vizquel her brothers had given her off the wall. Nick had tried to cover up by cleaning up the broken glass, then hiding the frame and the jersey with the intention of having the whole thing repaired.

Really, he should have just made the confession from the get-go.

Instead, when she came home and saw the jersey was missing and demanded to know what happened to one of her most treasured possessions, he'd stammered out some crazy story about how her brothers had stopped by and borrowed it because they wanted to take some pictures of it.

It wasn't Jazz's imagination.

He sounded just as uncomfortable then as he did now.

"What?" The single word tasted sour in

Jazz's mouth.

Nick pulled in a breath. "The people down at the morgue, they told Lindsey they can't be certain, that there are plenty of factors that go into looking at skeletal remains and determining if a woman has given birth."

"Yeah, yeah. Your friend Fred told me. Dorsal somethings and grooves and ligaments."

"Yeah, well, they took all that into consideration."

"And?"

He cleared his throat. "As far as they can tell, she never had a child."

"What?" It wasn't like Jazz didn't hear him; it was just that she couldn't believe what he said. She was convinced her theory was not only sound, it was brilliant. She was positive she was right and that this major piece of the puzzle would lead them to Bernadette's killer. "But it all makes so much sense, Nick. The learning disability, and Bernadette's obsession, and the poems. I haven't had time to tell you about the poems, but —"

"I get it. I really do. And I know just how you feel. There are times when I think I've really got ahold of a great piece of evidence, that it's going to make all the difference in

365

a case. Then when I find out I've made a colossal mistake —"

"Is that what you think this is?" Her voice pinged against the high ceiling and caromed back at her. "A colossal mistake?"

"I didn't say that."

"You sort of did."

"What I meant was —"

"It's all right. I get it." It wasn't easy to admit, but once her initial anger dissolved and left Jazz feeling cold and empty, she knew she owed him an apology. "I'm sorry. I overreacted."

"It's hard to get bad news."

Jazz sighed. "I just thought —"

"I know. Like I said, I get it. Hey, give yourself credit for coming up with a theory Gary Lindsey never thought of."

"That's a lot of consolation."

Nick laughed. "Would dinner tonight make you feel any better?"

Just thinking about it eased her disappointment. "It would."

"Seven?"

"No Police Patrolman's meeting tonight?"

"No dog training?"

"I can meet you somewhere."

"Nah. I'll pick you up. It's a beautiful day. I'm thinking dinner someplace on the water. Blue skies, sunshine, lake breezes. The cure for just about anything!"

Jazz wasn't so sure, but she knew it was worth a try.

She thanked him again, apologized again, and ended the call.

"Shit."

Eileen was just coming in from the hallway and she slanted Jazz a look. "Coroner?"

"No baby. Not as far as they can tell."

"Shit," Eileen echoed. "Where does that leave us?"

"Pretty much right where we were before last night. Nowhere."

The realization hung over Jazz all that afternoon just like the rain clouds had the day before. She faked a smile for the girls who stopped in on their way home, wished them a good Thursday evening, told them she'd see them the next day.

It wasn't so easy to keep that smile in place when Maddie fluttered by the office and leaned inside for a quick, "Adios, Ms. Ramsey!"

"Uh, Maddie . . ." Jazz knew — no, she felt it deep down in her bones — that the secrets surrounding Bernadette's murder involved Maddie. She had to find out more and she wasn't sure how to do it. She only knew she had to keep the conversation going, to keep it light and casual so Maddie wouldn't become suspicious. She got up and walked to the doorway. "Your mom coming to pick you up?"

At the same time she moved one step closer to the front door of the school, Maddie shook her head. "She's stuck in surgery and Dad's got a few more patients he needs to see before he can leave. He said I should take Uber home, but I dunno. It's kind of creepy, don't you think, getting into a car with someone you don't know?"

Jazz admitted it was. "If you need a ride —"

"No, no, I'll be fine." Maddie grinned and took another step toward the school's front door. "I'm going to . . . I'm going to get the Rapid downtown. That's what I'm going to do. And the bus from there. I'll call Dad along the way so he knows where I am."

"A good plan," Jazz told her. "But I know where you live. It's not far from my mom's house and I could use taking you home as an excuse to stop and see what she's up to."

"Nah. Thanks for the offer, Ms. Ramsey. But really, I gotta go. Don't worry about me. I'm good."

"You've been good. And happy." Jazz hoped the look she gave the girl was not as penetrating as it was friendly and interested. "You must really be enjoying summer school. You like your teacher?'

Maddie sidestepped toward the door. "Sure."

"And the other girls in Spanish class?"

"Si." She grinned.

"Except you were already this happy Monday morning, before that class ever started."

Maddie's smile froze and a color like blood stained her cheeks. "Is there . . ." She cleared her throat and moved the books she was carrying from her left arm to her right. "There's nothing wrong with being happy, is there? I don't think there is. And it's been nice talking to you, Ms. Ramsey. But I . . ." She glanced at the clock that hung on the wall in the hallway. "I really have to get going. I checked the Rapid schedule, and if I don't hurry I'm going to miss the next train. Bye!"

She heard Maddie's voice one more time when she excused herself around someone at the front door. The next second, Mark Mercer came around the corner.

"Hey." He stood there looking for all the world like he'd just been caught cheating on an algebra test. His hands flitted nervously over the front of his windbreaker. He rolled from foot to foot.

"You want to come in?" Jazz waved toward

her office.

He joined her near her desk.

"I've got . . ." He reached into his windbreaker and pulled out a folded sheet of paper, but he didn't hand it to Jazz, not right away.

"If she ever finds out, I'm dead meat," he said.

Jazz knew — she hoped she knew — exactly who he was talking about.

Exactly what he was talking about.

She darted a look at the paper. "Odessa Harper's resignation letter."

"Well, a copy," Mercer said. "And if Hyland the Harpy ever catches wind of the fact that I went through the personnel files —"

"Your secret is safe with me." Jazz crossed her heart. "I swear."

At the risk of looking way too eager, Jazz glanced at the letter again. "What does it say?"

Mercer frowned. "Not much. I mean, all the usual. I mean . . ." He handed the paper to Jazz. "Take a look for yourself."

Jazz unfolded the paper. " 'It is with the greatest regret,' " she read, " 'that I inform you that as of today . . .' " — she checked the date at the top of the paper and saw that it was just a couple days after Christmas break had started that year, the year Berna-dette disappeared — " 'I am resigning my position at Forestall, Clemons, and Stout. I appreciate the opportunities and experi-ences I had there and I wish the staff all my best.' "

"See, just like I said." As if it was actually his fault the letter wasn't more sensational, more revealing, Mercer grimaced. "Plain ol' resignation letter. Nothing fancy."

"Except . . ." Jazz read over the letter again. "It sounds . . ." She was talking more to herself than to Mercer, but maybe work-ing in a law office, he was used to that. He danced from foot to foot, watching her, waiting to see what she would do.

What she did was go to the cabinet where Bernadette's file was kept.

"The police took the original letter, but we kept a copy of course," she told Mercer, and then because he looked confused, she added, "Bernadette's resignation letter."

"Maybe they think the killer really wrote it."

"Maybe . . ." It wasn't polite to mumble, but Jazz couldn't help herself. Her brain was suddenly caught in a loop with no way in and no way out. She retrieved the letter from Bernadette's file, then sat down and smoothed it out on her desk next to the letter from Odessa.

" 'It is with the greatest regret,' " she read, " 'that I inform you that as of today I am resigning my position at —' "

"It's just like I said!" Mercer's groan betrayed his frustration. "There's nothing interesting in Odessa's letter."

Jazz looked up at him. "Except I'm not reading Odessa's letter."

She knew the instant he caught on. His expression settled. But only for a second. Then his eyes popped and he hurried around to stand next to Jazz, reading aloud along with her.

" 'It is with the greatest regret that I inform you that as of today I am resigning my position at St. Catherine's Preparatory Academy.' "

Jazz sucked in a breath and Mercer read on.

" 'I appreciate the opportunities and experiences I had there and I wish the staff all my best.' "

Jazz looked up at Mercer.

He looked down at her. "What does it mean?" he asked.

More confused than ever, Jazz shook her head. She tapped a finger on the copy of Odessa's letter. "I can keep this?"

As if the letter and the desk had suddenly

gone up in flames, he backed away from both. "I sure don't want it. As far as you're concerned —"

"I get it," Jazz promised him. "I don't know anything about how this letter showed up here at school. And I never saw you."

Mercer lumbered to the door. He stopped when he got there and looked back at Jazz. "Will it help, do you think? Will it help you find out who killed Bernadette?"

As hard as it was, Jazz had no choice but to admit the truth. "The hell if I know!"

Jazz was still thinking about the twin resignation letters at five when she cleaned up her desk and got ready to leave. She had a little less than two hours before Nick showed up at her house, and Wally to take care of before she could even think about leaving for dinner. She tucked the copies of both letters in her purse so Nick could look them over and maybe offer some opinion that would beat the *I have no idea what's going on* that had been whirling through her brain since Mark Mercer came and went.

That afternoon, Eileen really was at a meeting of the volunteers at the hunger center and Jazz was the last one at school. She turned off the office lights and grabbed the handle to close her office door. That was exactly when the phone on her desk rang.

She considered not answering. Whatever it was, it could wait, right? It was five and it was summer session, and whoever was calling, they'd think it was only natural she'd already gone for the day. They'd leave a message, and whatever they wanted, she'd deal with it in the morning.

Too bad responsibility was programmed into the Ramsey DNA.

With a sigh, Jazz slipped her purse off her shoulder, dropped her keys on the desk, and picked up the phone.

"St. Catherine's."

"Hi. This is Kate Parker, Maddie's mom."

"Doctor Parker, sure. This is Jazz. How are you?"

"Well, I'm a little worried. I just got home and talked to Scott."

Maddie's dad, Jazz knew.

"He tells me that Maddie told him she wouldn't be back until late tonight, that she was going to dinner with Della Robinson and her family." Before Jazz could say that Maddie hadn't mentioned it to her, Doctor Parker went right on. "But when I talked to her this afternoon, Maddie told me she was going to a movie with Tatum Lynch this evening. I know we shouldn't bother you with family things, but —"

"It's no bother, Doctor Parker. Really." She didn't need to ask, but it was only right to get the story straight. "You called —"

"Della's family and Tatum's. Yes. Both the girls are home. They told their parents they never talked to Maddie about getting together this evening. And we called Maddie, too, of course. Multiple times. She's not answering her phone."

Jazz didn't even realize her knees had collapsed until she felt the seat of her desk chair under her butt. "I don't want to worry you more, but when I talked to Maddie this afternoon, she told me she was taking the bus home."

"Scott . . ." He was obviously in the room. "Maddie told them at school that she was coming home on the bus."

Ice formed in the pit of Jazz's stomach and her mind moved a million miles an hour. "I'll tell you what." She congratulated herself for at least sounding calm. She didn't need to let the Parkers know that her insides looped and whooshed like she was on a roller coaster. "Why don't the two of you come down here. That seems easier than the three of us making phone calls back and forth while all this gets straightened out. We can call the police from here and —"

"The police?" Doctor Parker's voice edged with tears. "You don't think —"

"I don't know what to think," Jazz admitted. "But it doesn't hurt to get another opinion and it would be good to have an objective one. I bet the cops see stuff like this all the time."

"Yes, yes. Of course." From the way Kate Parker's breathing suddenly accelerated, Jazz could tell she was getting her purse, grabbing her keys, heading for the door.

They ended the call and Jazz called Eileen and told her what was happening. While she waited for parents and principal to arrive, she sat back and tried to make her heartbeat settle.

It was no use.

Of course it wasn't the first time a girl from St. Catherine's had lied to her parents about where she was going, what she was doing. It was dumb, sure, and most of the girls eventually realized that. But when it came to their social lives, teenagers were often thoughtless.

Except Maddie was responsible and considerate, a good kid, and Jazz couldn't imagine Maddie making her parents worry.

That was one thing that bothered her.

The other?

None of the other girls who'd lied about where they'd gone or what they'd been up to was so closely connected to a teacher who'd been murdered.

CHAPTER 23

She had trouble getting ahold of Nick — he told her he'd been in the shower when she called — and she didn't talk to him for a full ten minutes after she talked to Eileen, but he still managed to show up at St. Catherine's first. He arrived wearing a charcoal suit, a crisp white shirt, and a tie splashed with colors that reminded her of the yellow pansies and red geraniums planted in pots at the school's front door.

Damn.

He'd planned someplace nice for dinner. Someplace formal.

Someplace romantic.

At the same time disappointment stabbed Jazz's inside, Kate and Scott Parker arrived in a flurry of questions and tears and Jazz knew there would be other chances for nice dinners, other warm evenings. That was important, sure.

But not as important as finding Maddie.

As Jazz had done when she first talked to Kate Parker, Nick advised Maddie's parents to call the local precinct and get a patrol car over to the school. It didn't mean anything was wrong and there was no reason to panic, he was quick to point out, and Jazz couldn't help but admire the way he sounded so certain, so in control. He was calm and professional and that was just what the Parkers needed. He took charge, at least until two uniformed officers, both women, arrived and he turned Maddie's parents over to them.

Scott Parker was a tall man with pale skin and ashen hair. Kate was as big around as a pencil and she, too, was light haired and blue-eyed. Between the two of them, it should have been obvious they probably didn't produce a short, round, dark-haired daughter like Maddie.

Standing just inside Eileen's office with Nick, the principal, and the Parkers as they gave the police the pertinent details — Maddie's height and weight, what she was wearing — Jazz mumbled, "I should have known the first time I saw them."

"What, that Maddie was adopted?" The soft smile Nick gave her was supposed to make her feel better, but at the moment Jazz wasn't sure anything could. "Would it have made any difference?"

"No." She hated to admit it, and Jazz and Nick moved farther into Eileen's, the better to give the Parkers a little privacy.

"I didn't want to make any calls before the cops got here," she told Nick, "but I've been thinking about my friends in search and rescue. They might be able to help."

He signaled one of the officers, and she came over and gave Jazz the go-ahead.

The fact that three volunteers and their dogs got to the school within a half hour only proved to Jazz how dedicated her fellow dog handlers were. She was proud to be part of the team.

"So what do you want us to do?" Rick Randall had brought his springer spaniel, Lucy, and the dog sat at his side, her tail vibrating with the excitement of being put to work. "School top to bottom?"

Nick and the two uniformed cops agreed it was the best place to start and Eileen went upstairs with them and opened the door to the fourth floor while Jazz went down to the cafeteria along with a handler named Jane and her dog, Pedro, to make sure all the doors down there were open and they had full access to all the storage rooms.

Heading back to her office, she met Eileen

in the hallway.

"Your Nick called Detective Lindsey," Eileen said, and before Jazz could remind her he wasn't *her* Nick she went on. "Nick's in my office with the Parkers and the other cops. Lindsey said he'd be right here."

They walked along the hallway together. "I wish we could help." Jazz knew Eileen felt the same way; still, voicing her frustration made her feel as if she was doing at least something, anything. "I've been thinking about all that stuff in Maddie's locker. Maybe we missed something?"

"You mean some sort of clue about what Maddie is up to?" Eileen didn't need the plan spelled out. She ducked into the office, got the locker key, and a few minutes later she and Jazz stood again side by side in front of Maddie's locker. They opened it and congratulated themselves. When they replaced all of Maddie's papers, they'd obviously done a good job. This time, just like last time, that single cream-and-blue note card fluttered to the floor.

Jazz knew what it said inside. " 'Come from the silence so long and so deep.' "

Eileen remembered the words, too. She shivered. "Such a gloomy thing to write."

Jazz stared at the card at her feet. "From what I saw online, the poet is wishing her mother could come back from the dead and comfort her."

"Okay." Eileen reached up and grabbed the rest of the papers from the locker, then braced the pile against her chest. "How does that help us?"

"I'm not sure it does," Jazz admitted. "Especially now that we know my whole theory about Bernadette being Maddie's mom is bogus. But what I'm wondering is why this one note isn't tied up in the bundle with the rest of them."

Eileen dug through the pile and pulled out the notes tied with yellow ribbon. "And that one . . ." She glanced at the note card on the floor. "It's not dated like all the others, is it?"

"It's newer," Jazz decided. "Maddie hasn't even had a chance to tuck it away with the others."

"Who wrote it?" Eileen wanted to know.

Jazz thought about biting back what she was about to say, but there didn't seem to be much point. What mattered was finding Maddie, and if she looked like a fool for pushing the envelope, making the effort, putting words to the crazy idea that popped into her head, they'd never accomplish anything.

"Well, the poem is about someone coming

back from the dead," Jazz said.

For a moment, Eileen fell under the spell of the suggestion. "And Maddie has been awfully excited and happy," she said, then instantly stepped away from Jazz, and the very idea. "No! No way."

Jazz knew Eileen was right, but she still felt the need to defend herself. "You know I don't mean that literally. I'm not talking about someone rising from the dead like some sort of vampire."

"I hope you're not!" Eileen made a face and shook her shoulders. "What are you talking about?"

"What if . . ." It was no more than a glimmer of a thought, and a wild one at that, but Jazz tried to explain. "What if Odessa Harper is more involved here than we realized?" When she called Eileen about Maddie's disappearance, she'd also told the principal about the duplicate resignation letters so she didn't have to explain again. "That whole letter thing is just too strange to be a coincidence. And Bernadette was consulting her."

"Yeah, about suing us." Eileen's words were acid.

"But that's the whole point. If Bernadette thought she could actually make a case against us, she would have had to give

Odessa all the details."

"Like the fact that we thought Bernadette and Maddie were too close." Eileen nodded.

"And maybe even the fact that one of the things they did to keep in touch was write notes. Maybe Bernadette even borrowed the notes back so she could show them to Odessa. That would explain why the older notes are tied together."

The idea was tantalizing and that was too bad, because Jazz could see it still didn't make any sense.

"But why would Odessa want to send a note to Maddie three years after Bernadette's death and make it all about coming back from the dead? It's almost as if . . ." There was no breeze there in the hallway, so Jazz couldn't explain the icy chill that touched the back of her neck. "It's like Odessa wanted to fool Maddie into thinking Bernadette really was back. That she's still alive. Think about it. The DNA results on the skeleton aren't back. A girl as impressionable as Maddie might be holding out hope. If she thinks there's any chance Bernadette might not be dead, it does explain why she's been so happy."

"And it might explain where Maddie is."

"And why she's keeping whatever she's up

384

to a secret. If she thought she was going to find out —" They had already turned away from the locker and were on their way back downstairs, and Jazz froze. "What if she thought she was going to meet someone who could tell her what really happened to Bernadette?"

Eileen's face paled. "You think she's in danger?"

"I wish I knew."

Eileen went into Jazz's office to sort through Maddie's papers just as Rick Randall showed up with Lucy.

"Nothing and nobody," Rick said. "Want us to check outside?"

Jazz needed air. Maybe it would clear her head. "Can I come along?"

"Are you kidding?" Randall laughed. "When I'm with you, I feel like your dad's back. You've got his instincts when it comes to dogs."

It was the best compliment Jazz had heard in ages, and in spite of all the questions she had about Odessa Harper and Bernadette and Maddie, in spite of the worry that jack-hammered her insides, when she stepped out into the warm evening air she was smiling.

At least until Gary Lindsey stuck his head out the door.

"You can leave," he told her. "We'll take it from here."

Nick stood behind Lindsey and Jazz darted him a look, and his expression told her he didn't agree, but he wasn't in charge. "But —"

"Sister Eileen will be here to handle anything we need."

Jazz stepped nearer to the school. "But I —"

"We appreciate you getting your friends and the dogs here, but like I said, we don't need your help."

When Jazz got home, Sarah was pacing her front porch.

"School grapevine," Sarah said, and held up her phone. "Is it true? Maddie's missing?"

Jazz had spent the walk home grumbling to herself, and now she slammed her purse down on one of the two white Adirondack chairs on her front porch and propped her fists on her hips. "Yes, it's true, and that son of a bitch Lindsey sent me packing before I could do anything to help."

"You said he was stupid."

Jazz shoved her key into the lock on the front door. "Come on in," she told Sarah. "Only don't expect me to be very good company."

When Jazz got back from taking Wally out in the yard, Sarah already had a bottle of wine open. "You look like you need this." She handed Jazz a glass.

"I need to punch that jerk in the nose!"

"Not sure that's going to help." Sarah sipped her wine.

"It would make me feel better."

"Maybe dinner would do that?" Sarah suggested. "My treat."

Jazz juggled her wineglass in one hand while she dished up Wally's dinner. "I'm not hungry."

"I am." Sarah rooted through the cupboard and found nothing on her list of approved foods. "Come on, you'd be doing me a favor. And you can fill me in on what's going on."

As usual, Wally breathed in his food, then scampered over to Jazz to tell her he was ready for his after-dinner walk. She hooked the leash to his collar. "Coming?" she asked Sarah.

The three of them walked as far as the park, and that was usually far enough to make Wally happy. That evening, it wasn't nearly enough to relieve Jazz's anger, or the tension that strained her insides and made her breaths come in short, quick gasps.

"You could walk a little slower." Sarah scrambled to catch up. "I'm an art teacher, not a track star."

Jazz waited for her at the next corner. "Sorry. I just —"

Sarah put a hand on her shoulder. "I get it. I do. But running through the neighborhood isn't going to help. And it's sure not doing me any good." She looked down at her feet and the sandals encrusted with phony jewels that glittered in the last of the evening light. "These shoes are killing me!"

"Sorry," Jazz said again. "I'm just feeling so —"

"Frustrated. Yeah, I bet."

"And helpless. I think there's a connection between Bernadette's death and Odessa Harper, the attorney who was going to represent Bernadette in her case against the school. I think Odessa might be the one Maddie's gone to meet."

"And what did Lindsey say when you told him?" Sarah wanted to know.

Jazz spit out a curse. "He didn't give me a chance to tell him. I sure hope Eileen mentioned it to him. But what difference does it make, anyway? He won't listen."

"Nick would."

He would and the realization warmed Jazz inside and out even if it didn't raise her spirits. "I'll give him a call later. Maybe he can head over here when he's done at school and I can tell him what I'm thinking."

"What do we know about this Harper chick?" Sarah asked.

"Not much." They stopped at a corner to let traffic pass, and when Wally sat at Jazz's side she patted his head and praised him. "She quit her law firm at about the time Bernadette died. But her resignation letter . . ." They were walking past one of the popular bars and music washed over the sidewalk. "I made copies of both their resignation letters. I'll show you when we get back to my house. It will be easier than trying to explain."

"So she quit. And where did she go?" Sarah wanted to know.

Jazz shrugged. "No one at the firm seems to know. Or at least they're not talking. She lived here in the neighborhood. At least she did when she was working at the law firm. I looked up the address. It's that big blue house —"

"What?" When Jazz froze with the rest of the sentence unspoken, Sarah walked right past her and had to turn around and come back to look her in the eye. "What's wrong?"

"Nothing. Maybe something's right." She

handed Wally's leash to Sarah. "Take him home."

"Me?" Wally knew something was up. He jumped and barked. "You know I'm not very good with —"

"He's a puppy. How much trouble can he be?"

"Where are you going?" The truth dawned and Sarah's mouth fell open. "Odessa Harper's house?"

"It's not like I'm going to break in or anything," Jazz assured her. "I'm just going to walk by."

"Then Wally and I will walk by with you."

"You'd better not. Maybe I'll knock on the door. Just to see who's home." When Sarah opened her mouth to tell her this was as bad an idea as Jazz already knew it was, she held up one hand to stop Sarah in her tracks. "I'll just see if she answers, that's all."

"And if she does, what are you going to do, ask if Maddie's there?"

"Maybe." Jazz considered the idea. "That wouldn't seem so weird, would it? We're all concerned about Maddie. We all care about her welfare. It's only natural that I'd be looking for her."

The sun had slipped over the horizon and the street was bathed in pale gray light that made Sarah's face look ghostly. "And if this Odessa had something to do with Bernadette's murder?"

A shiver climbed Jazz's spine. "That's all the more reason for me to get over there and talk to her as soon as I can."

The house that had once belonged to Odessa Harper — and maybe still did — was one of the oldest in the neighborhood, a sturdy home built by the early New England settlers who'd come to the area from Connecticut to farm in the years after the Revolutionary War. The house had a small front porch and that most unusual of all Tremont features, a large yard. Unlike so many of the houses in the neighborhood, this one wasn't built smack up against the ones on either side of it. There was a picket fence (it needed paint) around the entire perimeter of the property, a wide stone walk leading up to the front door, a spacious yard planted with tall trees that probably dated to the establishment of the homestead, and snowball bushes all the way around the house. They were so overgrown, they must have kept any light from ever invading the downstairs windows. Not that it mattered. Not that night anyway.

All the curtains were closed.

There were lights on inside the house, though. Jazz could see their warm glow through the chink between the curtains.

Someone was home.

To her way of thinking, this was good news, but it didn't explain why an icy hand touched her insides and advised caution.

She sloughed off the thought. All she was going to do was knock on the door and see who answered. And if it was Odessa Harper? Then they would chat. About a girl who was missing from the neighborhood. Not about murder.

The thought firmly in mind — along with the reminder not to forget it — Jazz pushed open the gate and walked up to the house. She'd just raised her hand to knock when she saw a shadow slip across the curtains on the windows to her right. Another one followed it, a blocky splotch that didn't move as smoothly or as steadily as the shadow that preceded it but hopped and squirmed as if the very act of walking normally was somehow impossible.

It was a pleasant night, and the windows were open.

"Shhh." She heard the hiss from inside. A woman's voice? Or a man's? It was so low and so hushed, Jazz couldn't tell. "Did you see someone? Did you see someone at the gate?"

The only reply was a gurgle of tears.

Jazz's heart stopped. She fought the urge to pound on the door and instead flattened herself against the front of the house to make sure she couldn't be seen.

"Over here." It was the same voice she'd heard the first time. "Get moving. We'll sit here and wait another hour or so. Just until we know the coast is clear."

"But I can't . . . I don't want to . . . We can't do this. I told you, we can't do this." The words were edged with tears and despair, but the voice was unmistakable.

Maddie.

Jazz's heart pounded. Her breath raced. She reached for her phone to call Nick or 911, or both, but she knew she couldn't make a call from where she stood, not without being heard. She started down the steps, but in the dark, it was impossible to see a loose brick. Jazz's foot hit it and slid, then caught. She grabbed the railing to keep herself from falling, but her phone flew out of her hand and ended up somewhere behind one of the snowball bushes. There was no chance of finding it in the dark, and no time, either. Not when she heard the voice from inside the house again.

"Did you hear that? Did you hear something?" Before the voice had been low and furtive. Now it was louder, more frantic. "We can't wait. We've got to leave. Don't just stand there. Get moving. We've got to leave now!"

The lights in the front room flicked off and Jazz waited for the door to open, and when it didn't she realized Maddie and whoever she was with must have gone around to the back of the house. She raced toward the back door, and she was waiting there, poised and ready for when it popped open. Her plan was simple — she'd confront the person in the house. She'd demand to know what was going on. And there was no way in hell she was leaving without Maddie.

But the door opened.

And Jazz stood rooted in place, speechless and stunned.

Of all the people she had expected to see, she'd never thought it would be Bernadette Quinn.

" 'Come from the silence so long and so deep.' " The words whooshed out of Jazz along with every last bit of air in her lungs. They made sense now. So much horrible sense. It was just like she'd told Eileen. Like a poem about someone who had come back from the dead.

That dead woman reared to a stop just inside the kitchen door and dropped the duffel bag she'd been carrying onto the green ceramic tile floor. As if it was some kind of crazy reminder of everything that had been, Bernadette was dressed in an ankle-brushing gray-and-white-plaid skirt and a white blouse. Her hair was longer than Jazz remembered it. Her face was fuller and paler. She had a set of car keys in her hand.

There was no way she could be as surprised to see Jazz as Jazz was to see her, but she'd been caught off guard. That would explain why her eyes were wide and round, why her hands clenched and unclenched the keys and they clattered together. She wasn't expecting company, and she sure wasn't expecting Jazz to recover in a heartbeat and step forward, settle herself with her feet apart, and block the way out of the house.

"What's going on here?" Jazz demanded.

Bernadette opened her mouth to say something, but before she could a strangled sound came from the far corner of the kitchen where Maddie was folded into the space between the refrigerator and the dishwasher, her eyes squeezed shut and tears streaming down her cheeks. Her hands were duct-taped together in front of her. It was no wonder she wasn't able to walk without an effort; her ankles were bound, too.

"What the hell!" Jazz pushed past Bernadette and went to the girl. She put her hands on Maddie's shoulders. "Maddie, it's me: Jazz."

As if she wasn't sure it was true and she didn't want to find out it wasn't, Maddie slowly opened her eyes. "Ms. Ram-m-msey?" The words stuttered over a sob. "Ms. Ramsey, you found me!"

"I did." Jazz tightened her hold on the girl and inched her away from the wall. "And now I'm going to take you home."

"She's already home."

The words were pure venom.

Jazz gave Maddie a reassuring pat, then turned to face the woman Eileen and Jazz had thought was the victim they found on the fourth floor of the school.

Bernadette's eyes blazed. Her jaw was tight; her arms were close to her sides; her nose flared.

That's when Jazz knew. That's when she knew she was right.

"You *are* Maddie's mother."

Behind her, Jazz felt Maddie flinch, but

Jazz knew better than to take her eyes off Bernadette. She'd seen the same burning light a time or two in the eyes of an aggressive dog. She knew she couldn't show any fear.

"Who was Odessa Harper?" Jazz asked Bernadette.

"Odessa was the woman who stole my baby!" Bernadette's lips barely moved over the words. "She was the attorney who worked at the hospital where my Margaret Mary . . ." She looked at Maddie and tears welled in her eyes. She swept them away with the back of her hand. "Where my Margaret Mary was born. Margaret Mary . . ." When she took a step closer, Maddie whimpered and Jazz warned Bernadette off with a look.

Jazz wondered if Bernadette even noticed. Her gaze was focused over Jazz's shoulder, on the girl who was sobbing uncontrollably now.

"Margaret Mary and I were supposed to be a family. I was going to keep you, honey," she told Maddie, her voice suddenly as sweet as it had been rock hard only seconds before. "Don't you ever doubt it. You were such a surprise. Such a gift! And at first, I didn't know what to do about you. But after a while . . ." She pressed a hand to her stomach. "It didn't take me long to realize you were all I wanted in the world. I gave up my vocation for you. And I made plans. I'd work in a gas station, or a fast-food joint. I'd do anything I could to support us and keep us together. It was all that mattered."

"Then a couple days after you were born . . ." A single tear slipped down Bernadette's cheek, and this time she didn't bother to brush it away. It glimmered in the light from the ceiling fan that whirled above Jazz's head. "I was young and labor was difficult for me. I wasn't feeling well and they gave me something to help me sleep, and when I woke up . . ." She let go an animal howl. "The bassinet next to my bed was empty. You were gone. And that Odessa Harper, she came in to talk to me, as cold as a corpse. I told her my baby was missing, and she . . . and she . . ."

Her chest heaving, Bernadette pulled in breath after breath. "That bitch had the nerve to smile at me and tell me I must have forgotten that I signed adoption papers. She even had the nerve to show those papers to me and offer to make copies for me. But I didn't sign those papers. I never signed those papers!"

When Bernadette took a step closer, Jazz squared her shoulders and stood firm.

"I told her, Margaret Mary. But Odessa Harper, she wouldn't listen. Not even when I insisted. And then later, I heard from a couple other girls there at the hospital that the same thing happened to them. Don't you see?" For a moment, her gaze darted to Jazz, demanding that Jazz listen, that she understand. "Harper was running a baby-selling business. She was stealing children from young unwed mothers and selling them to the highest bidder."

Bernadette stamped her foot against the floor. "That Odessa Harper, she made money off parents who were desperate to have children. But the Parkers, they can't have Margaret Mary. They can't!" Her voice pinged against the oak cabinets. "Margaret Mary is mine!"

"And Odessa Harper?" Somehow, Jazz managed to keep the panic out of her voice. "What happened to her?"

Bernadette's laugh was edged with sarcasm. "What happened to her was that she had the misfortune of leaving her job at that shady hospital and ending up here in Cleveland. I needed a lawyer, I went to consult her firm —"

Jazz's mouth went dry. "And there she was."

"Talk about miracles! I don't think she

remembered me. Why would she? To her, I was just another baby producer, just another young girl who was alone and frightened and desperate. She agreed to take my case and I invited her to the school. You know," — Bernadette's lips lifted into a grin — "so she could look around and get a sense of the place, so she could better understand my grievances against St. Catherine's. Oh, I could practically see the dollar signs flash in her eyes. She'd done her homework. She knew the school had money. She knew if she could win my case, she'd get a nice chunk. Of course she came to the school."

"And the fourth floor?"

"That was genius, pure and simple. It was easy to wait for Eileen to leave the keys lying around and have a copy made of the one I needed. I just slipped the key off the ring and —"

"And didn't put it back where it belonged," Jazz told her.

Bernadette shrugged. "It hardly matters now, does it? It served its purpose. Once I had everything ready upstairs and that Harper bitch was in my classroom, I told her a story about the fourth floor, about how I sometimes would hold classes up there. She didn't know no one ever used the space. The stupid cow actually believed me." A sly

400

smile made Bernadette look like the predator she was.

Jazz's stomach soured. "The plastic sheeting, the extra clothes. Or did you put yours on Harper and change into hers?"

A shiver cascaded over Bernadette's shoulders. "No way I would ever put that evil woman's clothes on my body. I had clothes stashed upstairs, and I put those on her and tossed hers in the trash on my way home. And you know, I have Cammie and Juliette and Taryn to thank for the whole thing. I never would have thought of any of it if not for them."

"The angels."

Bernadette winced as if she'd been slapped. "Angels!" She spit out the word. "They are wicked girls and they did a wicked thing. All those months, I thought I was the recipient of a miracle, and then that day —"

"The day I found you crying in the chapel."

Bernadette nodded. "The little twits apparently don't have much of an attention span. They got bored with their little game. That day, I was in the chapel praying and I heard the voices again. It started out just like usual." A smile lit her face and Bernadette's eyes were dreamy. "They told me I was special to the Lord, that I was looked at with favor by the Heavenly Host. And then . . ." Her mouth twisted. "Those damned angels reminded me how they'd told me Alanda Myers broke up with her boyfriend. They told me they'd overheard Alanda on the phone with Seth. That's how they knew they broke up. They laughed at me. They mocked me. And after they did . . ." Her voice trailed off, her shoulders slumped.

"After they did, you lost your faith, and once you did that, you knew you had nothing else to lose." Another thought hit Jazz. "And you're the one who tried to steal Pumpkin out of Sam Tillner's yard."

"Whose yard?" Bernadette spit out the question. "It's been eating at me all this time. That man with my cat. That man with my house!"

"And you here, hiding out at Odessa's." Jazz couldn't help herself; she felt what was nearly admiration. "And it's all because you remembered Titus the cat, right? You thought about the switcheroo the girls had pulled on you. If you could manage the same thing . . ."

Bernadette's laugh was hard and sharp. "It was a gift! How wonderful that the Harper bitch and I were just about the same

402

height, just about the same weight. It was easy to dress her in my clothes and leave my cross on her. I had no need for it any longer. It all worked out perfectly. It was lucky no one found her before her flesh rotted completely. It gave me time."

Behind her, Jazz could feel Maddie's body tremble. She reached back a hand and touched the girl's arm. "Time to keep an eye on Maddie."

"What mother wouldn't? Only now those Parkers . . ." Bernadette's top lip curled. "They're going to steal her away."

"They're not stealing me!" Maddie screamed. She gasped and gurgled and her knees buckled and Jazz knew if they had any hopes of making it out of there, she had to get Maddie to keep it together. She turned and lifted the girl to her feet and kept an arm around her to keep her from collapsing again.

"I'm going with them!" Maddie screamed. "I'm going with them to Honduras because I want to. They're my parents and I love them. You were my favorite teacher, Ms. Quinn. You were always my favorite. But you're not my mother. Ms. Ramsey, Ms. Ramsey," she cried. "I thought it was so wonderful when I heard from Ms. Quinn. I thought I could meet her and we could talk and I could tell her what I've been doing and how much I've missed her, but now —"

"I know, Maddie. I know." Jazz shushed her. "It's all right now. Everything's going to be okay."

"It is not going to be okay!" Bernadette whirled toward the nearest counter, and when she whipped around again she had a knife clutched in her right hand.

Until that moment, Jazz hadn't been afraid. Now ice cascaded through her insides and her breath caught.

Bernadette's voice was quiet now, calm. Her face was washed with a color like blood and her expression was stone hard. "It's not going to be okay until I take my daughter away from here."

Jazz stood firmly in front of the girl. "I can't let you do that, Bernadette."

She waved the blade and it caught the light and flashed at Jazz.

"No!" Maddie screamed. "You can't hurt Ms. Ramsey."

Jazz knew the moment Bernadette was going to attack. Her eyes glinted and her tongue flicked from between her teeth like a snake's. Jazz only had a second, but she grabbed the closest thing at hand, a wooden cutting board. She held it in front of her like a shield, sure that it was no match for the knife.

At the same time Bernadette lunged, Maddie pushed Jazz from behind to try to move her out of harm's way. Jazz lurched forward and stumbled and the knife swished through the air near her ear and Bernadette screamed at the same time footsteps pounded against the back porch.

Then he was there like one of Bernadette's saints, out of nowhere, bringing salvation.

Nick had his weapon drawn and a look on his face that told Jazz he'd never back down, not an inch.

"Drop the knife," he told Bernadette. "You make one move toward Jazz or the girl, and I swear to God, I'll blow you away."

Bernadette Quinn, who should have been used to being dead by now, dropped the knife.

Between the cops and the media who swarmed the school, there was no room to breathe. Jazz gave her statement to Detective Lindsey. She gave it again to a uniformed officer who had her write everything down and sign. She told Eileen everything, of course, but when she talked to the Parkers she left out the part about the knife. For one thing, they didn't need to know their daughter had been in danger. For an-

405

other . . .

Jazz stood in the doorway between her office and Eileen's and watched Maddie sip an iced tea, her mom on one side of her, her dad on the other.

"She doesn't look bad, considering," Eileen leaned in close and told Jazz.

"She was very brave."

Eileen patted her shoulder. "Look who's talking."

"Nick's the one who saved the day. Poor guy, all he wanted to do was go to dinner tonight. Instead, he got a call from Sarah telling him what I was up to. Good thing, huh?" She glanced around. "Where is he, anyway?"

"Talking to some important-looking man in a uniform. Last I saw him, he said he'd be a while."

Jazz had thanked him, of course. Once Nick had Bernadette on the floor on her stomach and handcuffed, once his backup arrived and they calmed Maddie and stripped the tape from her wrists and ankles, Jazz had given him a short-and-to-the-point accounting of what had happened and had promised to explain everything in detail later.

All about Titus.

And the simple fact that Bernadette had

taken a book on forensics out of the library and none of them had ever questioned why.

"So, you think Odessa Harper really did trick Bernadette into giving the baby up for adoption?" Eileen's question snapped Jazz out of her thoughts.

She pushed off from the wall where she'd been leaning. It was the first she realized she was bone-tired. "I don't doubt it. We'll let the cops sort that out," she said. "For now . . ." Lindsey had asked her not to leave the school, not until they were sure she'd told them all she could, but for now, Jazz needed quiet. She needed peace. She told Eileen where to find her and went upstairs.

The chapel was dark except for the sacristy light and she slipped into a pew and focused on the red glow, letting the warmth of its light flow through her. She closed her eyes, took a deep breath, and did her best to make the tension flow out of her and the silence wrap around her.

At least until she heard a voice whisper in her ear.

"Jazz Ramsey, you make me crazy!"

Jazz sat up like a shot. There was no one next to her in the pew, no one behind her. She sucked in a breath and tensed, ready to jump up, ready to run.

Until she remembered the angels.

Her exhaustion suddenly forgotten, she turned in her seat and looked up at the choir loft.

He would have been impossible to see in that charcoal suit if not for the glint of his hair in the dim light.

"You should have called," Nick whispered near the wall, and the words ruffled Jazz's ear.

She couldn't help but laugh, and since she wasn't sitting near a wall that could carry her whisper, she spoke up nice and loud. "Dropped my phone."

"Poor excuse."

"Happy ending, though."

"Except for the part about you almost getting killed. You can't do that to me, okay? You make me nuts with poking your nose where it doesn't belong, and you make me nuts with your dogs and your training and your crazy family. And you know what else makes me nuts?"

She was almost afraid to ask and it turned out she didn't need to. His words wrapped around her, as warm as the light, as soft as the night air. "It makes me nuts knowing that I never want to live without you."

ACKNOWLEDGMENTS

Writers are lucky people. We get to create worlds and the people who inhabit them. We put words in their mouths, dreams in their heads, hopes in their hearts. And sometimes, we get them into plenty of trouble.

But we never do it alone.

When it comes to plotting and writing books, when it means getting those books out to the world, there is a team of people behind every writer. They are cheerleaders and sometimes, they are the ones who prod us and poke us . . . just when we need it.

My thanks to all of them.

My brainstorming group, Stephanie Cole, Serena Miller, and Emilie Richards, fabulous writers and great friends, always willing to bat around ideas and come up with new ones when the old ones peter out.

The terrific people at St. Martin's Minotaur, especially my editor, Hannah Braatan, and to Nettie Finn, Allison Ziegler, and Kaya Janas.

My ever-supportive agent, Gail Fortune.

And of course, my family. Thank you to Lucy and Eliot for (usually) leaving me alone while I work, and of course, thank you to David, who is my biggest cheerleader.

ABOUT THE AUTHOR

Kylie Logan is the national bestselling author of the Jazz Ramsey Mysteries, The League of Literary Ladies Mysteries, the Button Box Mysteries, the Chili Cook-Off Mysteries, and the Ethnic Eats Mysteries.

The employees of Thorndike Press hope you have enjoyed this Large Print book. All our Thorndike, Wheeler, and Kennebec Large Print titles are designed for easy reading, and all our books are made to last. Other Thorndike Press Large Print books are available at your library, through selected bookstores, or directly from us.

For information about titles, please call:
(800) 223-1244

or visit our website at:
gale.com/thorndike

To share your comments, please write:
Publisher
Thorndike Press
10 Water St., Suite 310
Waterville, ME 04901